# DIFFERENT
# SHADES
*of the*
# SAME COLOR

# DIFFERENT SHADES
## *of the*
# SAME COLOR

*Mima*

# DIFFERENT SHADES OF THE SAME COLOR

*iUniverse books may be ordered through booksellers or by contacting:*

*iUniverse*
*1663 Liberty Drive*
*Bloomington, IN 47403*
*www.iuniverse.com*
*1-800-Authors (1-800-288-4677)*

*Because of the dynamic nature of the Internet, any web addresses or links contained in
this book may have changed since publication and may no longer be valid. The views
expressed in this work are solely those of the author and do not necessarily reflect the
views of the publisher, and the publisher hereby disclaims any responsibility for them.*

*Any people depicted in stock imagery provided by Thinkstock are models,
and such images are being used for illustrative purposes only.
Certain stock imagery © Thinkstock.*

*ISBN: 978-1-4917-8608-6 (sc)*
*ISBN: 978-1-4917-8609-3 (e)*

*Library of Congress Control Number: 2015920919*

*Print information available on the last page.*

*iUniverse rev. date:   12/22/2015*

**Also by Mima**

**Fire**
**A Spark before the Fire**
**The Rock Star of Vampires**
**Her Name is Mariah**

**To learn more go to www.mimaonfire.com**

# Acknowledgments

Thanks to all the people who have supported my writing. As usual, I dedicate this book to those who never quite fit in and with consideration of my protagonist, I specifically dedicate this book to all the people with open minds, open hearts and who want to make the world a better place.

A special thanks to my mom, Jean Arsenault for her love, support and of course, helping with all the f*cking edits – we did it!

I would like to dedicate this book to Mary Butler; a wonderful lady who always supported and encouraged my writing. This one's for you;-)

## Chapter One

It was like a scene out of a bad reality show. The awkward tranquility of the evening surrounded them both, comforting their every step as the gentle waves made an uncommitted attempt to touch Natasha's bare feet. The full moon beamed down on Cliff's face, causing an angelic glow in his eyes, as he gently clasped her fingers and guided her along the water's edge. Her heart should've raced as he droned on about the significance he had in her life; actually, it did, but for entirely the wrong reasons.

Was this the moment she was supposed to be living for? Having a reflective evening walk along the beach with a saint, someone who claimed to have all the answers? Was she supposed to cling onto his every word like some kind of pathetic fool? Was she supposed to be grateful at his meager and uncreative attempt to shake up her world?

Clifford Rook gave – what he thought to be – a compelling explanation, but she simply couldn't listen. Nothing he said fit what she had in mind for the future. She felt herself blocking his proposal – although, to be fair, it felt more like a strong suggestion than a request.

Natasha Parsons felt numb. What he suggested felt more like a trap: as if the walls were closing in on her and she was feverishly attempting to find the door to get out. It made her angry and resentful. It frustrated her. However, attempting to explain this was to no avail. Apparently she just wasn't herself these days: the days since her accident.

*Then who the fuck was I before?*

In reality, the accident that everyone spoke of had been her own doing, but it was enjoyable how people continually tried to make light of her actions, as if she were a kid that tripped on her toys and toppled over. It wasn't exactly that innocent and they knew it.

No longer listening to him talk, she was abruptly brought back into the conversation when he suddenly stopped and reached for her other hand. Facing her, he was gazing into her eyes and all she could focus on was the tiny, white crumb on the end of his nose.

Wait - it was a bit of food, right? She couldn't stop staring at it. It was impossible to hear his words or even take him seriously, as this repulsive morsel seemed to spring up in front of her eyes and she caught herself frowning and threw an awkward smile on her face.

He stopped talking. What had he been saying? It couldn't be what she thought.

"I.." She paused and blinked rapidly, hoping to discourage tears from forming in her eyes because it would be a sign of weakness; and the last thing she wanted at that moment, was to seem vulnerable. "I don't know what to say."

"I'm hoping you'll say yes," His smile was sincere, if not feeble, as the glow from the moon suddenly highlighted his pasty, white complexion. His washed out hazel eyes gazed at her, while Cliff's dark hair moved with the gentle breeze that had suddenly picked up. He looked insistent and anxious, while she felt like running away. It wasn't a situation where one felt she could say no.

*Fuck!*

Anxiety filled her core, almost causing her to not be able to breathe. She had never been so afraid in her life.

*It isn't supposed to be like this, is it?*

Clearing her throat and looking away, she suddenly had an impulse to giggle at the absurdity of this situation. This was clearly someone's idea of a sick joke; it couldn't actually be happening. She looked back into his solemn, loving eyes and had to start a coughing fit in order to conceal her laughter.

*It's a dream. It's a joke. It can't be real.*

"Natasha?" She could hear concern running through Cliff's voice and she coughed even harder, causing the laughter bubbling up within her to feel like a volcano that was about to explode. Finally managing to get back into control, she looked into his eyes.

"Would it be okay if I gave this some thought?" She managed to ask the question with a straight face, batting her long eyelashes, with an upward glance that were deceitfully innocent.

"Okay." He made a short step back and his face showed no expression. She waited in hopes that he would give her more information, but he just shook his head. "I understand, but please don't take long."

"Yes, well, I do appreciate you being so understanding." She once again felt anxiety bubbling up from within her, but managed to catch it in time and put it in its place.

"I realize it's a lot to take in." He gave her a sympathetic grin and she found her eyes once again revert to that fucking thing at the end of his nose. Instinctively, she wanted to reach out and whack it off his face, but she had found out from a previous incident that people don't usually appreciate such a gesture. She was overly conscious of her behavior these days and thought about each word and action before allowing it to enter the world. Since hitting her head, Natasha felt as though she were under a microscope.

"I understand." These were the only words that cropped up in her mind and they appeared to satisfy him, as he let go of one of her hands and guided her away from the water.

The Vancouver beach was eerily empty that evening, as she glanced in the general direction of her apartment building. Momentarily relieved that they were leaving – Cliff suddenly halted and sat down on the cool sand, next to their sandals. Assuming she was supposed to do the same, Natasha cautiously sat down. Realistically, the late spring evening was a bit chilly for her liking, but her tongue felt frozen in her mouth, as reality came to light.

"I'm sorry, I'm not feeling well," She suddenly announced as the world seemed to stop and her arms felt heavy, as though they were about to pull her entire body to the ground, not allowing her to rise again. The doctor in her knew that this was a reaction to a stressful evening.

"I should be taking you home soon," He gently commented. Feeling uncomfortable, she diverted her eyes toward the ocean. "I've given you a great deal to think about."

"Just give me a moment, if you don't mind?" Natasha closed her eyes and drifted back to only seconds after getting the news. They were still in the restaurant and unable to digest the words, Natasha looked for a distraction. She found one at the next table.

The sexy stranger's dark eyes had penetrated through her, as he looked past the chubby blonde lady who sat across from him. The distinguished, Hispanic man sent her subtle messages of attraction that she quickly recognized. It was the way he licked his lips, while staring at her, rubbing his fingertips softly over the rim of his wineglass – she felt herself lost in the possibilities.

She wanted the stranger, suddenly feeling an intense lust filling her body, as she gazed at him in such an obvious way, that it was amazing that Cliff didn't notice.

Without thinking, she pointed toward the back of the restaurant and after excusing herself, Natasha casually gestured toward a bathroom that was down a long hallway and behind the kitchen. He followed her and within minutes, she was crushed against the wall, his mouth on hers as he entered her and she gasped in pleasure, encouraging him to pound into her harder and harder, her legs awkwardly wrapped around him with only his body and the wall for reinforcement. She was glad the music was loud enough to drown out her loud moans, as waves of pleasure erupted throughout her body. She had never felt so alive.

The encounter was over as quick as it began, but it was perfect. She felt the orbs of pleasure continuing to run through her body, as she made her way back to the table. Her dress and hair back in place, as was the man at the next table, she returned to her seat as if nothing occurred.

Now sitting on the beach, she once again fantasized about having sex with the stranger. For a brief second, she could smell him, taste him, feel his hands running over her thighs – but then, Cliff's voice pulled her away from reliving those enticing moments again.

Grudgingly, she brought her attention back to him,

Taking a deep breath, her eyes blinking rapidly as her mind slipped out of denial, Natasha found her voice. "I need some time to think."

His eyes widened, his head tilted forward slightly into a nod.

# Chapter Two

Before the accident, Natasha Parsons barely had time to enjoy her amazing view of English Bay. She would give it a quick glance on her way to and from work, but that was about it. Now, she couldn't imagine a day without sitting and gazing at the beautiful British Columbia coastline. She didn't care if people thought it was peculiar that she had her couch facing a huge window rather than something more conventional, like a television. This was her version of nirvana.

Not that life was very fast-paced and exciting since the accident. In fact, most mornings she would awake feeling disappointed to leave a magical dream world, where she was flying through the air or having sex with a celebrity. It took her sick leave to remind Natasha about the emptiness of her life.

Perhaps that was a little dramatic. After all, she was a doctor, right? The profession that seemed to drive egos - a status that her family loved more than she did - gathering the instant respect based on a mere title.

The truth was that she was a general practitioner who worked in an office with three other physicians. Their relationship was professional — much different from what you might see demonstrated on a weekly hospital drama series — there were no office romances, nor would Natasha even consider the thought. The entire environment was stuffy and serious. Status mattered to them; she could tell.

It wasn't exactly glamorous. Natasha spent most of her day listening to little old ladies complain about how they couldn't poop, or emotionally insecure people wishing to find an answer to their problems in a pill bottle. Sure, there were many people with legitimate complaints, but there were just as many who had self-diagnosed long before they made it to her office, often assuming the prognosis was much harsher than it was in real life.

The reality was, of course, that usually the simplest, most logical and boring diagnosis was true to their ailments. Most spots, lumps and bumps aren't cancer, few coughs are pneumonia and most symptoms wouldn't lead to death.

The truth was that the human body is amazing. It wants to heal itself. In fact, it's usually people who get in their own way – the garbage they eat, their sedimentary lifestyles, the drugs and alcohol that they over consume, the lack of sleep, the inability to properly deal with stress – but no one wants to hear that information. They want a magic pill. They want to hear it's absolutely not their fault - to blame their families, their boss, the devil – anything to avoid accepting responsibility for their own health.

Just before the accident that put her on a month long sick leave; she had a visit from one of her hypochondriac patients. This lady was in the office every week. *Every week.*

For months, it was stomach issues that gave her a range of symptoms from diarrhea to general discomfort. The patient dramatically insisted that she could die because the pain was so severe. It was disrupting her entire life and causing her misery. She believed she had everything from celiac disease to stomach cancer; the list went on and on and required her to go to more than one specialist.

They found nothing.

Eventually the same woman came back with 'blaring headaches' that made her life intolerable. They gave her great discomfort, made it impossible to sleep, and made her life unbearable and miserable.

"How's that stomach?" Natasha had interrupted the woman's rant and she appeared stunned and fell silent for a few seconds. "You were having so many issues, is that no longer a problem?"

"Well, obviously not," The woman grumbled, the lines in her face seemed to deepen even more with a frown, followed by clear frustration that rang through her voice. "I hardly think the two are related."

"Maybe not." Natasha attempted to hold her own annoyance under wraps. It had been a long, draining week and this woman stuck on her last nerve.

*I definitely need a fucking vacation.*

"It appeared to be an ongoing problem for a long time, I felt the need to ask-

"This is so typical of doctors," The defiant patient griped, pushing a strand of her faded, red hair behind one ear, as the wrinkles around her mouth made her expression appear harsher than necessary. "You don't listen. I'm talking about my severe headaches and you only want to talk about my stomach. Were you not listening to anything I just said?"

"I did, however-

"I believe it's your age. I know everyone says you're terrific, but I think you're far too young and inexperienced to truly diagnose anyone properly. That's why I asked to go to a specialist to make sure I had a clean bill of health." The woman continued to rant, her eyes growing red and she appeared to be fighting off a tear that was forming in her right eye.

"They push you young people out of medical school so quickly, just to make us happy that there are physicians available. You're no better than the veterinarian where I bring my cat."

Taken aback, Natasha opened her mouth to say something but was too stunned to talk. A flash of anger shot through, something that wouldn't have been the case in the early days of her career, when she would've instead fought off tears. However, now, these words didn't carry the same meaning as they once did and in fact, they had no meaning at all.

*Well, you fucking cow-*

Studying this woman's face, the many lines and deep wrinkles that etched her jaw and cheek, it occurred to her that perhaps they were as much an indication of her health as anything. People didn't find these lines only from being in the sun too long or failing to moisturize, these deeply set indents almost appeared to be painful, connected with pain and fear in the patient's eyes. Her nails were bitten down to the skin, her arms were lean and frail and her hair limp, dry and dull in appearance. There was a darkness that surrounded this woman, who suddenly looked regretful of her words, something that tended to happen if Natasha didn't respond too quickly to absurd comments.

"I... I..." The patient continued and for a brief second, Natasha thought she was going to apologize, but it was as though she suddenly had a flash of her original thoughts and regained her power. "I don't feel that you're equipped or interested in helping me with my health issues."

"And you feel that perhaps your cat's vet would be better equipped?" Natasha was careful to show assertiveness in her voice, yet no judgment or wrath in her presentation. Opening her large, blue eyes to their maximum size, she tipped her head and gave the woman a compassionate, upward glance, aware that this might help her to drop her defenses.

"I...I guess I-

"You know," Natasha spoke gently, yet abruptly cut her off yet with a touch of condescension in her voice. "Vets are doctors too and also spend a lot of years studying in school, so you have a valid point. Of course, I think they choose animals because they're easier."

The patient looked embarrassed and so, Natasha continued, still choosing her words cautiously.

"Their owner take them to a vet when they notice they aren't well and the veterinarian diagnosis them and gives them a shot or maybe some medication for their condition to make them feel better..." She noticed the patients face becoming calmer, more tranquil and with her own soft and calm voice, Natasha added, "... or puts them to sleep, anyway,"

She hurried through the latter comment as if the patient across from her didn't suddenly have a horrified expression on her face. "The point is that the process is a little more complex when dealing with a human. People read all sorts of crazy things on the Internet or watch a doctor show and diagnose themselves."

The patient fell silent and appeared slightly unnerved.

"Maybe I should umm...."

"Are you sleeping well? Any stress in your life?" Natasha continued, ignoring how the patient's eyes briefly jumped toward the door. "Changed your eating habits? Those glasses, are they new?"

"I got new glasses a few weeks ago, but-

"Then I would recommend you return to your Optometrist because it kind of sounds like you have the wrong prescription."

The patient nodded, said 'thank you' and left.

Realistically, Natasha worked a thankless job. People only respected you when you made them better. Suddenly you were the magician! You were God! They all loved you. They sent you Christmas cards and talked highly of you to friends.

It was when you didn't say what they wanted to hear, that it was a whole other story.

For example, people never wanted to hear that they had to change their diet. They fought that advice as if it were unheard of to cut out their breakfast cola or not munch on a bag of potato chips while staring at the television. It was unheard of to cut down on their meat consumption and forget about telling people that vegetables weren't just products that mothers pushed on their plate in order to assault their taste buds; their body needed them.

Few seemed to take her advice seriously and if they did, it rarely lasted. The initial shock scared them, but then things went back to normal. Friends and family often the culprit, insisting that the doctor was exaggerating and that you 'only live once'. It was hard to explain to these people that the quality of their lives diminished with their poor choices, not to mention that their life might be much shorter than they wish, if they continued bad habits.

It was senseless telling people information if they weren't open and sometimes, Natasha felt like a hypocrite. It wasn't as if she never had pizza for breakfast or hadn't got pissed at a few parties during university. Life happens, but it's about balance.

She had her accident that same weekend. Her hypochondriac-vet patient from earlier that week would've had something to say about it, had she known the details. Fortunately, Natasha's family was powerful, politically connected and therefore, the word of how she got hurt would

never come out, even though it took place in a public venue. It wouldn't leave the hospital or the room she spent the hours leading up to her social faux pas. It was about image. It was about what other people thought. It was all about status; just ask her mother.

Cynthia Parsons had sharp, hazel eyes that could cut through anyone and although that had intimidated most people, she only made Natasha giggle – which was exactly what occurred that particular night in the hospital room. Her mother glared at her and sharply told her that 'this was no joking matter' and in turn, Natasha laughed at the exaggerated seriousness in her expression.

"Why is she behaving this way?" Her mother snapped, her comments directed at the delicious Indian doctor that had treated her in emergency that night. He was looking over some test results – God knows they had done enough tests – his brown eyes held skepticism as he glanced toward Cynthia. As usual, Natasha was lost in her own realm of thoughts.

*He has a hot body. I wonder what he looks like naked. I find brown guys so primal and-*

"…occasionally personality changes, but let's not jump to conclusions yet." His brown eyes dashed from Cynthia to Natasha's face, almost as if he wasn't sure what to say in the presence of another physician.

"Frontal lobe trauma can change elements of someone's personality," Natasha immediately knew what he was referring to, even though she had been lost in her own thoughts and missed most of what he just said. "But it's unlikely cause I feel exactly the same. I think I can go home now."

She started to get out of bed, but her mother had other ideas. "I believe you need to stay put until the doctor says otherwise."

"Mom, *I am* a doctor and I-

"You people truly do make the worst patients don't you." She shook her head and glanced toward the hot, Indian man across the way. He clearly wanted to get the hell away from them both and muttered something how it 'wouldn't be much longer' and slid out of the room.

Natasha was left with a deflated fantasy and a pissed off mother.

"What the hell were you thinking, tonight?"

Natasha felt the glee of the last few moments drain from her body. There was simply no dignified way to explain how she hit her head.

# Chapter Three

The adult thing to do would've been to return his telephone calls. Unfortunately, he wanted to discuss the accident. She did not.

*Why can't he go back to wherever he came from in the first place?*

Natasha wasn't even sure where Clifford *did* come from; he seemed to suddenly appear in her life and had been around ever since that day. He continued to hang around, like a persistent fly that somehow became trapped in a home and circled around excitedly, as if to slowly torment people to the brink of insanity. He didn't appear to understand that he had no place in her life; but then again, weren't those the ones who hung around the longest? Weren't those the ones who never got the subtle hints that others thought were painfully obvious?

She had a great deal on her mind and certainly had no time for Clifford and his mad delusions. Even when she made clear indication that she wasn't ready to embark on the suggested journey, it was as though her wishes merely passed over his head, like clouds in the sky. He didn't want to hear it.

Originally, she made a modest attempt at suggesting that they 'take a few steps back', to think about things a little more clearly. It was best to not make any harsh decisions yet. After all, weren't those the ones people tend to repent later?

Clifford's eyes seemed to fade as he listened to her words, slowly shaking his head, reminding Natasha of the patients at work who didn't want to hear what she said. How could she be compassionate toward his wishes, yet assertive at the same time?

Shame flowed through her heart and Natasha had a brief regret, perhaps she should go along with what he wanted. Perhaps she had no option but to give in to faith, as he suggested. Perhaps she was being headstrong. Natasha reluctantly agreed to go to dinner with him again.

And so, they went on a date - for lack of a more appropriate term. She chose a popular chain restaurant that was not only recognized for its great food, but also for having some of the most attractive waitresses in the city. Glancing at Clifford's face upon walking in the door, Natasha briefly wondered if the deprived man ever left his small universe. His eyes stared at the beautiful women flowing by, carrying large plates of food, wine glasses and bottles of beer; a smile glued to their faces, almost as if they were youthfully ignorant of being objectified; but hey, it was fun and why not? Natasha mused wryly.

*He would have his head shoved between their tits if he thought it could happen; just like every other straight man.*

She managed to suppress a grin, as they were directed to a table near the back of the room. It was a busy evening, the hum of voices united with the glorious, unmistakable scent of perfectly crafted meals was enough to fill anyone with delight: even Clifford.

"Can I bring you a drink?" The young woman who served their table had a naivety about her that was unexpected; given the fact that her shirt was opened just above her belly button, exposing her voluptuous caramel skin that managed to peak out perfectly, without flowing out in a sleazy kind of way.

*How does that happen? If I wore a shirt opened that far, it would be an awkward fucking mess, rather than sexy.*

"How do you do that?" Natasha threw in the light-hearted question that likely should've stayed in her head; but perhaps this display would embarrass Cliff just enough that he'd avoid her in the future. It appeared to be working, as she noticed a hush at the table when she pointed at the woman's cleavage.

"I mean, I know you *obviously* have more to work with there than I do," She let out a giggle and rolled her eyes, as she pointed at her own, small bustline. "Most people do, but I'd look like a fool if I wore my blouse opened like that. It wouldn't be all sexy and cute, like when you do it. You know?"

The table was silent. Dead silent. Natasha was pleased as she gave Clifford a quick glance over; she felt the awkwardness from her impromptu question. Her eyes returned to the waitress, who appeared totally at ease; if not a little flattered.

"Thank you! You know, you could do it as well, the key is to have a great push-up bra and fitted blouse," She insisted, as if they were two girlfriends hanging out at the mall. "But look at you, you're so tiny. You can wear anything and look fabulous."

"Oh, well, thank you honey!" Natasha traded smiles and waved her hand in the air. "Aren't you sweet? I just-

She broke off and quickly glanced across the table at Clifford. She was satisfied with the deer and headlight expression on his face, and decided to stop her train of thought.

*This should do the trick.*

"What do you have on special today?"

The rest of the dinner didn't go much better. The original awkwardness seemed to extend throughout evening, only easing when the waitress returned to check in or drop off some food. Then her and Natasha would start chattering again, much to Clifford's discomfort. Of course, the Bellini helped and although she had made a rule to drink less since the night of the accident, being with Cliff seemed to be the exception.

As it turned out, she kind of enjoyed making him uncomfortable. It didn't stop him, however, from attempting to regenerate an old conversation that was already getting pretty old. She simply didn't want to talk about the future; especially the future that he had in mind. It wasn't what she wanted and yet, he couldn't seem to see things from her standpoint.

"You don't understand," She persisted between her sips of the Bellini, barely nibbling on her Calamari; it was difficult for Natasha to digest her food when her stomach was jumping around anxiously, something she tried to hide from Clifford. She had to convince him that she was

right. There was no way he could leave the restaurant without agreeing with her decision.

In the end, it didn't happen.

"Natasha, you know it's not as simple as you make it sound," Clifford attempted to lay it all out for her, his words were mild, gently gliding across the table and slithering under her skin, like an electrical current traveling through her limbs. She didn't want to admit to seeing his point. That would suggest defeat and she wasn't ready to give in yet.

"I know, but please," She heard the emotion in her voice and instantly stopped talking. This wasn't what she had expected at all. Her cool, confident exterior was starting to fall apart and it was necessary he didn't see the vulnerable side of her.

Too late.

"I recognize that you're scared," He reached out and softly caressed her finger and the kindness in his voice was unmistakable, as she bit her lip and looked away. "But sometimes what we fight against the most is what is actually the best thing for us. What appears big and scary isn't really that bad. I think you will see that-

"Anything else for you this evening?" The Latino waitress returned with her perfect, Hollywood smile and expressed no reluctance to interrupt. It was almost as if she knew that Natasha couldn't breathe and needed a lifeline at that very instant.

Maybe she was an angel.

Natasha mused and stiffly sat back in her seat. Shaking her head no, she quickly grabbed and tossed back the rest of her drink. An uncomfortable Clifford sat across from her and shook his head. "No, I guess we're done here for tonight."

Had he not added the 'tonight' at the end, she would've felt better, but it simply meant that their discussion would continue again in the future. She would have to find a way to avoid him at all costs. Even if it meant doing something desperate or crazy, there was no way that Natasha could speak to Clifford. She couldn't have another conversation like they had that night. It was emotionally exhausting and her arguments were becoming weaker by the moment.

*Everyone has a breaking point. I can't allow Clifford to find mine.*

# Chapter Four

"So, do you still have your pussy?" Her voice purred through the phone line, immediately followed up by the girlish giggle that always caused Natasha to smile, even though she knew the question was intended to shock. Pieces of paper were rattling about in the background and there was a slight echo in the room.

Natasha could almost picture her sister sitting on the edge of her chair, laptop shoved aside, while she doodled on a random piece of paper. It didn't matter if it was a flyer, a receipt for a $500 dress or notes for her latest article, Vanessa had a habit of drawing everything from a simple cartoon image to something more complex, often expressing her mood at the time. She did so in an almost trance-like state without ever checking what was on the other side of the paper.

As a teenager, Vanessa once composed a drawing of a very well endowed naked man while chatting along on the phone, totally unaware that the other side of that specific piece of paper was a list of blood work their mother had to get done the following morning. It didn't go over very well.

"Yes, Clifford is still around." Natasha's answer was somber, if not slightly mocking in tone. She felt as though she should scold Vanessa for her catty comment, but she understood why her sister assessed Clifford in such a manner. He lacked a backbone and was kind of a pussy, all matters considered.

*Not that I want him to have a backbone. That would only proof* fatalistic *to me.*

"So he just isn't getting the hint?" Vanessa's voice erupted into a giggle and more paper could be heard being shuffled around, as if she were looking for something to sketch on as she gossiped.

Natasha sat back on her couch and looked over the beautiful, Vancouver horizons and listened to the slight hum of the refrigerator in the next room. Shaking her head, she finally answered. "No, he's definitely not taking the hint." She decided it was easier to play along, since her sister didn't know the whole story on Natasha's unwanted companion. "And with him, chances are he never will."

"And with him," Vanessa abruptly added. "With *him*, you have to remember that is the key part of that statement. Stop being so hippie dippy and just get rid of him. You aren't being clear and assertive enough, Nat."

"I was assertive plenty and I'm not hippie dippy," Natasha took a firm stand, although she wasn't even sure herself. She understood where her sister was coming from, however the problem was much too complex. "I simply feel like it doesn't matter what I say anymore because it just comes back to the accident. Everyone seems to believe that if I make a decision they dislike, it must be cause I hit my head."

Another giggle erupted on the line, her sister being the only person who found the whole incident to be completely hilarious. "Well, it was quite a situation." Vanessa flipped from her Canadian to a Southeast Asian accent. "You brought *great* shame to our family."

Natasha joined her in a hearty laugh, recognizing that it was simply Vanessa's oddball way of making fun of her own Cambodian heritage. Having been adopted from the Asian country a couple years before Cynthia Parsons' unexpected pregnancy with Natasha, the two often noted that they were closer than any blood siblings.

"As if I am the only one who has brought disgrace to the family," Natasha observed teasingly, as a smile swept across her face. "You've done some pretty naughty things yourself over the years too, Van, if I recollect correctly."

"I have, this is true, but I've managed to keep my indiscretions private," Vanessa spoke with her usual stream of confidence. "But, I got to tell you, that accident is going to be tough to top, little sister. I'd have to be pretty clever to cause such a scandal, especially at an important event like Uncle Kramer and the Crazy Redheads political hootenanny."

Natasha felt an impromptu explosion of laughter bubble up from her belly. Her sister had a way of making reference to people by almost anything other than their actual names. Aunt Sylvia had gained a title of 'the crazy redhead' after going through several shades of reddish hair color throughout the years, while exhibiting some very bizarre and erratic facial expressions. Uncle Arnold, or 'Kramer' had inherited his name after Vanessa saw a picture of their dad's brother as a teen and noted how he resembled the famous television character.

"Yes, indeed," Natasha finally regained her bearings and continued their conversation as if it were totally serious. "I do think that when the fundraising flyers went out, they did refer to it as being a 'hootenanny'. Except I guess you got it mixed up, sister darling, it is actually mom's side that is all redneck. Dad's side is the refined Vancouverites."

"Ah, yes, how could I forget?" Vanessa spoke quickly, a trace of sarcasm in her voice. "I'm the 'dirty, uncivilized Cambodian girl' but yet, mom's kissing cousin and hick relatives from that little shit town in Alberta are somehow more civilized? How many times was that thrown in my face?"

Natasha felt her smile dissolve, as she recalled the heartless remarks that had been made toward her older sister throughout their childhood. In a heated or drunken moment – sometimes the two together – their mother would make an occasional 'slip' on how Vanessa should be more appreciative of everything their family had done to 'save' her from growing up in 'a filthy country and eating bugs for breakfast'. How many times had Natasha witnessed the tears in her older sister's eyes, as her spirit deflated and in silence, she would leave the room? Over the years, her response to the same remarks would turn cold, detached and it was rare to see a hint of hurt in her deep, brown eyes.

"Vanessa, you have to let that go," Natasha's voice was comforting, nurturing and her compassion heavy, as she spoke into her iPhone. "She's ignorant. She shouldn't have said those things to you."

"She shouldn't have *thought* those things." Vanessa snapped, but Natasha knew the anger wasn't directed at her, so didn't take offense.

"I know," Natasha agreed and felt tears burning her lids, her nose starting to run, but she quickly stopped, knowing that her sister wasn't looking for sympathy. "You're right. You're right. That was wrong. She shouldn't have thought those things, but you can't hold on to this anger. You should be proud of your roots. It's what makes you *you*."

"I want to go back," Her sister's words surprised her; although they shouldn't have, because she had shown interest in returning to her country of origin many times. As a teenager, Vanessa and their mother often had screaming matches over the topic and Cynthia Parsons assumed that Vanessa's interest in going back linked to some form of disrespect toward the family who took her in. Natasha understood that she just wanted to learn about her own heritage, see and experience where she came from and learn about the family who had given her up for adoption. Their mother had forbidden her from ever going back.

"You should." Natasha lovingly insisted. "You've got to go."

"I don't know, Stephen thinks that I won't find what I'm looking for, if I do go." Vanessa referred to her husband, a man she met in college. Thoughtful, serene, Vanessa's husband was not the sort of man who discouraged anyone from their goals, which made Natasha concerned that perhaps he knew something that they did not. He was a teacher, certainly well educated; perhaps he recognized that there was something his wife would discover there that would break her heart.

"You've wanted to go since you were ten," Natasha gently reminded her. "I think that says something." Then, attempting to lighten the mood, she added, "I mean, you're an old lady now Van, come on, you should know your own mind."

"I'm not an old lady," Vanessa grumbled through the telephone line. "I'm a few years away from 40 and who says that 40 is old anyway?!"

"Well, I guess I've been told," Natasha heard her voice lift to the original tone in their conversation, while she smiled into a nearby mirror. Her dark blonde hair falling into her pale, ashen face, as she tilted her head then quickly looked away. The scar was still rather prominent on her forehead, almost in the direct center; the wound was healing nicely but would never completely go away. A year from now, she knew it would be a fine, clean line that was hardly noticeable at all; but she would always remember its significance and-

Her heart filled with sadness, something she quickly pushed aside.

"Exactly," Vanessa said, her speech suddenly became introspective. "Isn't it odd though, how we generalize people according to their culture, age or religion, when we're all just a different shade of the same color? Yet, people use these accusations as if their weapons."

"Not that I'm innocent of it," She continued. "I just did the same with half our relatives, but it doesn't make it right."

"Our *family* isn't right," Natasha insisted.

"So have you heard from Arnold and Sylvia since that whole ordeal," A touch of humor returned to Vanessa's voice. "I can imagine your little scene must've made interesting dinner conversation the following day."

"I think the fact that I got hurt may have taken some negative attention away from me."

"I'm sure they believed that you deserved it," Vanessa said, with a smile in her voice. "Probably why mom played up how you had all those stitches, how she was watching you for a concussion…"

"Well, I did have a minor concussion because I did lose consciousness for a few minutes or seconds," Natasha stumbled through her sentence. "I'm not sure. It was too embarrassing."

"Yet everyone acts like it was a minor hiccup," Vanessa teased. "As if you weren't caught-

"Yes, I know," Natasha cut her off and laughed. "I think I'm cursed."

"If you weren't then, I'm sure the crazy red head has put a hex on you about now," Vanessa insisted. "If she doesn't, maybe the pussy will put a curse on you."

"Clifford would never do that," Natasha said with a giggle following quickly behind. "And stop calling referring to him as my pussy! I mean, he's not that bad…he's just…"

*How the fuck do I finish that sentence and why am I defending him?*

"You're right, Nat," Vanessa suddenly sounded oddly serious. "We shouldn't be insulting all the pussies out there."

# Chapter Five

※ ❈◈❀❂❀◈❈ ※

"You know, we're pretty lucky," Natasha observed from the passenger seat of her sister's Jeep convertible. It was a Saturday afternoon and the two were heading back to Vancouver after an impromptu road trip with no particular goal. It was hardly unusual for them to take off for their own private escape from everything – Vancouver, their families, careers, problems – just because they needed a break. It allowed them to bring some perspective into their lives, while soaking up the sun at the same time.

"We are?" Vanessa leaned sideways to turn down the radio, never removing her attention from the road for a second. Pushing back a strand of hair that had pulled free from her ponytail, she looked peaceful and relaxed. Always beautiful, Vanessa wore a simple, white blouse and modest gray shorts; her caramel skin was accented by her gold Ray-Bans and a gentle swoop of pink lip-color. A glint of sunlight briefly caught on the gold watch that Stephen had bought her for their tenth anniversary the previous year.

"Of course we are!" Natasha spoke enthusiastically as she signaled toward the mountains that loomed over the city. A warm breeze flowed over her, as the sunlight touched her face. "It's a beautiful day, not a cloud in the sky and we managed to escape our complicated lives, even if for a few hours. Isn't that reason enough?"

"Isn't this around the time when you begin to dread returning to your 'real life', " Vanessa teased, as the Jeep slowed down to follow the traffic ahead of them. A quick glance at Natasha, she shook her head. "Good thing I suggested you cover that scar before we left the house today. You'd think I was the doctor here."

"I never thought about it. It's funny because the scar is there every time I look in the mirror and yet, it's almost like it's not there. Does that make sense?" Natasha said while self-consciously touching the bandana that she had wrapped around her head on the way out the door earlier that day. At the time, she hadn't given it much thought, but now that Natasha sat adjacent to a carload of attractive men, she suddenly felt ridiculous.

"No, Nat, nothing you just said made sense," Vanessa spoke seriously and suddenly broke out into laughter that nearly came out as a hiccup. "But what would I expect, you hit your head, right? According to mom and dad, you're a totally different person now, someone who makes observations about how lucky she is while wearing a hippie bandana."

"Do you think I look like a hippie?" Natasha glanced down at her loose, flowing white shirt that she put on over a bikini top, ripped jean shorts and braided wedge sandals. A quick glance in the mirror at her bandana and sunglasses answered her question. "I guess I sort of do look like a hippie, don't I? Is that cool anymore?"

Traffic began to move forward and Vanessa continued in the flow as she unsuccessfully attempted to hold back her laughter. "Nat, you are so different. This is so *not* you!"

"Why does everyone keep saying that?" Her words came out in a long whimper that almost proved Vanessa's point, since she wasn't one to have a whiny attitude. Was she different now?

"I don't see how me changing a bit here and there has anything to do with hitting my head," She hesitated for a moment. "And I'm the doctor, I know about frontal lobe damage and yes, it can affect someone's personality but it's usually more extreme. You know, the patient acts overly impulsive or sexual or…whatever."

"Oh, so maybe you hit your head before the night at the Kramer's politician shindig? Is that what you are telling me?" Vanessa teased her as she continued to stare forward, a smirk on her slender lips. "Cause technically the impulsive sexual behavior occurred before you hit your head, right??"

Natasha didn't reply at first, but instead reached for her bottle of water. "Do you think I'm a terrible person?"

"No!" Vanessa sharply replied. "Of course I don't! Don't listen to what mom and dad think. If they had their way, I would be a submissive little Asian girl who didn't speak her mind and you would be married to some rich snob."

"But I did make a pretty stupid mistake," Natasha slowly opened her bottle of water and took a sip. "They have a right to be mad."

"Oh fuck them!" Vanessa bluntly remarked. "Why do you even care what they think? The whole fundraiser is a sham. It's a joke."

"I can't disagree with that," She confessed. "I-

"And you gotta get rid of The Pussy," Vanessa continued, shaking her head in confusion. "I don't even get where this guy came from and why you still have him around?"

"It's hard to explain-

"Well, you should anyway."

The two young women fell silent as they got into the city and a sense of dread filled Natasha. Her life was still up in the air. She wasn't working for a few weeks, still 'recovering' from an accident that her family wanted to pretend didn't happen, instead focusing how she 'changed' since it occurred. Cliff didn't accept what she wanted and wouldn't go away. Her sister didn't realize what was going on and unfortunately, Natasha couldn't tell her the whole truth.

Glancing at Vanessa, she smiled. "Thank you for taking me away from it all today. I really needed it."

"Hey, today wasn't just for you, Miss Center of the Universe," A smile crossed her lips and still keeping her eyes on the road, she reached out, her fingers gently touching Natasha's arm. "Sometimes I need an escape too. I'm fortunate that the bulk of my life is okay, although lately, I feel as though something is missing."

Natasha opened her mouth to speak, but before she had a chance, Vanessa cut her off.

"And don't say a baby, cause we both know that isn't it," Her words were gleeful and caused Natasha to laugh. Since getting married, their mother had bombarded Vanessa with questions on when she would finally 'settle down' and have a child or two. The couple wasn't ready and weren't even certain it was something they wanted. "Mom's already addressed that topic."

"Hey, she knows she's got no chance with me," Natasha quickly remarked. "So she's grasping at straws."

"It isn't like she likes kids anyway, she hated us."

"She didn't hate us," Natasha shook her head. "She is...I don't know."

"Afraid of how we represent her?"

"Maybe, a little bit," Natasha nodded. "I think you're right."

"I know I'm right, little sister."

Natasha was relieved that they didn't go back to the topic of her uncle's party three weeks earlier. Although she was having an easier time laughing about the whole thing now, she still felt a little sensitive about the night. It wasn't like she was a kid in her first year of university; she was an adult. It wasn't appropriate behavior, especially for that specific function.

"Do you think I drink too much?" Natasha asked her sister. "I'm trying to see why I did it." She pointed to her forehead, even though she knew it was unlikely that Vanessa was looking in her direction. "I can't even explain it."

"Why do you feel the need to explain it?" Vanessa shrugged. "You were living, Nat. That's what you are supposed to be doing. I mean, it probably wasn't the best time or place..."

"See, that's what I mean? Why did I choose *that* time and place?"

"To rebel? To react?" Vanessa said before quietly pondering her thoughts for a few minutes. "Because you were stressed out?"

"Maybe." Natasha replied sorrowfully and looked out the window. They were now back in the city and getting closer to her apartment building.

"Look, it doesn't matter, the point is that you need to forgive yourself and let it pass," Vanessa said as she turned the Jeep down Natasha's street. "Shit happens. It's done. You can't turn back. It's a funny story and I'm not making light of it cause I know you were hurt, but you're okay, right?"

She pulled the Jeep up in front of Natasha's apartment and put it in park. Pushing her sunglasses to the top of her head, Vanessa turned toward her. "You are okay? You would tell me otherwise?"

"Yes," Natasha said after a short hesitation as she unfastened her seat belt and pulled her sister into a hug. A gentle coconut scent filled her lungs as she felt Vanessa hug her back, before she moved away. Grabbing her phone, a quick glance brought her back to reality. "Oh fuck! Well, it was a great day."

"Who is it? The Pussy?" Vanessa asked with a snicker.

"No, it's dad. He wants to come see me."

"Oh shit."

"I haven't talked to him since that night."

"You may as well get it over with, Nat."

"I know," She agreed and slowly opened the door of the Jeep.

"Let me know how it goes."

"I will," Natasha climbed out of the vehicle and landed on the pavement. Closing the door, she smiled at her sister. "Thanks Van."

She simply smiled in return, glanced in the mirror and pulled forth from the curb. Natasha slowly made her way into the building and thought back to that night at the posh hotel down the street. If she could turn back time; would she?

# Chapter Six

Her dad wasn't the only person trying to contact her that day. In the elevator, Natasha discovered another message from Cliff; it had been one of several attempts since their last conversation, a few days earlier. Her fingers shook as she deleted it and inhaled a tear that was threatening to leap from the corner of her right eye. Biting her lip, she pushed the unpleasantness aside and decided that she could only face one battle at a time; the first was with her father.

Back in her apartment, she cherished a few still moments to reflect, to stare out the window at the beautiful beach and to consider what to say when he arrived. Nothing came to her. If only she understood her recent actions, but Natasha was confused about everything lately and wasn't able to put it into words. She hid from others how disorientated she sometimes felt, how strange the woman in the mirror seemed to her, even though there were fragments that she knew all too well. No one would understand and the last thing Natasha wanted to do, was to alarm her family.

Natasha's thoughts were cut off when a buzzer abruptly alerted her that someone was at the door. Jumping, she never grew accustom to the shrill sound that interrupted the silence. For the amount of rent she paid, one would think they could throw a more pleasant interruption to let her know that someone was at the door, rather than a noise that sounded like a fire alarm.

*Fucking money gluttonous landlords, probably got a deal on this model.*

Pushing this last, unexpected thought from her mind, she checked the main entrance to make sure it was her father and promptly let him in. He arrived at her door much in the same manner he would to meet a new real estate client; formal and fake. In fact, she was surprised he didn't reach out, shake her hand and introduce himself, because everything else about his manner sent the message that he was there for a serious matter. There would be no coddling or hugging his little girl. In fact, the last time he hugged her was when she graduated from medical school, years earlier.

"Hi dad," She heard the voice of a little girl when she spoke. Gerald Parsons stood tall in the hallway, well over 6 feet in height, with a strong presence that could not be dismissed. His smile was relaxed, his blue eyes studying her, as if not completely sure of what to say. He was handsome, once with dark blond hair similar to Natasha's, but today it was a salt and pepper, which only seemed to accent his eyes more intensely. It made him somehow seem more accessible, less intimidating and maybe even-

*He cheats on mom! Oh my God, why hadn't I seen it before?*

There was no evidence or explanation behind this random thought, just a feeling that hit her like a ton of bricks. He was charming and in the past, had arrogantly admitted that this was part of his sales tactics in real estate. His focus had always been women. She knew many women who found him appealing and several who had even commented on his looks over the years. At the time, she had taken the comments to her own ego's door, somehow accepting that he was merely an extension of her, rather than an object of desire.

*He probably has some twenty year-old whore stashed away somewhere.*

Stunned by her own thoughts, she opened her mouth to talk and nothing came out. Instead, she stopped and signaled for him to go into her apartment. Where the hell were these ideas coming from? It never, ever would've occurred to her that their dad would cheat on their mom: until that minute. She felt the impulse to run to her phone and text Vanessa.

"Umm..come in dad, I just put on a pot of coffee," She pointed toward the kitchen, where the percolator was making the gurgling noise associated with a completed pot.

*I even buy his favorite kind of coffee! What the fuck is wrong with me?*

"I have to send a text quickly."

"That's ok," Her father gave her his smooth, relaxed smile and started toward the kitchen. "I'm going to make myself at home and grab a cup."

"Please do," Natasha attempted to sound natural, but discovered a glimmer of anxiety in her voice. If he noticed, there were no indications, as he sauntered into the kitchen and started going through her cupboards.

*He's been here a million fucking times and always opens the wrong doors.*

Grabbing her phone, she didn't hesitate to text her sister.

*Do you think dad cheats on mom?*

A minute later...

*Dah.....*

Then,

*Wait, are you just figuring this out? Remember when they had your graduation party? Your friend with the fake tits said how hot he was and you brushed it off? I told you something was up there.*

She had. It was true. Yet, it never sunk in until that moment.

Feeling pretty stupid and naïve, Natasha bit her lower lip and sat her phone back down on the coffee table and put on a bright face as she entered the kitchen. Her dad was leaning up against the cupboard and sipping on his coffee.

"You must've inherited your great taste in coffee from me, Nat," He gave her a gentle smile and took another drink.

*Maybe I've also inherited some of your less desirable traits along with it.*

"Want to come into the living room?" Natasha chose to ignore both his last comment and her thoughts. Without bothering to make a cup of coffee for herself, she headed into the next room and could tell he was right behind her. "So what is going on?"

"I thought I should drop in on my way home. We haven't had a conversation since your uncle's fundraising night," His words somehow sounded sharper, causing a tension below her neck and she winced, feeling the heaviness of early suddenly return. Sitting on the couch, she decided to remain quiet.

"So, how is your head?" His question seemed to ease the tension as he glanced toward the scar.

"Fine, it's healing nicely."

"And you? How are you feeling?"

It felt like a loaded question, but she decided it was best to be brief. "I'm fine."

"So, about the party," He put his cup on the small table in front of them and she found herself staring at it, noting that he ignored a coaster that was less than an inch away. His voice held a hint of anger and although it was subtle, she could feel it in his words.

"Your uncle was a little concerned about your demeanor that night and to be honest, so am I."

She remained silent. He waited; as if he knew this was the place where Natasha would normally apologize. This time, she did not.

"What was that about?" Although she could see a touch of frustration, a smile attempted to curl his upper lip. "I mean, it was hardly appropriate behavior for an adult woman, a doctor, let alone at her uncle's political fundraiser. There are so many reasons why you acted strangely, that night."

She remained tight lipped.

"Your mother and I were discussing it and thought maybe you were working too much. Years in university, studying hard to become a physician and trust me, I know the pressures of school. When I was in university it wasn't exactly an easy road, plus the hours since are long and exhausting, just as they are for you as a physician," He paused for a moment. "I suppose in your situation, it's normal that the pressures could get to you and push you too far. We all lived through times when we went a little over the edge and I know there were several times when your mother had to visit a psychologist and it's nothing to be ashamed of-

"Dad, I'm not crazy." Natasha heard the words shoot out of her mouth.

"I'm not saying crazy," He put his hand up in self-defense. "I'm proposing that you're feeling the strain of your lifestyle and maybe you need some extra time to…relax, maybe look into some anxiety medications or talk to someone. I mean, you literally deal with life and death every day and hey," He shrugged dramatically. "I would likely do something crazy like you did at the party, if I were in your shoes. Things happen."

Natasha was stunned by his suggestion. He thought she was mad!

….it would give you a chance to get away from it all, time to think..."

"What?"

"Your aunt's place? In Alberta?" He repeated his words. "I was thinking maybe you should go see them, get out of town for awhile and relax in the country."

*He wants me out of the city so I don't embarrass him or uncle Kramer while he is trying to make headway in the political arena. With the election coming up, he's scared I will do something to mess up his campaign.*

"Ah, God, mom's redneck relatives?" Natasha shot back, noting the shock in her father's eyes. She never talked back to him. Never. "No thanks!"

"Natasha, they aren't exactly 'rednecks', we aren't talking a reality television show. I meant the country air might do you some good," He calmly recommended, his blue eyes attempted to seduce her into agreeing with him. Was that how he picked up the women he screwed on the side; his power of persuasion and his innocent, manipulating eyes? "They do live in a rural area in Alberta, it's pretty quiet, obviously nothing like Vancouver, but I think you would enjoy it."

"I seriously doubt it."

"Look, I'll set it up for you," He rose from the couch, briefly glancing at the abandoned cup on her table. Did he ever finish coffee that she prepared for him? Suddenly her mind jumped back to all the times she threw out an almost full cup of coffee that he left sitting on her table, as if she were a waitress who was supposed to clean up after him. "And I will get back to you in a day or two."

He headed for the door, leaving her stunned.

*He ignored everything I fucking said and is going to do what he wants anyway!!*

"Dad!" She jumped up from the couch and rushed behind him, almost tripping on a shoe. "No, I didn't say-

But he was already opening the door, disregarding her words when she caught up. Natasha opened her mouth to say more, but felt as though she were slapped in the face when she saw Cliff standing on the other side.

Without giving it a thought, she heard herself loudly proclaim, "Fuck! Not *you* too!"

# Chapter Seven

❦

Both men seemed to be stunned by her comment. Oddly, her father acted more taken back by her reaction than Clifford. Suddenly, Gerald Parsons seemed much smaller than when he first arrived, shrinking beside Clifford, he was no longer as intimidating. Opening his mouth to comment, he then closed it tightly and shuffled uncomfortably, as if he was too stunned to talk. It was a side of her father that Natasha didn't recognize and for a second, it made her feel more powerful.

Meanwhile, Cliff's face was expressionless. His hazel eyes eased from her face to Gerald Parsons', as if trying to understand the situation. He remained tight-lipped and relatively serene, as heaviness filled the room, making it almost impossible for Natasha to breathe. In his silence, he said a great deal.

Such arrogance! Both of them were trying to control her in their own way. Clifford had hoped to take advantage of her 'confused' state after the accident to draw her further into a whole new world, while her dad wanted to push her out of town! It hadn't been evident to her until that moment, as they both stood there with awkward expressions on their faces. Her father was the first to talk.

"Natasha, you clearly don't mean that, sweetheart." He gingerly pointed in Cliff's direction; a smile attempted to curve his lips, but didn't quite reach. His apparent shot at helping Clifford out went unnoticed.

"You're upset and I totally understand, ever since your accident you've been acting very strangely, so-

"I'm not acting strangely," Natasha heard her own voice abruptly cutting off her father, something she probably had never done before in her life. She felt tension collecting in her expression, while her eyes shot darts through both of the men who stood before her. "Just because I'm not behaving how you think I should, doesn't mean something is wrong with me."

"Come on," Her father eased into a patronizing smile, another thing she hadn't recognized until this moment. How many times had he done the same thing in the past and she had misread it? He quickly glanced at Clifford, who seemed unmoved. "You obviously aren't yourself. You would never talk this way to Cliff or me, for that matter."

"Dad, you've only met Cliff once before, so how would you know how I talk to him? I mean, really? You don't know anything about him," She pointed in his direction, returning her gaze to Gerald Parsons. "A five minute conversation a at coffee shop hardly qualifies you to make such an assessment."

"Which is," She continued, briefly looking into Cliff's eyes, then back at her father, as he stood in the same spot, mouth opened ajar while his eyes were lost in a state of confusion, "probably what you do in the real estate world, but in the real life, it's not the same." She paused for a brief moment. "You guys think that I'm crazy, but I'm beginning to think that it is the other way around."

"Natasha," Her father's voice set the same tone as when she was a child and had dropped crumbs on the kitchen floor. "Come on, that's hardly fair…"

"It's hardly fair to insinuate that I'm 'not myself' since the accident, as if that is necessarily a bad thing by the way, but I can't point out that you both are trying to control my life? Maybe you need to go visit mom's redneck relatives in Alberta and spend some tranquil time in the country and Cliff…"

Not yet sure how to finish that sentence, she felt a momentary flash of compassion, but disappeared as quickly as it arose. "I don't even know

what to tell you. How dare you come into my life and attempt to turn it upside down, steal it away from me as if nothing matters."

"Natasha, I think you're being a little dramatic," Her father's comments sounded more like a relentless attack, as if he was letting her know this conversation was not over. "Whether you want to believe it or not, you're a well established doctor who's respected in the community and you can't start acting erratically or it'll ruin the reputation that you worked so hard to build. I think you should consider that a little more carefully in the future."

"Dad, I highly doubt it's my reputation you're concerned about," Natasha remained strong in her bearing, even though her heart was pounding wildly while her face grew hotter by the moment. "My reputation is fine."

"So far, only some of your extracurricular activities might affect it," His eyes blazed in fury, challenging her and for a moment, she almost felt herself cave. Taking a deep breath, she turned her head.

"Why don't you worry about your own extracurricular activities, dad, and I'll worry about mine."

The words tore through him like a lightening bolt and he immediately deflated, shrinking back in shame, he said nothing and walked out the door. Clifford appeared crestfallen, stumbling forward as if she had invited him into her apartment.

"Cliff, I'm sorry, but I think you should go home."

Shutting the door, she leaned against it and felt moisture collecting under her bra, as her heart raced fitfully and tears suddenly sprang to her eyes. She knew that she had done the right thing, said the right words, but yet she suddenly was left feeling exhausted and drained, as if the two men had stolen the last bit of spirit she had for the day. Locking the door, she dragged her body across the room to sink into the couch, where she stared at the horizon.

Her tears were dedicated to everything that day had brought with it: the realizations about her father, her disappointment when coming to terms about the man he really was and intense loneliness that stemmed from her disconnect to her blood family. Not that it mattered that Vanessa was of no biological connection, but it still felt strange to be a universe apart from the family you were born into, almost as if *she* were the adopted child, rather than her sister.

Natasha also had some regret about her manner of dealing with Clifford. She should've allowed him inside the apartment and had an honest conversation with him, since he had been more than reasonable with her. He wasn't the bad guy in this situation. It wasn't fair how she attacked him. However, at the moment, his unexpected arrival was the straw that broke the camel's back. It was about the timing, she resolved. Timing is everything.

A smile rose to her lips when Natasha wondered if he was still standing outside of her door, with that dumbfound look on his face. It was cruel to think that way, but suddenly she didn't care. She was tired of society, her family and friends telling her how she was supposed to act; what was right and what was wrong. It wasn't a matter of living by a moral code, creating by someone outside of one's self, but surviving with what felt right.

Thinking back to her earlier question to Vanessa, she grabbed her phone and checked her messages. Slightly surprised to not notice anything new from Cliff – from either right before or after his impromptu visit – she felt a void that Natasha wanted, yet now didn't know what to do with, creating a discomfort she hadn't expected.

Taking a deep breath, she scanned her messages. She found one from her mother, several more from Vanessa inquiring about her visit with dad and finally, another from an old friend she hadn't spoken to since the night of her uncle's fundraising campaign.

Exhausted, Natasha dropped the phone on the couch and stood up, discovering that her right leg suddenly felt heavy, as did her arm. Fear caused her to freeze on the spot, knowing exactly what this meant. Feeling tears burning in her eyes, she fell flat back on the couch and as sounds that resembled that of a wounded animal escaped from her lips; loud cries shook her entire body as she crumbled and watched the dark clouds once again roll in outside her window.

*It's already happening.*

Staring out the window, a moment of serenity blanketed her body, suddenly making her feel secure. She was protected. No one could hurt her. It was going to be okay.

A new text message interrupted her thoughts. Natasha glanced at her phone to discover that her sister was once again attempting to get in touch with her.

*Are you ok?*

A smile crept on Natasha's lips, it astonished her what a strong connection they had; that in her silence, her sister sensed her sorrow in that moment.

Picking up her phone, she bit her bottom lip and replied.

*No, but I will be.*

# Chapter Eight

The next morning was another story. Natasha awoke to sunshine streaming in her window, turning her bedroom into a place of peace and tranquility. She felt a bit groggy at first, as if hung over from a wild evening of drinking rather than an emotional night of crying agonizing tears, followed by bouts of anger, followed by more tears. Finally, exhaustion had won over and she fell into a peaceful sleep that brought with it, dreams of her running on the beach.

*Hmm…that's a good idea. Maybe I will do that later.*

Ever since the accident, she had to put aside her usual exercise routine, knowing that it was important to allow her body time to heal.

*After all, haven't I pushed my luck enough these days? I've already embarrassed the family without someone discovering my body passed out while running along the Seawall. I mean what would people think, right? That I'm an addict misplaced from the downtown eastside?*

Oh, the Downtown Eastside! That had been a touchy subject a few years ago. After her training had been complete, Natasha's first instinct was to work in this poverty stricken portion of Vancouver, assisting those who needed it the most. Perhaps she had been slightly naïve about how much positive she could infuse in the area that many had long given up on. How many times had her father avoided even driving near Main and Hastings, uninterested or perhaps, not caring about the many people lying on the streets, lost in their own underprivileged existence.

Drugs, prostitution, mental illness; all trademarks of one of Canada's poorest neighborhoods and something that was often the topic of jokes to the ignorant.

Not that she always had such an open-minded position in the matter. Her family had shown interest in helping those in need, but only if they were able to keep at arm's length of the actual people. She grew up assuming that those who lived in the impoverished area were there for a reason – poor life choices, laziness, and stupidity – this was the impression her parents had used to segregate their class from those they viewed as beneath them.

Vanessa was the person who opened her eyes. Working on a story about poverty and homelessness for a national magazine, she decided that the best way to get a true portrait of the desperate situation was to speak directly to the people in one of Canada's poorest neighborhoods, a place that was practically in her own backyard. She mainly spoke to women – many of which were prostitutes, heavily addicted to drugs or alcohol – all of which were receptive and honest about the miseries of their everyday lives. They talked about their concerns, the dangers and brutality that they often faced, along with the heartbreaks that surrounded them on the street. Many were desperate people who slowly fell off the grid, forgotten by society, mimicked by those who held no compassion or understanding of their situations.

Feeling grounded by the experience, Vanessa told the story of having a long conversation with a young Cambodian woman named Andrea. Like Vanessa, she was also exacted from an improvised community as a baby; however that's where their similarities ended. Andrea was addicted to heroin and performing sexual favors in exchange for money to sustain her habit. She talked about years of sexual abuse from her 'white father' until the age of 16, when she ran away with a boyfriend who promised her the world. It didn't exactly turn out as she had expected.

After disclosing painful stories in exchange for some money and her favorite meal at McDonald's, Vanessa was astounded and saddened by what Andrea told her. When their interview was finished, she didn't hesitate to embrace the young woman and express her gratitude to her for being so candid. Vanessa then asked why she felt so comfortable telling her so many private details.

Expecting to hear that it was their shared ethnicity that made the young, homeless woman so forthcoming, she was stunned when Andrea turned to her and with a vacant smile, gestured toward the streets where she lived and responded.

"I have nothing to lose."

Vanessa sobbed as she retold the story to Natasha, who was also disturbed by the reality they had been sheltered from as children. This stirring account was a form of encouragement to Natasha to continue her studies in order to later serve the Downtown Eastside, even if it was a little bit; she wanted to make a difference. Of course, once Natasha finished school and announced these intentions at her graduation party, her family quickly insisted that she reconsider this decision. It was better, they insisted, that she got her feet wet at a 'nice' downtown office, before plunging into the hardships and despair that the downtown eastside would introduce into her life.

Naively, possibly a little frightened and vulnerable, she stupidly agreed with her parents and eventually took a job with a group of pretentious doctors, that were more interested in talking about their next exotic vacation than serving those in need. They weren't interested in helping the world, but helping themselves, and she decided it made her feel like she was guilty by association. She grew resentful, then depressed.

Feeling released from those chains that had kept her hostage for the last few years, Natasha suddenly felt a burst of energy on that Sunday morning and impulsively turned on her music. The relaxing vibe of "Stolen Dance" flowed through her apartment, as Natasha danced round in a long, white T-shirt that barely covered her childlike, pink underwear and short, tanned legs. Her dark blonde hair gently caressed her shoulders as she moved, the soft waves occasionally reaching out to touch her face, quickly falling back into place, only to return again, as she moved to the music.

She was a terrible dancer. It was an on-going joke between her and Vanessa, who would practically be in tears from giggling each time she watched Natasha dance; whether it were across her apartment floor or the dance floor of a popular night club. It was something she now exaggerated to make even worse, simply to see her sister laugh.

Not everyone shared her sense of humor. Natasha had an ex-boyfriend who made great efforts to instruct her how to dance like a 'normal human being' before they attended a wedding together. Of course, in sheer rebellion, she endured his lessons then danced in her usual, moronic way at the reception. He walked off the floor when she started shaking her head around in a ridiculous manner, actually causing the middle-aged woman nearby to tap her on the shoulder and ask if she was okay.

Her father intimidated her and insisted she not dance at any family functions. Ever. Natasha agreed with reluctant obedience.

Nearly as bad as her dancing, was her singing. The worst possible combination, as Vanessa insisted, was when Natasha decided to do both together. Of course, Natasha only sang the chorus because she rarely knew the remainder of the song and it was always off key. In fact, she hadn't realized how bad her singing was until Vanessa recorded her rendition of "Lucy in the Sky with Diamonds" and played it back to her.

She was terrible. Natasha was stunned. Briefly filled with sadness and disappointment, she then saw the humor; it was *so* terrible, that it was hilarious!

So now, the ongoing joke was how Natasha was planning to audition for one of the reality shows based on either singing or dancing. It often sent Vanessa into an automatic hysterics, while managing to personally insult others. One lady actually ragged her out for not taking it seriously and how she was, in turn, insulting all 'real artists who work hard to make it'. To that, Natasha rolled her eyes and laughed.

It wasn't that she didn't respect artists; it was that she thought anyone who took themselves that seriously, were up for a rude awakening. Just ask the doctor in her office that looked down at patients who came in with STIs and ranted about how 'easy' it was to practice safe sex, so why weren't people doing it? That was, until she came into Natasha's office one day and discretely confessed she had contracted syphilis.

She appeared to be in shock that she, a doctor, could also be a normal human being as well.

The morning escaped Natasha, as she danced around, turned on the coffee, then returned to the living room to dance around some more, repeating the song again and again. Finally, exhausted, she allowed the songs to change and returned to the kitchen to pour a cup of coffee. Inhaling it, she cringed a bit, deciding it was quite strong; then again, wasn't it always that way? Hadn't she just filled her cup with a lot of milk and sugar to hide the bitter taste of the overpriced coffee? Hadn't she mindlessly bought it because her dad insisted it was the best?

Glancing at the empty coffee cup in the sink, the one he had neglected the night before, she couldn't help but feel some resentment. Opening the cupboard door, she plucked out a container of coffee that her father loved so much and threw it in the trash.

"Today, I shall buy a new kind of coffee," She said out loud, her thoughts suddenly interrupted by the doorbell. "But first, I shall answer the door."

She giggled and assumed it was her sister dropping by, as she often did on Sunday.

It wasn't Vanessa. It was her mother.

"Natasha, you shouldn't be opening the door dressed like that," Cynthia Parsons gave a disapproving look at the long white T-shirt that was barely hiding her butt and glanced at a nearby clock. "It's almost noon, shouldn't you be getting dressed soon?"

Giving a casual shrug, she turned and walked toward the couch, making sure that her shirt lifted, displaying her barely covered ass. "I'm on sick leave, I didn't realize I had to have such an organized schedule."

Sitting down, she watched her mother's forehead wrinkle in a frown, the rest of her face quickly falling in line. "I dropped by to talk to you about your trip to Alberta."

"My what?" Natasha snorted and started to laugh. "What's this trip you speak of?"

"Your father and I think it would be good for you if you got out of town for a few days. I think a break from the city would be exactly what you need," A smug smile attempted to take over her lips, but seemed to fail. "It would be a nice time of year, especially in the country. Beautiful weather, the flowers coming out...."

"All things that happen here in Vancouver too." Natasha couldn't help but remind her.

"With less...confusion and noise of the city." Her mother continued.

Biting her lip, thinking of the various choices in front of her, including the many text messages sitting on her phone from everyone from fair-weathered friends to her nemesis Clifford, Natasha stunned both of them when she nodded and said. "Ok, I'll do it."

# Chapter Nine

※♦♦

She said it, but she didn't actually mean it. Sure, it crossed her mind that some time out of the city would be nice, but a hick town in Southern Alberta didn't exactly carry much appeal. In truth, Natasha scarcely knew her relatives that lived there, so it would be incredibly awkward to spend time with any of them, let alone stay in their homes.

Although Natasha had traveled there as a child, the trips were limited to funerals or a rare visit. Cynthia Parsons often denied where she came from and Natasha thought it stemmed from shame. Her family was hardly the most sophisticated group of people on the planet and although nice, they looked at Cynthia and her children as if they were aliens that landed from some other planet.

The last time she had been to Hennessey, Natasha was a teenager. She remembered asking her mother if the long, curious stares were because she was dressed differently than everyone else. Was it because she stood out? At the age of 17, she desperately wanted to fit in and was sensitive to local town folk's probing eyes, as she and her mom walked through town.

"No, they just don't know you," Her mother's response was blunt, if not slightly humored. "They're attempting to figure out who you are."

"Do they need to know who I am?" Natasha heard the irritation creep into her voice, as she self-consciously glanced in the direction of an old man who did nothing to hide his curious stares. "Is it any of their business who I am?"

Humor touched her mother's lips, an unexpected smile uplifted the corners and she sniffled. "No, but they like to believe it's their business."

"But mom, they're looking at you the same way," Natasha muttered, moving closer to Cynthia, as if she were to somehow protect her from their probing eyes. "And you used to live here."

"Maybe they don't know me anymore either." She muttered back and turned into a small grocery store.

At the time, Natasha took her statement literally, rather than concentrating on the fact that perhaps her mother was a whole new person now, after spending years in one of the largest cities in Canada. What made her move? When did she reach this decision? It was rare for Cynthia Parsons to even reference her life before moving to British Columbia. Why was she so secretive?

These questions were never asked and the answers weren't volunteered. That particular visit to the town was brief, her mother signed some sort of family papers and they left the next day. Since both her grandparents were dead, Natasha assumed their visit had to do with property or something of that nature. It hadn't occurred to her to ask about that either.

She had, however, met her aunt Flora and found her interesting.

Flora was vastly different from Cynthia Parsons. She wore jeans and a T-shirt, rather than dressing to impress (then again, her mom was working at the bank at that time and probably didn't possess a lot of 'casual' clothing) and her dark blonde hair, pulled back in a messy bun. She had bright blue eyes, similar to her sister's and a kind smile that radiated in a way that put Natasha automatically at ease. Then again, Flora was an elementary school teacher at the time, so clearly had a kind heart to work with kids. She had since taught high school and was now retired.

The house she lived in once belonged to Natasha's grandparents and somehow landed in Flora's lap after they passed away. There was some sort of confusing story regarding an ex-husband that Natasha wasn't privy to, but apparently upon breaking up with him, her aunt moved into this house and did a few, small renovations. She enjoyed her life in the country; growing a cute little garden in the summer and cross-country skiing in the winter, she seemed content with the serenity of the rural area and although asked Natasha questions about her life in Vancouver, she didn't show a sincere interest when she suggested her aunt come for a visit.

"Flora's too busy," Cynthia insisted, almost as if answering for her older sister, rather than leaving her to sit with the possibility. An awkward silence followed and Natasha couldn't help but to feel that she somehow had crossed a line.

Flora had no children, but apparently there was still a whole lot of other relatives that Natasha hadn't met; second or third cousins, great aunts, people that she barely heard of and certainly never laid eyes on, so it would be extremely awkward to spend time with complete strangers, even if they were related.

Vanessa was stunned to hear the news.

"Was that a joke?" She sounded aghast through the phone. "Are you going to this little shit town to visit Aunt Flow and the others? How hard *did* you hit your head?"

"Calm down, don't worry," Natasha gleefully insisted. "I told mom that because I wasn't in the mood for an argument that early in the day. I have no interest or intention of going anywhere. I want to stay here, in my little apartment for the next couple of weeks, then get back to work and my normal life."

"Your life has never been normal," Vanessa insisted breathlessly and Natasha could hear traffic in the background, including the sound of a bus taking off nearby. "Don't think mom is going to let this go."

"Well, even if she doesn't, she can't force me to go there. It's not like I'm fucking seven."

"I know but still, she has a lot of time on her hands now that she retired, so she might push it farther." Vanessa cut out briefly and then continued, "If you do go, don't stay long and for God sakes, don't drink the Kool-Aid."

"Okay mom's family is bad, but they are hardly a cult."

"Don't be so sure, I've heard of cults here in western Canada."

45

"I think that's like, actually here, in BC," Natasha insisted and wandered toward her living room window, gazing out at the bright blue skies, a sudden beep pulled her back into the moment. "Oh wait a sec, Van, I have another call."

Glancing at her phone, she saw the name Clifford Rook flashing. Ignoring it, she sighed and returned to Vanessa. "Never mind, its just Cliff on the other line. I don't intend to talk to him. I think I was pretty clear last night."

"You've said that before."

"But this time, I think he may have got it."

"I think you've said that too."

"Well, regardless, I don't plan to talk to him."

"Sounds like a good idea." Vanessa agreed and suddenly her voice was clearer, as gentle music flowed in the background. "But the Pussy is pretty persistent."

"I know, but there's nothing he can say to change my mind," Natasha suddenly felt a bit light headed and made an excuse to end the conversation. Gingerly sitting on the couch, she shut her eyes and took a deep breath. Reaching out, her hand leaned against a pillow, hoping her balance would return. After a minute or two, it passed.

Her phone vibrated and she slowly reached for it, unsure if she was ready to face the world once more. Clifford had text her several times in the last two days. She deleted them. The next one was from her mom.

*I will make the arrangements and get back to you later. Is tomorrow too soon?*

Natasha let out a short laugh and deleted this message too. It wasn't necessary to answer it. She wasn't going anywhere.

The last one was from her friend Stella. She wanted to see if Natasha was 'up' for some shopping. The idea of walking through a mall seemed so meaningless to her now, just an empty activity that stole a portion of her day. She deleted this message too.

Returning her phone to the coffee table, she decided to sit on the balcony and read. When Natasha was working, it wasn't uncommon for her to require almost a year to finish reading a book. It was frustrating, but she just didn't have time to herself between her downtown office and shifts at the hospital. Sometimes it felt like people were sick more than they were healthy and it was overwhelming and sadly, not as satisfying as she would've thought while in medical school.

She was well into a chapter when she heard a knock at the door, causing her to jump and automatically resent the visitor that was taking away from her relaxing afternoon. Wasn't that what her doctor had recommended she do during her time off? Relax?

To her dismay, she found Cliff on the other side. He managed to slink by the security entrance, as if it was a step that he ignorantly felt justified in skipping. His persistence frustrating, she felt her body drain to exhaustion as soon as their eyes met.

"What are you doing here?"

"I thought we should talk," He responded evenly, no emotion in his voice.

"Look, I'm sorry about last night." She paused for a moment and noticed he was walking toward her, as if she were actually going to let him in the door. Anxiety crawled through her spine. "My father was here and he…he unnerved me and I-

Not sure how to finish this sentence, Natasha sensed that somehow Clifford already knew what she was going to say.

"I can't talk right now because I have to pack."

"Pack?" A wrinkled formed on his forehead and eyes narrowed, as if trying to determine if she was telling the truth. "Where are you going?"

"To see family in Alberta."

"Seriously?" Clifford's eyes widened in humor, while his lips fell into a relaxed grin. "The relatives in the country?"

"Yes." She snapped defensively, even though her original tone had been gentle, somewhere along the line it faded away. "Please, go home."

He looked crestfallen as she slowly eased the door close. Her heart sunk, knowing that what she did was wrong, but Natasha felt as though she were deep in the ocean and struggling to swim to shore. She didn't know how else to survive.

Glancing out the peephole, she watched as the defeated man walked away.

# Chapter Ten

"Did you ever find out what the Pussy wanted the last time he was there?" Vanessa asked, a slight echo in the phone suggested that she was in her home office. Unlike most writers, she didn't have a room full of books and papers. She kept everything filed away and the room almost empty, claiming that having 'too much stuff around' distracted her, making it difficult to finish her assignments on time. With no pictures on the wall, furniture, limited to her chair, desk, a small filing cabinet and some very basic office supplies, the room was almost bare.

"No," Natasha leaned back on her couch, her feet on the coffee table and her eyes closed. "I guess to talk."

"You know, he seems harmless, but you got to be careful. He could be crazy," Vanessa insisted, her voice continuing to echo, the sound of shuffling papers soon joined a hint of concern that unexpectedly grew in her voice. It was so unexpected that Natasha's eyes sprang open and a chill ran through her spine, as she gave a quick glance around her apartment. "I don't want to scare you, but you don't know with people. Sometimes the littlest thing can make them snap."

*Like hitting their head against the wall and getting a slight concussion?*

"Clifford is harmless," She said, but Natasha lacked conviction and therefore wasn't able to convince either her or Vanessa that it was true. After all, up until the last few days, he hardly left her alone; the texting had not completely subsided. It wouldn't either.

"He's not accepting your decision and I don't like that," Vanessa was persistent and it was difficult to argue her point. Not that Natasha could exactly divulge the truth in the matter. If she ever did, Vanessa would think it was *her* that was crazy, not Clifford.

"It doesn't matter, I'm taking off today for Alberta, so I won't have to worry about him showing up at my door while I'm there," Natasha said airily, in hopes of returning the conversation to its original vibe.

"So when did this happen?" Vanessa said with a giggle following her words. "When did you suddenly decide that you want to go to this hick town? The last time I checked, you had no intentions on leaving Vancouver for the remainder of your time off. You don't expect me to believe that you're sudden change of heart is to avoid your stalker?"

"He's not a stalker, just a little too..."

"Persistent? Emotional? Crazy?" Vanessa said, her voice lifting slightly with the last word. "Or is it cause you let mom and dad bully you?"

"I didn't let anyone bully me," Natasha attempted to defend herself, but secretly wondered if that was true? She quickly dismissed the idea, refusing to give it another thought. "I suddenly realized that this was the universe's way of telling me that maybe I need a break from Vancouver. You know, with everything that has been going on lately-

"What has been going on lately is that you are suddenly discovering that our parents have constantly manipulated you," Vanessa said, her voice overflowing with confidence and assertiveness. "You have to start doing what you want, not allowing them to guilt or bully you. You need to start living the life you....

Although Natasha knew her sister meant well, there were times that she was almost doing the very thing that she accused others of doing. She knew Vanessa loved her and only wanted the best, but there were times when she was as pushy as the others, except her encouragement was usually in a slightly different direction. Still, it was a push that Natasha didn't need. It was hard to think clearly when there were too many voices talking at the same time. Perhaps this trip to the country was exactly what she needed.

"...he was right too, the best advice I ever got." Vanessa finished her sentence and Natasha found herself suddenly very alert, wondering what she missed.

"Absolutely!" She enthusiastically agreed and a smile curved her lips. "I promise to work on that, Van."

There was a hesitation on the other end of the line, followed by, "Well, that's good." Another hesitation followed and silence.

"Okay, well, I should go and finish packing. Mom's taking me to the airport in a couple of hours and I'm only half ready."

"Text me and let me know what is happening," Vanessa continued her instructions. "When are you coming back?"

"I'm not sure. I haven't booked anything yet, I wanted to keep my options open."

"Good idea!" Vanessa said with a stamp of approval in her voice. "That way, if you hate it, you can come back anytime and if you...find it relaxing, you can stay longer. When do you have to return to work?"

"Two weeks? Maybe two weeks and a few days?" Natasha glanced around the room, but was unable to find a calendar close at hand. "Anyway, I would rather play it by ear, as you say. Who knows? Maybe that country air will do me good."

A snicker could be heard on the other end of the phone and Natasha mindlessly joined in.

"Stop that!! Hennessy isn't that bad!"

"Sure, when you are talking about a bottle of cognac," Vanessa said, referring to a popular liquor brand.

"Are you kidding, that's the kind of thing that got me into this mess in the first place," Natasha said, thinking back to the many drinks she had on the night of her uncle's political fundraiser. Alcohol tended to get her in trouble.

"Fine then," Vanessa agreed, another giggling following. "Be careful and text me when you get there and let me know what is happening."

"Will do."

The next few hours were a blur. Trying to decide what kind of clothing would be appropriate for Hennessy was a challenge: was May a warm month in Alberta? How should she dress? Should she take along some skirts or stick with jeans? She didn't really want to fit in, but at the same time, she didn't really want to stand out. This was what Natasha hated about packing. It was deciding on what she would actually need and wading through an endless 'what if' list in her mind.

Outside of her professional life, Natasha hated to make decisions. The possibilities for everything in life seemed so endless and the analytical part of her wanted to go over every possibility carefully, in order to make the right decision. It didn't matter if it was packing for a trip or buying a car (which is one of the main reasons why she did not have a car yet) each decision was agonizing and stressful. She hated it.

Not that it mattered that day. Once Cynthia rushed through the door and announced that they were going to be late, Natasha made some fast wardrobe decisions, while her mother checked that everything in the house was unplugged, locked up or turned off, before they dashed out of the apartment and into the car downstairs. Although her mother was clearly stressed as they practically flew to the airport, Natasha calmly pointed out that they *did* manage to get there on time and all was well.

Her mother gave her a quick, unexpected hug and hurried her away to drop off her luggage.

Natasha compared navigating an airport to being in a complicated maze; mindlessly going through all their procedures, moving forward, to go through yet another one until you were finally able to board a plane at the end of it all. It was another reason why she hated to fly so much. Busy airports were chaotic, packing the correct amount and kind of clothing was stressful, not to mention deciding on the destination, when to go and what you could and couldn't have on your carry on. Was it just her imagination, or did that seem to change all the time?

Once on the plane, Natasha felt more relaxed. Seated next to the window, she would be able to enjoy every moment of the flight; the takeoff, as they bolted into the air, watching the world become smaller beneath them and floated among the fluffy, white clouds. It was her idea of heaven.

Vanessa was the opposite. She loved to travel, didn't mind airports, but hated being on a plane. They made terrible travel companions or great travel companions, depending on how you looked at it.

Awaiting the takeoff, she reached in her pocket for the iPod Shuffle she had rushed back into the apartment to get before leaving – something that her mother had not appreciated and grimaced, biting her lip in frustration, even though it only took another half second to grab and rush out. Slipping the buds in her ears, she pressed the middle of the tiny, pink device, filling her ears with the relaxing nature sounds that helped to center her during times of stress. She actually carried the device with her at work, occasionally slipping into the bathroom and listening to a few seconds of the tranquil sounds, in hopes of getting into a better frame of mind and spirit.

On instinct, her eyes flew open as a young woman that Natasha recognized as having an intellectual disability, sat beside her. She appeared to be ushered in by an older lady, with dry, graying hair pulled up in a messy bun. She had lines on her face that appeared harshly etched on her chin and forehead while the woman's cheeks were smooth, yet sagging at the same time. She avoided Natasha's eyes as she sat down, while the young woman didn't stop staring.

Quickly turning off and removing her iPod, she turned to the young woman and smiled, "Hi!"

The girl continued to stare at her, transfixed and then her eyes glanced down at the shiny iPod. "Is that yours?" Her voice lifted with the last word, as if it were unbelievable that Natasha could possess such an item.

"Yes, it is," She awkwardly smiled. "I thought I-

"Can I have it?" The girl posed the question, as if it were completely normal to do so, reaching for the pink iPod, just as the guardian abruptly spoke up.

"Cassie! No!" She was sharp, alarming Natasha as much as the young woman, who quickly drew her hand back.

"That's fine, don't worry-

Natasha attempted to speak, but her words were quickly cut off.

"Cassie, we talked about this earlier," The older lady acted as if Natasha wasn't there, not even glancing in her direction, she scolded the young woman and then leaned back in the chair and closed her eyes.

Cassie gave Natasha a helpless look before linking her hands together and quietly sitting in her seat.

Feeling awkward, Natasha twirled the cord around the small device, sat it on the tray she had pulled out to place a book on and decided to simply enjoy the rest of the flight. Staring out the window, Natasha found herself absorbed in the take off and finally the beautiful clouds that floated along side the window. Feeling completely light, she turned her head and reached for her iPod – but it wasn't there.

Pushing the tray back, she looked for her iPod; it wasn't on the floor and when she unbuckled her seatbelt and stood up, it wasn't between the seats or anywhere to be seen. Glancing toward the young woman beside her, she was a quite pale, purposely avoiding Natasha's eye.

Sitting back down, she anxiously checked her pockets, carry on and the floor once again. People across the aisle were looking at her curiously, while the older who sat on the aisle seat appeared to be sleeping. The disabled girl kept turning her head to avoid Natasha's eyes, swallowing hard, she pursed her lips together and her cheeks grew pink.

"Did you see my iPod?" Her question came out much harsher than Natasha intended, causing the older lady's eyes to fly open and the people across the aisle to turn their attention toward them. "It was just sitting on the tray," She pointed to the table she had already pushed back into place. She briefly considered that maybe that point would be held against her. "Now it's gone."

The young woman now had tears in her eyes, while the older lady beside her glared at Natasha. "Are you accusing Cassie of taking it?"

"Well, it *is* missing and she tried to take it earlier, so it *is* a possibility, right?" Natasha heard the words flying out of her mouth, followed by a gasp from across the aisle, just as the flight attendant was walking by with a drink in her hand. She stopped.

"Is everything okay here?" She gave her professional smile, her deeply tanned skin glowing along with her dark, burgundy lipstick.

"I'm missing my iPod and earlier, this young woman was attempting to take it," Natasha spoke with confidence, although she was quickly getting the sense that her side was that of the underdog. Heavy stares in her direction suggested that *she* was the one who was out of line. However, the many lectures Vanessa gave her about being more assertive were finally kicking in, although possibly, not the best time.

"She wasn't going to take it," The older lady loudly snapped. "She only wanted to see it. Cassie may be disabled, but she does know right from wrong. She would never take anything."

That's when the tears arrived. Both the old lady and Cassie started to cry, the stewardess continued to smile, not breaking out of character, while everyone around her seemed to suddenly be alert to the situation. Some were standing, trying to get a better view, while others were muttering amongst themselves. Natasha felt as though the entire plane was closing in on her, while her heart pounded in fury. She wasn't feeling embarrassed. She wasn't even feeling victimized. She was feeling complete, black fury and when Natasha looked into Cassie's eyes, she obviously knew it too.

Reaching into her pocket, Cassie pulled out Natasha's iPod and threw it on her lap. Then she let out a loud cry, as if she had been physically attacked and wailed for the rest of the trip.

# Chapter Eleven

"So the little retarded girl tried to steal your iPod?" Flora Johnson let out a short laugh from the driver's side of the truck, as she followed a stream of vehicles out of the city limits. Natasha was only half listening to her aunt's inappropriate comment, as she abruptly pulled a jacket out of one of her bags and squeezed it through her seat belt. When she left Vancouver earlier that day, it was beautiful and warm, but Alberta was a whole other story. Almost as soon as she arrived, the clouds swept in.

"Are you cold, honey?" Her aunt expressed concern and automatically reached over to turn up the heat. Warm air started to shoot through the vents and gently caressed Natasha's face, just as she pushed both of her arms through the jacket and pulled it together underneath the seatbelt. "This rainstorm came out of nowhere. Hell, I'm not even dressed for it."

Natasha silently glanced at her aunt, who wore a blue blouse, a pair of jeans and Puma sneakers. In contrast, Natasha was wearing a pair of tan shorts and a loose, white T-shirt and sandals. Neither of them was dressed for the sudden blast of rain that hit the windshield.

"Thanks, the heat feels nice," She shyly smiled at her aunt.

As soon as Natasha arrived in the crowded airport that day, she had been overcome with anxiety; what did her aunt look like? It had been over ten years since they saw one another. People streamed past her in every direction, while she remained firm, frozen in place, suitcase in hand, like a lost child. Fortunately, a smiling face appeared in the crowd and she instantly knew it was her aunt.

"Well, here's hoping the weather improves before we get to Hennessey," She continued to ease through the traffic, which was getting pretty slow at this point. Reaching toward a collection of dials, Flora turned on the radio.

*Country music? Just fucking shoot me now!*

"Umm…hopefully," Natasha said and planted a smile on her face. She felt her body start to relax for the first time since arriving.

She stared at her aunt. There were vague resemblances to her own mother; the way Flora smiled without managing to wrinkle the skin around her eyes, as if her entire face brightened up. She definitely wore less make-up, maybe mascara and concealer, if any at all. Her eyes were larger than Cynthia Parsons and Natasha knew from old photos, that it was her aunt that was the more attractive of the two during their teenage years.

Flora carried a relaxed position that could be sensed immediately, something Natasha assumed had to do with being from a small town. She seemed like somebody who would've been a hippie in her youth – carefree, open-minded, rather than guarded and stern, like Natasha's mom. In many ways, the two women couldn't be more different.

"So you did get your iPod back?" Flora smiled as she asked the question, squinting her eyes, she reached for her sunglasses and pulled them on. "For such an overcast, dark day, you wouldn't think I'd need my shades."

"You wouldn't think," Natasha said as a grin crept on her face; she suddenly felt so relaxed and carefree. Away from the world that she was usually trapped in; it was like being a rat in a maze, except the maze was her apartment and each time she got to her door, someone in her family was on the other side… or Cliff.

"Oh, yes, I did get my iPod back," She went on to tell the whole story, describing how *she* became the airplane's pariah after the intellectually challenged young woman attempted to steal it. Fuming once again, feeling as though she had been judged and treated unfairly, it kind of irked her to see her aunt displaying a vacant grin as she watched the road ahead. "The girl tore it out of her pocket and threw it at me, as if *I* did something wrong."

"And you can't say anything because then you'll be a bitch and accused of picking on the special needs girl?" Flora said as she shook her head, acknowledging the situation. She continued to grin, but her lips were stiff as if there were subtle indications of anger sifting through her face and collecting together in her mouth, waiting to express a sentiment; but it never came out.

"I know, right?" Natasha heard an influx of a teenaged girl in her voice and suddenly felt ashamed. She glanced out her window at the clouds that continued to darken the skies, even though the rain was subsiding. Noting all the vehicles that surrounded them, she felt somewhat claustrophobic, but she forced that thought aside

"Everyone's always got to be politically correct all the goddamn time," Flora added, now removing her sunglasses and throwing them on the dash. "I get that and it's fine, but that little girl shouldn't be taking your stuff. I don't care if she has a disability. Right is right and wrong is wrong. I use to see it in the school system all the time. Some kids were spoiled and are never told 'no', therefore they go out into the world and think that those rules don't apply to them.".

"I bet you saw some fucked up things in schools," Natasha said, without feeling the need to cherry pick her words, a sense of freedom flowed through her body. She stretched her legs over her bag on the floor, her shoulders flapping down in comfort. "I mean, do you think kids are more spoiled? Like, say, more than ten years ago?"

"Well, they're a hell of a lot more spoiled than they were when I began teaching in the early 80s, that's for sure," She nodded and her face became quite tense as she signaled and switched lanes, speeding past a string of slow moving vehicles. "These city people can't drive."

"You should be in Vancouver," Natasha grunted and her aunt's face automatically relaxed, crinkling into a smile. Nodding her head, she seemed to agree.

"I have no doubts about that."

"Have you ever been to Vancouver?" Natasha asked, yet she already knew the answer. Her mom's family never came to visit. At least, not that she could remember.

"No."

"Why not?"

"Well, I wasn't ever invited," Her aunt answered honestly and she leaned her head slightly to the side. "Not that that is any excuse, it's a free country and I could've gone there anytime. I guess I didn't feel welcomed by your mother." She paused for a moment. "I probably shouldn't be saying that to you, but I don't believe in sugar coating things. That's the God's honest truth."

"No need to sugar coat with me," Natasha replied and she automatically felt even more at ease. "If anything, I feel the same way. I don't know if it's my mother or Vancouver in general, but I constantly feel like I'm saying or doing something wrong. As if I have to watch exactly what I say and it's-"

"Confining?" Her aunt finished the sentence and nodded. "It is, isn't it?"

"Yes, definitely." Natasha laughed and glanced out the window as Flora's truck sped past cars, trucks, vans, everything. She felt so free and alive in that moment. It was strange in a logical sense that she felt comfortable with a woman that she barely knew, but yet, maybe it wasn't so strange at all, when she thought about it. Natasha didn't fit in with her family – or at least, she hadn't thought so until that day.

Vanessa was obviously the exception, but then again, her sister was adopted and in many regards, sometimes Natasha felt like she was as well.

The two chatted for the entire drive to Hennessey; talking as if they were catching up rather than learning about one another, until the signs for the small town began to pop up.

"So we are almost there?" Natasha inquired, noticing how the traffic had long disappeared, the roads were down to two lanes, as they entered a quaint little town with minimal traffic – actually, minimal everything. A few stores on 'Main Street', a couple of café style restaurants, a bar and a variety of little businesses were scattered as they drove on through.

They were silent as Natasha took it all in and felt as though she would have the entire town memorized by the time they reached her aunt's house.

The people were different; she saw that right away. The guys were what Vanessa would refer to as 'real men' rather than the 'metrosexual wimps' that she insisted were taking over Vancouver. Was it possible that the men here were actually taller and stronger? It kind of seemed that way at first glimpse

They passed an attractive guy on a bicycle, but unlike Vancouver, he didn't arrogantly try to bully the car out of his way, as if he owned the road but instead drove along with the traffic, doing his best to go out of the way.

*Interesting.*

Natasha watched an overweight woman walking out of a corner store, with a family of chubby children following her down the street. They were each licking an ice cream cone, while one child was far behind the others, looking sad and displaced. Chocolate ice cream was sliding down his arm and dripping on the pavement. The mother didn't seem to notice.

"Are there a lot of families here?" Natasha asked.

"Not really, a lot of families are moving into the city. There's not a great deal of work here, so they can't afford to stay."

Natasha just nodded. People were poor here. She could see it right away. It wasn't because they were dressed in shabby clothing or that they were lying on the streets like the homeless in Vancouver, but she felt a sense of hopelessness when Natasha looked at them. It was the older cars that lined the street, including one with duct tape across the fender, apparently as a form of repair. It was the storefronts that were faded, tattered and in need of a new coat of paint. It was all of the little things added together.

The seemed like practical people who didn't get caught up in the superficial and ridiculous status of her own home. It was truly humbling.

*These are the people who would be living on the downtown eastside if they were in Vancouver.*

"Are there a lot of poor people here, Flora?'

"I think there are poor people everywhere," Flora spoke practically, as they slowly came to the end of the 'busy' section of town and Natasha noted how houses were more spaced out, the farther they drove. "You don't have to be rich to be spoiled and you don't have to be poor to be deprived."

Natasha just smiled. She was so right.

# Chapter Twelve

~⟡~

Strangely, it wasn't until just before arriving at Flora's house, that Natasha considered the possibility that she had been exiled into the country. Not that this should've been a surprise to her; after all, she had caused a great deal of embarrassment to her family. A few people from the party knew how the political candidate's niece had hit her head, but chances are they wouldn't spill the beans.

Things happen.

Of course, she didn't want to hurt Flora's feeling by asking such a question, as if to suggest that her home was an unbarred prison. Chances were good that her parents had hatched the plan and didn't even let Flora in on the truth. They were both manipulative, particularly her father, who had a way of making people think that his ideas were their own.

Grabbing her cell, she sent a quick text to Vanessa.

*Have I been exiled to the country?*

No reply.

She was probably busy.

"So here we are," Flora said as they drove up to the familiar farmhouse that rested on a beautiful property, surrounded by an array of tree varieties (not that Natasha was much of a horticulturist, so she wasn't sure of the kinds) with a healthy green lawn and flower beds randomly scattered throughout the front yard. There was a tire swing hanging from a gigantic tree and although it looked quaint from a distance, Natasha suspected there were a number of gross, yucky things living inside it, so there was no way she would ever sit on it. "Might be a little different than you remember it."

"Yeah, wasn't there a barn over there," Natasha pointed behind the house, noting that it appeared to be an extension on her vegetable garden.

"Yes, we decided to tear the barn down years ago," Aunt Flora replied as she put the truck into park and removed the keys from the ignition. Opening the door, she slipped out and Natasha hesitantly did the same. She wasn't sure why she was feeling apprehensive about being on the property, but something was making her feel uncomfortable. It was no longer raining but a strange chill swooped through her body, causing an involuntary shake that she could feel right to her toes.

Reaching out, she took hold of the truck door for support and briefly closed her eyes, before opening them again and shaking her head. The heaviness in her right leg returned and for a moment, Natasha feared she wouldn't be able to walk. Fortunately, her aunt didn't seem to notice that anything was wrong.

Pulling herself together, Natasha ignored the fact that her legs felt a bit wobbly and turned back to see Flora grabbing her suitcase from the front seat. "I'm sorry, I could've got that, I-

"Nonsense," Flora gave her a compassionate smile and reached out, gently patting her arm. "You are my guest and I'm happy to help with your bags."

"I don't want to seem like a princess who can't even handle her own luggage."

Flora wrinkled her forehead and lifted one eyebrow. "Why would I think that?"

Natasha couldn't answer the question with anything but a shrug and hesitant smile.

*Why do I think that way?*

As they walked up to the house, Natasha forgot her awkwardness and took in the peacefulness of her environment. Flora's house was located along a quiet road with only a few houses, therefore eliminating most of the traffic as well. As a result, there was stillness that she wouldn't have either known or appreciated when she last paid a visit, at the age of seventeen. Back then, she had been so wrapped up in her own problems, that Natasha simply didn't appreciate her little escape from Vancouver.

"Long time since you've been here," Flora commented, almost as if she had read her mind. She reached out to unlock the door and they went inside.

Any apprehension that Natasha felt upon arriving was quickly erased, as she entered a bright, beautiful kitchen. Everything was gleaming, fresh, clean, perfect. It wasn't an expensive apartment that was cramped, such as where Natasha lived or the overpriced home that her own parent's chose, just a comfortable country home that was simple and unpretentious. A glass vase with fresh daisies sat in the center of a small, wooden kitchen table that appeared to be the same one as with her last visit. It was old, rustic and perfect, at the same time. The rest of the kitchen looked pretty modern in comparison; a dishwasher, new model of refrigerator and stove, not to mention hardwood floors that appeared quite new, with no marks or stains.

"I love your place," Natasha said, while her head turned in every direction, curious about her vacation home. "It looks the same, but kind of different at the same time."

"I bought some new appliances" Flora said as she sat Natasha's oversized suitcase upright and closed the door behind them, motioning toward the floors. "Then I did some renovations after me and the ex broke up, which was just what I needed at that time."

Natasha was curious about the breakup, but didn't want to ask. She barely remembered her uncle Paul, other than the fact that he was away a great deal with his work. Had she ever met him?

"Anyway, let me show you around and see how much you remember," She said while removing her shoes and Natasha took off her sandals. "I don't have a dining room, but I have a pantry, if you can believe it." She opened a narrow door in the far corner of the kitchen and Natasha followed her, peeking inside. It was full of flour, chocolate chips and various other items that suggested her aunt enjoyed baking. She wasn't a big woman, so obviously she didn't eat a lot of her own treats. "It's nice to put extra supplies in here." She pointed farther back and Natasha noted an array of everything from toilet paper to soaps and bottles of water. "The house is big, but small at the same time, so I don't have a lot of space to put extra supplies."

"You have a lot of supplies." Natasha observed.

"Well, when you live out of the city, it's good to stock up when you can," Flora commented as she shut the door. "Plus everything costs more here, so when I'm in the city, I tend to pick up extras if I see a good sale."

"Smart." Natasha smiled. She was hardly a bargain shopper, so admired her aunt's frugalness.

"Here's the living room," Her aunt pointed toward the next room. Natasha noted that although it was wide in size, the ceilings were a bit lower than in the kitchen. Entering the room, she instantly sensed the special moments that the walls must've witnessed; all the Christmases, laughter, tears, passion. There was so much character and although it obviously was modernized, there was a still a touch of simplicity to it that made her instantly feel at ease. It had character.

"Let me show you the upstairs," Her aunt pointed to a stairway that was almost hidden by a wall. They were narrow, but a railing jutted out and reached to the top floor. She started to follow her aunt up and then remembered her suitcase at the front door.

"I'll be right back, I'm just going to grab-

"Just get it later," Her aunt seemed to read her mind again and proceeded to rush up the steps. Natasha did the same.

The top level also appeared to be small – that was, until you entered any of the rooms. The first was a bathroom that was likely not much larger than her own at home, but it was so bright, so fresh and beautiful that Natasha thought she could probably live there. The window was open a jar, letting in the springtime air. The walls seemed to reflect the limited sunlight that came from outside, while an antique style tub looked inviting. Sparkling, clean: her own bathroom at home seemed like a drugstore shelf after a riot.

"I love this," Natasha pointed at an old-fashioned style, white bowl that sat on a separate table from the sink.

"It's been here for years," Flora said and grinned. "The funny part is that we sure love looking at them now, but if we had to use it to wash up like in the old days, we wouldn't find them so adorable then."

The two women left the bathroom and headed toward a bedroom. Judging by the size and clothes on the queen-sized bed, it was clear this was Flora's room. Long, flowing curtains moved in the gentle breeze, while everything in the room appeared to have its place and looked so comfortable. A delicate, yet adorable wicker chair sat in the corner, with a reading lamp beside it and a stack of books were heaped on the floor.

"Don't mind the mess in here, honey," Flora gestured toward the room and Natasha almost laughed out loud.

*If only she saw my bedroom most days. It looks like a bomb of clothes went off in the fucking middle of it.*

"And here is your room," She said, swiftly moving forward and opening the door to a slightly smaller room, with a double bed covered in a beautiful, white comforter that almost looked too pretty to actually use. It appeared to be a homemade. Natasha moved closer and touched it.

"Wow, this is beautiful," She remarked and glanced back at Flora, who had pride in her face. "It looks like someone made it? Was it you?"

"Oh hell no," Flora said with a quick, unexpected laugh. Shaking her head, she moved ahead. "I like beautiful things, but I don't make them. I bought this at a craft store a few summers ago. The lady who was selling it obviously had no idea how much it should've cost, cause I got it for a steal."

"Wow, that's good! I hope I don't spill anything on it," Natasha cringed a bit, considering how she had tripped over a shoe earlier that morning and dropped a cup of coffee on her couch. Jesus. She would have to be very careful in this house.

"Nat, don't even worry about such a thing,"

Noting that Flora called her by the same nickname as her sister, she smiled to herself.

*Van hates it when anyone else calls me 'Nat'. She would die if she were here!*

"This is a beautiful room," She glanced at the lone, tall chest of drawers that she probably wouldn't use during her visit, as well as the closet beside it. A long mirror was positioned on an otherwise, empty wall opposite the bed and in the corner, sat a chair resembling the one in her aunt's room, with a reading light on a table beside it.

"If you want to rearrange anything, go ahead. I have the table over there, but maybe you would prefer it beside the bed. There is only one on the right side. It's totally up to you."

Natasha didn't have the heart to tell her that she probably wouldn't be there long enough to worry about it. She feared that her aunt thought she was moving into long-term, but then again, maybe she just believed in being a good hostess.

"You know what? It's perfect. I don't want to change a thing," Natasha insisted, as she walked around the room, inspecting every corner. "It's so homey."

"Well, it's your home for as long as want to stay." Her aunt started to move out of the bedroom and into the hallway. "I'll go get your suitcase."

Before she could argue, her aunt was out of the room and halfway down the stairs. Smiling to herself, she noted that the air was a bit stuffy and decided to open a window: and that's when she saw him. Tall, muscular, tanned, handsome – and walking up the walkway to the front door!

*Fuck! He's moving too fast. I want to see more!!*

Hurrying out of the room, she halted after hearing voices downstairs. The mystery man was in the house and talking to her aunt. Slowing down and quietly walking down the stairs, it was her hope to overhear some of their conversation and discover something about the man that maybe she could-

Stunned by what she saw through the peak hole where the stairs opened up into the living room, she halted and looked out. The gorgeous, very young man she had just seen walking into the house, was kissing her aunt while grasping her breast through her blouse.

# Chapter Thirteen

❧❧❧❧❧❧❧

It wasn't that she believed her aunt Flora shouldn't have a boyfriend. That wasn't at all the case. It was just weird that he seemed to be barely out of high school and groping her much older aunt in the next room. No judgment. She pretended to not see a thing.

Was she being a prude?

It was afterward, when the introductions were made and Flora gave him a chaste tap on the bicep – the huge, bulging biceps – referring to him as the 'boy' next door, that made it kind of creepy.

"Chase helps me with some of the handy work around the house – you know," She said with a sheepish smile on her face. "Cutting the lawn, fixing a leaking tap, repairing a broken cabinet door….

*…fucking your brains out….*

"… You know, things like that." Flora continued and avoided Natasha's eyes, as she wandered to the cupboard and pulled out the identical bag of coffee that had, until recently, been in her own kitchen.

*The fucking same coffee dad always drinks. Seriously? Why does everyone drink this overpriced crap? Don't people out here in the boonies drink the gigantic cans of the cheep stuff?*

Turning her attention back to the town stud, Natasha couldn't help but question how exactly this…. *arrangement* started. Of course, it wasn't difficult to figure out *why* it got started. The man was absolutely hot. She wasn't keen on his look - he had this kind of dimwitted expression that she felt was a turn off - his body, however, was phenomenal. The tight T-shirt showed off everything – the bulging arms, the sleek chest and a stomach she would've snorted coke off: if she *were* that sort of girl.

He wore jeans and she found her eyes staring at his groin. Was there a bit of a bulge down there?

"…coffee, right?"

Her aunt was asking her a question. Noting that only Chase seemed to notice her wandering eyes, she turned her head as if she had done nothing wrong and went on to confidently answer the question.

"Yes, I would love a cup of coffee."

"No, honey, I was wondering if you have this brand in Vancouver?" She held up the familiar bag and shook it around.

*I live in Vancouver. Not in the middle of fucking nowhere, of course we have it.*

"Oh yes, that's my dad's favorite." She pranced past Chase and noted that he was checking her out as much as she was checking him out a moment earlier. It was probably hypocritical that she found herself a little irritated by his preying, perverted eyes, but she didn't care.

*You were practically finger fucking my aunt in the middle of the kitchen, just ten minutes ago. This is unsettling.*

"It's a lovely brand," Her aunt acted as though it were utterly believable that her much younger 'handyman' would stop by on a Saturday afternoon, out of nowhere, to enjoy a cup of overpriced coffee. Natasha decided to play along.

*Van is going to die when I tell her this shit!*

"You know," Her aunt rambled on nervously and for a moment, Natasha couldn't help but feel bad for her. She probably hadn't expected the weak-minded moron to show up at the door, all sexed up and ready to pound her ass, only to learn she was tied down with a relative from out of town. "I only drink coffee that is recognized by the fair trade organization. Chase was telling me about a documentary on coffee growers around the world. You wouldn't believe the inhuman treatment and modern day slavery that includes kids."

"Really?" Natasha replied with sincerity in her eyes, casually glancing back at Chase, who smiled and nodded.

"Most people in the western world are completely ignorant about what is happening in these poverty stricken countries, in order for us to have a good cup of coffee." His voice was as smooth as honey and Natasha found herself melting in it.

*I'm officially a jerk. He's just a good guy and so what if-*

"...only right since Flora taught me so much in school." He gave a moronic laugh and helped himself to a coffee mug in the cupboard, automatically knowing exactly where to find one. "God, it seems like just yesterday."

Natasha glanced at her aunt who had a prideful smile on her face.

"Oh, you taught...Chase in school?"

"Yeah, she was my math teacher in high school," He said with a wicked grin, while the two lovers shared a look that made Natasha's stomach topple around anxiously.

*Oh my fucking God. This is really happening. He is eye fucking her right in front of me.*

"Oh, ah, that's lovely," Natasha muttered and glanced toward the coffee pot that couldn't possible drip any slower, than made an excuse to run upstairs for a moment.

In her room, she grabbed her cell phone and started texting like crazy.

*Aunt Flow is fucking this young thing. You wouldn't believe it!*

A few seconds later.

*Wow! Good for her.*

And then..

*Wait, they aren't related are they?*

Natasha almost laughed out loud, but quickly covered her mouth.

*It is sick enough that he's younger than both of us, probably 25, super hot and she used to teach him in high school. Hello?*

And then..

*Ahh...yeah, that's kind of fucked up. Are you sure?*

*I almost walked in on them when they were kissing and he had his hand on her tit.*

Nothing

Nothing

*Come on, Nat. Stop fucking with me. Ha ha…good one, you almost got me!*

Natasha bit back laugher.

*I'M NOT FUCKING WITH YOU. I swear to God! I thought he was going to fuck her right in the kitchen and she made him stop, saying I was upstairs.*

And then..

*I don't have a good feeling about your being there. I may have to come get you.*

*Wait, Van. I just got here. I will keep you updated.*

Rushing toward the stairs, Natasha suddenly stopped and slowed down. Remember, of course, that she didn't want to walk in on an unsavory moment. Well, unsavory for *her*.

But all was calm when she reached downstairs. Flora and Chase were drinking coffee at her kitchen table and her aunt quickly gestured toward the cabinet.

"There's more coffee. I left it for you, so fix as you please."

"Ok, thanks," Natasha attempted to act normal, but as she hurried to the cupboard and reached for the coffee pot, her sister's comments were still dancing on the edge of her brain. She had to act normal. She had to remain calm. She had to stay in control.

"So, how is your wife doing with the new job?" Her aunt asked and Natasha almost spilled the entire pot on the counter, but managed to stop her arm from shaking. "Bet she's enjoying it."

*He's married, a hundred years younger than Flora AND fucking her? What the fuck is with these people?*

"She's doing great," Chase answered enthusiastically. "The church is such a big part of our lives, that it only made sense that she take the job when the Reverend asked her to work for him.

Gingerly putting in the sugar and cream then taste testing her coffee, Natasha was slow to turn around because she was about to break out in laughter. This place was more dysfunctional than her life back in Vancouver.

In fact, it was oddly entertaining.

Joining them at the table, she merely smiled and took it all in.

"Chase's wife Audrey, is such a dear," Her aunt airily commented, as if her married, former high school student wasn't feeling her up a few minutes earlier. "Always bringing me little treats like homemade jams and fudge."

*If she knows you are fucking her husband, she probably is putting cyanide in them.*

"I'm lucky to have such thoughtful neighbors."

"Aha…" Natasha bit her lip and managed to calm herself enough to ask the next question that crossed her mind. "So where is…Audrey today?"

"Oh, she's pretty tied up with the twins." Chase said with a grin. "Three kids under the age of five keeps her pretty busy."

*Not you, obviously.*

"Sometimes she just wants me out of her hair," He let out a rather stupid little laugh and exchanged an intimate smile with Flora.

*Three kids under the age of five, she probably wants you out of more than her hair.*

"Oh, I see." Natasha smiled and nodded, continuing to bite her lower lip.

"So, what about you, Natasha," His tone was sincere and kind, something that brought her shame amidst her cruel thoughts about him. "Tell me about yourself. Flora says you're from BC?"

"Vancouver," She nodded and cleared her throat. "Born and breed."

"And you're a doctor?"

"Yes," She answered and noted how his intense brown eyes studied her face. "I'm a general practitioner."

"That must be so fulfilling." He smiled sweetly and leaned inappropriately close to her. She could practically feel the heat pouring off his body, making the little hairs on her arms to stand up and she quickly looked away.

*I'm going to fuck this guy.*

# Chapter Fourteen

*Jesus Christ!!! What am I thinking?*

Automatically leaning away from her aunt's boy toy, Natasha cringed at the thought. What the hell was wrong with her? How hard had she hit her head? There were so many reasons why she shouldn't hook up with this guy – married, with kids, fucking her aunt– it was best to stay under the radar and away from this idiot. Didn't her aunt notice how Chase was looking at her, practically salivating at the other end of the table. Glancing toward Flora, who absently stared into her coffee cup, Natasha wondered if she just saw what suited her in the moment.

"So, what sort of work do you do, Chase?" Natasha asked, thinking that maybe it would be a good idea to throw in a casual question while sipping on her coffee, hoping to finish it quickly and make an excuse to go upstairs and call Vanessa. "Besides, handy work?"

He slumped in his chair and fiddled with the handle of the coffee cup. "I was working at the local gym until it shut down about a month ago. Now I'm staying home with the kids until something else comes along." He avoided her eyes and briefly reminded Natasha of an uncooperative teenager. "Audrey has a pretty secure job, so we make out okay for now."

"Good thing Audrey has you," Her aunt suddenly piped up, a compassionate smile on her face and her eyes communicating something completely different. "It's so hard to be a working mother of such young children."

"She's a saint."

"Such a beautiful soul," Her aunt insisted with a smooth voice and probing eyes while Chase appeared stoic. "She's lucky to have you."

Natasha managed to suppress a giggle by taking a huge gulp of her coffee, then grabbing a napkin to wipe her mouth.

"You guys will have to excuse me, I just remembered that I was supposed to phone my sister when I got here," She said with nervous laughter in her voice, as she eased out of the chair and slowly pushed it forward toward the table. Grabbing her half-empty cup of coffee, Natasha rushed toward the sink, where she dumped the remains. Rinsing her coffee mug, she exchanged a gentle smile with her aunt before rushing upstairs. "She gets worried since I had my accident."

"Understandable," Her aunt nodded. "Take your time."

Back in the guest room, she collapsed on her bed and covered her mouth in order to suppress the laughter that arose from her throat. Squeezing her eyes closed, it occurred to her that all things considered, it shouldn't have been funny. Was this actually happening?

*How hard did I hit my head?*

Composing herself, she noted the murmur of voices downstairs and made a mental note to keep her voice at a whisper when she called Van. Grabbing her phone, she felt a laugh, jump out of her throat much like a hiccup. Biting her lips together, she phoned her sister.

"What the fuck?" Vanessa's voice seemed to jump out of nowhere, almost without the phone ringing at all. There was a subtle echo in the background, indicating that she was probably in her home office. "Were you shitting me when you said that Aunt Flow was fucking the local yokel? Are you sure you didn't misread the situation?"

Natasha got up from the bed and started toward the window, "I'm totally, 100%-

"Oh, Nat...cut...ah..." Her sister's voice broke up and Natasha immediately rushed back to her starting point on the bed and gradually sat on the mattress. "I think you have a reception problem."

"I can hear you now!" Natasha heard her voice come out both louder and more abrupt than expected. She noted that downstairs, both voices had stopped speaking.

*Were they making out again?*

"It's cause you're in the middle of nowhere, Nat," Her sister reminded her. "When Steve and I go out to those rural areas to camp, we always have the same problem. It's working right now, so don't move."

"I won't!" Natasha said and took a deep breath; suddenly feeling suffocated by this small town. In a much lower voice, she said, "And everything I told you is true, Aunt Flow-

"You're cutting out again," Vanessa cut her off in a nagging voice, causing Natasha to wrinkle her forehead in frustration.

"I said, everything I told you-' Natasha spoke loudly and suddenly realized that perhaps she should cool her heels, before she yelled out that their aunt was fucking the neighborhood handyman. "I mean, yes, it is as…beautiful here as I thought it would be."

"Oh, so they're close by and you can't tell me the juicy details." Vanessa's voice was suddenly clear as a bell, as laughter flowed through it and Natasha felt her anxiety drift away. It sounded like she was in the Jeep.

"If there are any," she spoke sternly in reply, "I certainly don't want to know about them,."

"Is he there right now," Vanessa inquired. "Is he really young? Hot? Does he look like he has-

"He's definitely younger than us," Natasha muttered into the phone, casually looking over her shoulder. Why hadn't she closed the door behind her? It would look too obvious if she did now, plus if she moved again, the call could be dropped. "He's married with something like three kids."

"Whhhhhhh….are you kidding me? Aunt Flow picked a married cowboy to ride? Wow, I guess loose morals aren't just for the city folk," A gentle giggle followed. "Are you sure you should be there? You're not going to get into some kind of trouble, are you?

"I haven't so far." Natasha reminded her.

"You've only been there a few hours."

There was silence on the line.

"I'm going there," Vanessa said, suddenly sounding very serious.

"It doesn't matter," Natasha insisted in a whisper. "Look, I don't even know-

"Oh, you are cutting out again." Vanessa said and Natasha held her breath and attempted to stay as still as possible.

And that's when she heard it; the distinct, yet the careful squeak of the couch. The almost too silent room below was suspicious enough, but then she heard a soft, suppressed moan that most people probably would've missed. Natasha didn't.

"Oh my God!" Natasha muttered into the phone. "I think they are fucking downstairs."

"No way!" Vanessa loudly replied as laughter blasted through the phone. "See, you had me for awhile, I *really* believed you, I thought-

"It's true," Natasha hissed into the phone. "I'm sure they are fucking downstairs now. I can hear the couch springs and....sex noises. I mean, they're trying to hide it, but the house is really quiet."

"What?" Vanessa continued to laugh. "Oh my God! You're telling me the truth? Go look!"

"I can't go look."

"Go look!!! You got to go look." Vanessa insisted. "Take a picture and send it to me."

"Are you mad???"

"Yes and no." Vanessa said and let out a loud yelp of delight. "Do it!! Go do it. You gotta do it! For me, Nat. Do it."

"Okay, I will hang up and *try.*"

"Ah!!! I love it." Her sister squealed in delight.

Fortunately, the thick carpet of the upstairs provided Natasha with enough support that her feet were nearly silent, as she slowly moved across the floor. She was like a cat, sneaking about, as she lurked toward the steps, her iPhone ready to take a photo at any moment.

Her heart racing in anticipation, she bit her lip and slowly eased down the first step, then the second, by the third, she could hear them much better. The chair in the corner was definitely the pleasure zone and she raised her phone up as she finally peaked around the staircase, she got the picture so fast, that she barely had time to register what she saw.

Back up the stairs, as mildly as she went down, Natasha headed to her room and opened up the photo. Just as she imagined, Flora was on the handyman's lap, her long shirt hiding much of their activity, including most of her naked ass, as she rode the cowboy. One pant leg was draped down Chase's leg and hanging lifelessly on the floor, the other still on her leg, as if to suggest it was an impromptu and rushed encounter. His head was leaned back, eyes closed, unaware that a photo was taken.

Could she actually hear them getting louder downstairs or was that her imagination? Did she hear a zipper being pulled up?

*I'm upstairs and they are seriously doing this?!? Is this some kind of bad dream?*

She quickly sent the photo to Vanessa before calling her back.

"Oh my fucking God! You actually did it," Vanessa cried with delight on the other end of the phone. "I can't believe you actually did it!"

"You told me to," Natasha insisted as irritation ringing through her voice, as she protectively hunched over her phone. "Now do you believe me?"

"You do realize that this is going to happen the whole time you're there, right?"

"I don't want to realize that."

"I'm coming to get you."

"You-

"Sit tight and try to keep out of trouble." Vanessa suddenly sounded very serious. "I don't have a good feeling about you ... being there."

"What's that suppose to mean, I-

"I will be there soon," Vanessa cut her off then she hung up.

Staring at her phone, Natasha saw a new text message. This time it was from Clifford.

*I have to talk to you. You can't put this off much longer.*

Natasha's forehead wrinkled as she glared at the phone. This was the last thing she wanted to deal with at that moment.

*I'm not home. We will talk when I return.*

# Chapter Fifteen

Sitting on the edge of the guest room bed, she couldn't move. It was barely 6 pm and already, the day had been a series of upsets that hardly made for a relaxing holiday. Her body was like a rock that stubbornly sat at the bottom of the sea, wishing to do nothing more than to catch the algae and the rubbish floating around - maybe an occasional sinking ship with its victim's bodies falling around her, condom wrappers, pink panties and stuffed animals. Then for some reason, she started to play a SpongeBob song in her head.

*What is wrong with me?*

It was when she started to imagine a conversation with the lovable cartoon character that Natasha briefly wondered about her sanity; but after considering the events of her day, it probably wasn't such a stretch.

Forcing herself off her bed, Natasha felt hesitant to leave her room, uncertain of how to face the aunt that she barely knew, to pretend she hadn't just witnessed a potential letter to Penthouse Forum. Holding her head high, she took a deep breath and walked downstairs to find her aunt sitting at the kitchen table, coffee in hand, glancing at a flyer.

*...after fucking my much younger, married neighbor in the living room, while my niece (who I barely know) was upstairs making a phone call, I like to settle in with a relaxing cup of coffee and see what Wal-Mart has on sale this week....*

"Oh, Natasha, there you are," Flora piped up, showing no shame in her eyes as she gestured toward a flyer on the table, as she took another drink of her coffee. "I was cleaning up and found this menu for a local pub and thought you might be interested in heading over there for dinner?"

Natasha felt an awkward smile creep on her lips, as she glanced at the chair that had originally been occupied by Chase. Opening her mouth to talk, her tongue was unable to move; not that she had an opportunity to respond, before Flora spoke up again.

"Chase went home for dinner. Audrey is a real stickler about having it right at 6 pm," Flora spoke evenly, gesturing toward a nearby clock and Natasha took advantage of the informality of the conversation to get back into the awkward groove. Oddly, she was the awkward one, not the other way round.

"I suppose," Natasha stuttered along as she pulled out a chair and sat down, noticing that her aunt's eyes were cast on her face. "I guess when you have that many children, you have to live by a very strict schedule."

"Yes, Audrey's father was in the military too, so she likes to run her household in the same, strict fashion." Flora gestured toward the kitchen window, Natasha assumed in the general direction of the couple's house. "That's okay, I was about to suggest that we go get some food. I would've cooked something, but the afternoon kind of slipped by, didn't it?"

"It did." Natasha felt a grin slip on her lips and had she less self-control, it likely would've developed into laughter. She briefly wondered if she was an unaware participant in some variation of the television show *Candid Camera*. "Dinner sounds nice. I am getting a little hungry myself."

"You will love this place," Flora started to rise from the chair and Natasha mindlessly did the same. "Burgers as big as your head."

"Wow… that's a… pretty big burger," Natasha said with a totally fake smile. She wasn't much of a meat eater and certainly possessed no interest in eating a gigantic, greasy hamburger – but there would certainly be something else on the menu. "Sure, let's go."

The drive to the pub was short and Natasha took in her surroundings along the way. This time she discovered a lot of farms, mostly appearing to be slightly run down and faded. There was something depressing about seeing an old barn, presumably once full of life and promise, now crippled and old, preparing to die.

A few people walked along the road, some with kids in strollers, while others rushing along with an iPod in their ears, as if they were trying to somehow leave themselves far behind. Natasha noted that Flora waved at many people in passing cars as if they all were friends, which was an interesting change of pace for a city girl. Natasha couldn't remember the last time she waved at a passing car. There was that one time she waved at a tour bus of a well-known rock band, but that was a whole other matter.

The pub was slightly larger than the hole in the wall that Natasha was expecting; loud, obnoxious, country music met them in the doorway and made it difficult to hear anything her aunt said. Natasha followed her to a table at the back and did her best to ignore the probing eyes that didn't seem to have any awareness of when staring became rude.

Natasha reluctantly took her seat, noting that Flora seemed completely comfortable in this setting, grabbing a menu that had gravy splattered on the front, she started to browse. Doing the same, Natasha saw the words 'We got beef' and then a listing of hearty dishes that included steaks that should've fed an entire household, not just one person, followed by a list of burgers that included an entire meal between the buns. It was a bit intimidating to someone who tended to avoid meat, but she was willing to play along.

"Oh, a birthday burger, that sounds fun!" Natasha commented, looking at the list of food that came along with it. It sounded like reasonably sized burgers, fries and a slab of cake.

"Oh no, honey, that's a children's meal."

*Really? A child can eat all that food?! Good fucking Lord.*

However, glancing round the room, Natasha quickly noted that most of the pub patrons were quite husky and probably could easily down one of these massive steaks. She was exhausted just thinking about it.

"I-I don't know what I want," Natasha continued to stare at the menu, noting that her aunt had closed her copy and placed it on the table. "I'm not a big meat eater-

"Well, you can get breakfast all day too," Her aunt interjected and turned the menu page, to indicate a selection of meals usually favored in the morning. At that moment, a nice omelet and coffee sounded somewhat comforting.

As it turned out, they didn't make omelets. Fried, over easy, over hard and scrambled was the only options. Natasha chose over easy and bacon, some toast, why not? That sounded refreshing at this point in the day.

"It's pretty busy," Natasha yelled over the music, glancing around at the few empty tables, while people continued to pour into the bar.

"There aren't many places to eat in town," Flora managed to communicate with ease over the music, that somehow seemed to grow louder by the minute. "Sometimes they have live entertainment later in the evening, it's a pretty happening spot with the young people, although, most choose a bar over there." She pointed toward the window. "The kids in town kind of run between the two places"

"Interesting." Natasha commented, unsure of what else to say.

"This place has the best food in town, though," Her aunt continued. "You always get nice, big helpings, well worth your money."

She wasn't kidding. When Natasha's food arrived, her eyes widened while her stomach rumbled. The plate was huge and contained two eggs, several strips of bacon, four slices of toast, a scoop of beans, two sausages, and a slice of ham and huge portions of hash browns.

"Oh, I just ordered the small breakfast," Natasha grinned self-consciously. "I..I.."

"Oh, this is the small breakfast, dear," The young waitress gave her a whole hearted smile and then proceeded to plunk down a huge steak – or at least half a cow – in front of her aunt. Flora looked at the piece of meat, much in the same way she ogled Chase earlier that day.

Staring in disbelief as her aunt started cutting the, what appeared to be, very rare steak, Natasha couldn't resist the temptation of the food that sat in front of her. The smoky aroma of bacon alone, was making her mouth water, her stomach growl and she hesitantly started to nibble on her food. Soon, she was sampling everything on the plate, brushing off the potential for a heart attack later that night, but simply enjoying the luscious food that was presented to her.

*If Vanessa could see me now...*

On impulse, she snapped a photo of her food and sent it to her sister.

To say she could consume the entire plate of food, would be a lie – but she certainly was able to make a huge dent in it. Feeling heavy and lethargic, she noted that Flora ate about the same quantity, leaving some pink meat sitting alone in the middle of the plate.

Feeling tired and uncomfortable after all that food, Natasha felt as though there was almost no air left in the room. The crowd of people was continuing to rise and where food was the theme of the evening when she arrived, it was now exchanged for huge mugs of beer, the boisterous voices challenged the music that seemed to get increasingly louder, faster and continued to have a country theme.

She wanted to leave.

Glancing at the next table, she was somewhat appalled when the redneck - who had grown increasingly louder throughout the night – dragging over a chair from another table and proceeded to prop his leg up on it, as if it was a reasonable thing to do in a public place.

*You're in a restaurant doucebag, not in your fucking living room. Why don't you unbutton your pants and start farting while you're at it.*

On the other side of the table, Flora talked – about the quality of the meal she had just eaten, telling her local gossip about people across the bar and sharing tales of her youthful adventures in this same establishment.

"I had to behave to a certain point, since I was a high school teacher," Flora volunteered with a salacious smirk on her face. "But often, I would be out partying with the parents of my students and well, what happens in the bar, stays at the bar."

Well, truth be told, Natasha knew this to be true – except exchange 'bar' with 'hotel banquet hall' – but it all came down to the same thing, didn't it?

As the noise level rose, she was relieved when her aunt finally suggested that they head home. Exhausted, Natasha confessed that she desired nothing more than to crawl underneath the covers and get some sleep. It had been such a long day.

"Maybe tomorrow we can go for a hike or shopping, whatever you want to do," Her aunt suggested on their way home, while Natasha struggled to keep awake. "It's your vacation."

"It doesn't matter, whatever you-

"Well, who is that now?" Her aunt cut her off, squinting, her eyes focused on down the road as they came close to her house. "There is a vehicle of some kind in my driveway."

Relief filled her heart. Had Vanessa managed to get there that fast? Had she said she was on her way or was planning to leave? Natasha couldn't remember. Surely, she would never make it that fast!

"My sister said she might-

"No, it's a man," Her aunt cut her off just as they arrived at her driveway and turned in. Natasha felt her mouth fall open in a stunned surprise, as they drove by a dumbfound Clifford.

# Chapter Sixteen

Flora's truck barely had time to stop when Natasha flung open the door and hopped out. Suddenly wide-awake from her food coma, she was seething at the sight of Clifford. His eyes vacant, he stood tall and lanky, wearing an ugly brown and yellow polo shirt and khaki pants, as if he purposely picked out the most pathetic outfit in his closet in order to make her feel sorry for him. He was the human equivalent of a sad dog trying to get petted. Even his subcompact car looked pitiful beside Flora's pickup truck. Hatred filled her body.

With both guns blazing, she approached him with such fierceness that he appeared to be startled, causing her to briefly feel sorry for him. Then she thought of what he was there for and all her compassion disappeared.

"What the fuck are you doing here?" Natasha fumed. Failing to demonstrate some restraint, all the anger from the previous days and weeks was unleashed at that moment. She felt like an animal, clawing from her deepest emotions, unable to keep back an ounce of ferocity. It came from a place within her that she hadn't realized existed, deep in the pit of her stomach, it raised triumphantly, with little regard to how her reaction may have also reflected her sanity.

It was unreal. That entire day already felt like an ongoing joke and she was the dumbfound victim, but this final event took the cake.

"How the fuck did you find me? Are you tracking my phone?" Natasha asked as her heart raced furiously and electricity ran through her arms. She had a strong desire to reach out and throttle the bastard. "What the fuck is wrong with you?"

Before Clifford had a chance to reply, Natasha felt a warm hand on her arm and turned to see her Aunt Flora. Standing beside her, an automatic presence of calm enveloped Natasha and she somehow felt safer. She wasn't used to having someone on her side, support was a rarity in her life.

With concern in her eyes, Flora clearly was trying to read the situation, glancing between her niece and the stranger in her driveway. "Do you know this man, Natasha?"

"Yes," Natasha snapped in Clifford's direction. She then returned her attention to Flora and with a shaking voice, she continued, "He won't leave me alone."

"I only want to talk to her Ma'am," Clifford spoke to Flora as if Natasha was a child that couldn't speak for herself, which only infuriated her more.

"I'm here, asshole," Natasha snapped while pointing at herself. "Why are you talking to her and not me?"

"I only wanted-

"OK, let's step back a bit here," Flora cut off Clifford by putting her hand up, as if to indicate for him to stop. Turning her full attention to Natasha, she inquired, "So, if I'm understanding, correcting, you've already communicated to this young man that you don't want to talk to him?"

"I've been telling him forever, but he won't leave me alone!" Her last word came out as a high pitch cry that seemed to alarm the three of them; it was full of desperation and fear. She suddenly felt faint, as if her limbs were heavy, pulling her to the cold ground and there was an odd, unexpected comfort to that idea. She almost felt herself giving in to it, but something stopped her.

"So, how did he know you were here this weekend?" Flora asked with skepticism in her eyes, as if she thought Natasha had somehow relayed the information on the sly. This only caused her anger to increase.

"I don't know! He always seems to know where I am," Natasha shot back and automatically filled with guilt for being so unruly toward her aunt. Fortunately, Flora appeared unscathed by the attitude slung her way, her eyes returning to Clifford's face.

"How did you know she was here, young man?" She asked. Natasha noted how her aunt's normally friendly blue eyes were now narrow, coldly fixating on the topic of her niece's rage. "And why are you here, on my property, uninvited?

"I… I found out from her mom," He answered, nervously shuffling his weight from one foot to another, with a wide-eyed expression, as if anticipating that it would lower everyone's defenses. He continued to concentrate his attention on Flora, as if she was the parent of a helpless child, who couldn't think for herself.

Meanwhile, Natasha felt her anger only reignite from the news that her mother was somehow involved in this mess. In truth, she only met Clifford once and totally misunderstood their relationship. Most likely, she regarded him as someone who might neutralize her hyper and sometimes, irrational daughter. Was that what was going on here? Had she sent him out to-

"…..her own good," Clifford was now looking at her and Natasha realized she had tuned out, missing most of his response to the question. Her aunt was watching her closely, as if expecting a reaction and Natasha wanted to sink into the ground.

"My own good?" She sputtered out, but quickly considered that she should've left it alone. Her aunt didn't have to know about this situation. Not that she would believe it, even if Natasha told her. No one would.

"Do you remember our conversation a couple weeks ago?" Clifford asked. His voice was easy, gentle, as he cautiously stepped back, his face remained neutral in expression. His eyes roamed her face and she felt a sudden pang of guilt, as calmness took over her body. She suddenly felt light, as if she could float up into the sky and over the clouds. She had no anger. She had no sadness.

Suddenly feeling awkward, she chose to say nothing. They both knew the answer to that question. Unspoken words travelled from her eyes to his and Natasha swallowed back her emotions, knowing that it wasn't the time or place to put them on display. Getting angry didn't change the facts. It wasn't Clifford's fault. She had put herself in this circumstance.

Natasha felt tears running down her face, each almost to her chin before she recognized she was crying at all. Truth had a way of pursuing her and no change in the destination would ever change that fact.

She felt her aunt's gentle hand on her back and her body being pulled into a quick hug. Stepping back from Flora, she noted that Clifford now stood before her, his eyes imploring her to accept the truth. She just couldn't do it. Not yet.

"My mother had no right to tell you where I was," Natasha said through her angry tears and she felt Flora give her arm a squeeze, giving her the strength to continue. "I can't do this right now."

"Natasha, I understand that you're scared-

"Clifford, No!" Natasha felt deep pain running through her tears, as she moved away from him, desperately shaking her head. "Please, no!"

She sensed movement to her left and turned to see Chase walking onto Flora's property. He appeared taller, his chest puffed out as if he was the great protector, taking care of the local women. Normally, this would've annoyed Natasha, but in that moment, it felt charming and sweet.

Looking past Chase, she noted a husky blonde, standing on the step next door, staring in their general direction. Her expression wasn't necessarily one of compassion or caring, simply full of cynicism. Maybe she had a right to feel that way.

*To an outsider, it would look like I'm insane.*

"….see if everything was all right?" Chase called out to Flora, his muscular chest protruding from the rest of his body, his face no longer carrying the tranquility and childlike innocence of earlier that day. Natasha glanced once more at Audrey, who rolled her eyes and went back into the house.

"We have a bit of a situation here, Chase," Flora spoke sternly. Small wrinkles formed around her eyes, as she glared in Clifford's direction. "This man obviously doesn't get that when a woman says no, she means no."

Natasha immediately recognized that her aunt chose the worst possible words to answer Chases' question. Without having time to finish her explanation, the two of them watched in stunned silence, as Chase grabbed Clifford by his shirt collar and drew him forward.

"When a woman says no, she means no asshole," His words were abrupt, direct and to the point and Clifford looked frightened for his life, while Flora rushed forward to grab Chase's arm.

"No!! Don't do it!" She interjected with a smooth, yet assertive tone that seemed to neutralize the situation. "I'm sorry, I didn't word that the right way. I mean they're having some kind of disagreement."

Chase let go of Clifford, but continued to glare at him. Clifford slowly eased away from Chase, not hiding the fact that he was clearly frightened of the strapping Albertan. "Then what are you doing here?" Chase challenged Clifford. "You weren't invited, were you?"

White as a ghost, Clifford shook his head. "I obviously made a misjudgment."

"You obviously did." Flora agreed, standing between the uninvited guest and Natasha, almost as a shield. "Now, I would appreciate it if you leave my property."

"I...I will." Clifford gave an apologetic glance at Natasha, who felt a minuscule moment of compassion, but it faded away quickly. Getting into his car, he wasted no time shooting down the driveway and back onto the road.

It almost seemed as if Chase were turning toward her in slow motion, a seductive grin barely touching his lips. His eyes were glazed as if coming down from an adrenaline rush; it was almost sexual and hypnotic. He somehow seemed bigger, almost like an animal that was growing in size just before fighting off an enemy. Yet there was a trace of excitement, his nipples hard under the flimsy material that covered his chest. It was extremely arousing and had there not been a captivated audience, she-

"....was here waiting for us," Her aunt was relaying the entire story to Chase, which nodded in understanding.

Natasha felt a chill pass over her body. It wasn't over.

# Chapter Seventeen

❦

She calmly thanked Chase for his concern and aunt Flora for her support then wasted no time rushing into the house and upstairs to the guest bedroom. There she calmly closed the door and automatically glanced into the mirror. It displayed the reflection of a woman who was nearly unrecognizable. Her hair wild from the humidity, her eyes filled with a combination of fright and sorrow, she resembled someone who had just entered the insane asylum.

The bandage she occasionally used to cover the scar on her forehead always stood out, like a scarlet letter reminding her of the how she got hurt in the first place. Natasha's face looked old, no longer that of a young woman, but someone who had lived a long, difficult life full of challenges and fatigue. It was an image that alarmed her and tears sprang from her eyes, now reddened and swollen.

Collapsing on the bed, her body exhausted after the ordeal that had just taken place, she silently cried into the gentle, soothing blanket beneath her. Running her hands over the comforting material, Natasha suddenly had the impulse to go to sleep and leave the day behind. She wouldn't change her clothes or get rid of her makeup, just stay in that exact position until the next morning.

But then she thought of her mother and her role in this whole mess.

Had Clifford really contacted Cynthia Parsons in order to find her? Was it merely a story to cover up the truth, that perhaps he was always aware of her location? Remaining calm, she concluded that perhaps this was her paranoia kicking in after a very long day.

Without giving it a second thought, she grabbed her phone and hastily called her mother.

"Hello darling, how are you enjoying Alberta?" Her mother's voice was too cheery, briefly causing Natasha to wonder if she was drunk. After all, it was Saturday night, wasn't it? Didn't her parents usually go to an expensive restaurant and attempt to give the impression that they still had a real marriage on the weekend?

A loud, booming voice in the background was clearly coming from a microphone. It took her another moment to realize that it was her uncle Arnold speaking. She couldn't make out his words, but she instantly knew it was one of his political events, where he attempted to win over some votes - or as Vanessa said - encouraged people to drink the Kool-Aid.

*That's why she wanted me out of town this weekend! She thought I would go to Uncle Arnolds's fucking shit show and somehow humiliates him! I was exiled to the country like some shamed creature.*

Suddenly she forgot about Clifford.

"What's going on? Where are you? Is that uncle Arnold talking?" Natasha couldn't control her rage. The fact that she had been shipped away to the country on the weekend of another political event – as if she would want to fucking attend it anyway – only added fuel to the fire. It was as if she were the embarrassment of the family, much like a kid who's locked in the attic so that the parents could hide their shame.

"What?" Her mother's voice found a nurturing tone, as her heels loudly snapped to indicate a fast dash to another room and uncle Arnold's voice started to drown out in the background. The line was silent and for a brief second, Natasha thought Cynthia Parsons had either hung up on her or the call had been dropped.

"Are you there?" Natasha felt her anger grow and she began to bite her bottom lip. Her available hand immediately reached for the bandage on her forehead, feeling a sense of ease as she touched it.

"Yes, I am," Her mother's voice was now shrill. An echo indicated that she was probably in a washroom or somewhere out of hearing range of anyone important. "Your uncle Arnold had a last minute thing tonight and of course, your father and I are here to support him."

"So is that why I'm here this weekend?" Natasha boldly asked, her heart racing furiously, just as it had a few minutes earlier during her conversation with Clifford. Why was everyone else trying to control her life? Even more so, why had she allowed it? "So I won't be there?"

Silence. As if she were being ignored, her mother finally spoke.

"I thought I was doing you a favor." Cynthia's voice was smooth, calm, as if she were entirely innocent in the matter. "I thought somebody should try to save you from yourself and your... crazy notions since you hit your head. I thought getting away from the city would be good for you, especially before you return to work."

Natasha was stunned. She didn't even know where to start with that statement; not that she had a chance to say anything before her mother spoke again.

"I know you'll be mad at me for saying this, but you haven't been yourself since hitting your head and to be honest, you weren't exactly showing adult behavior before either." Her words were curt, hardly the soothing and mothering tone Cynthia Parsons had used at the beginning of their conversation. Although it shouldn't have bothered Natasha, she felt a sinking feeling in her stomach. "You know that one of your dad's sisters is bipolar and it does run in families. I hate to ever think that-

"I'm not bipolar, mom!" Natasha couldn't keep back her fury. It was the most manipulative that her mother had ever been, trying to suggest that her mental health was questionable. Her anger continued to howl like a raging lion, but she couldn't help but think that the Band-Aid had been ripped off her family and the truth was seeping out.

"Honey, no one ever wants to think that they're bipolar." Her mother's voice was condescending, direct and cut like a knife. To suggest that her daughter was mentally unstable felt like the ultimate sign of deception. Natasha hated to accept it, but she also started to question her sanity at that very moment. Then again, maybe that was the plan all along.

"I'm a doctor, mom." Natasha curtly reminded her. "I believe I know the signs of bipolar – not to mention the fact that it's highly over diagnosed – but, it's an extreme mental disorder. I don't fall in that category."

"Because history has proven that you can be impulsive and out of control," Cynthia sneered and pain shot through Natasha's head. Rubbing her eyes, she felt the urge to cry more angry tears, but quickly swallowed back her true feelings. "What took place at your uncle's last fundraiser proves this fact. I'm not certain if the stress of your workload is getting to you or if something else is going on in your life, but your behavior that night was not how a rational, sane person acts."

Natasha opened her mouth to talk, but the words wouldn't come out. She felt deflated, suddenly tired. Her arms were limp, almost causing Natasha to drop her phone.

"I suggest you try to get your act together now before you make a complete mess of your life."

The line went dead.

Her mother hung up on her.

Dropping the phone on the mattress, she ignored the lurking text messages and instead closed her eyes, allowing her memory to slip back to that night. Her fingers gently moving over the cloth bandage on her forehead, her thoughts shifted to the large room where the fundraiser had taken place.

The event took place at an expensive hotel in the upscale end of the city. Rich people floated through the room, stuffing her uncle with pre-election day bribes. The man was essentially nothing more than a puppet on a string; it was only a matter of who would hold those specific strings that was the real mystery.

Her uncle was a snob. He didn't believe in helping people unless they were making over $100 000 a year. He didn't worry about poor people and had openly discussed 'cleaning up' the downtown eastside. In other words, he desired to take away the visually unappealing side - or the realities of Vancouver - so that rich assholes like him didn't have to see the poverty and hopelessness that truly did exist in their community.

The most pressing matter to Natasha was that Uncle Arnold wanted to close a supervised injection center. This was a place where addicts were provided with clean needles in order to prevent the spread of diseases such as Aids and Hepatitis. It also allowed some of society's most vulnerable people the opportunity to receive counseling from those who understood the miseries of addiction: those who understood that drug use was a little more complex than simply making a 'bad decision' in life. Many people applauded such a resource in the community and saw the benefits. Her uncle wasn't one of those people

Nevertheless, when Natasha attempted to discuss this with him at the fundraiser, he laughed and ushered her away, as if she were a wide-eyed child who simply didn't understand what she was talking about. He discredited her in front of several men in expensive suits – some of which were really listening to her plead her case – ignorant to the realities of what these people were up against. In her uncle's mind, this center encouraged drug use and recruited young, impressionable people into its doors and that simply couldn't have been further from the truth.

She had volunteered at these centers and knew there was no pride walking through the door, people weren't strolling in off the street, wanting to find out how to get high and the idea that anyone would seriously believe that, was preposterous. Desolation and disassociation were what walked into those doors and detachment walked out. It was an empty life, but this center was the lifeline offered to those who wanted to stop and in some cases save those, who would OD at the location. It was more than someone like Uncle Arnold could ever understand.

So, maybe she did what she did as a form of retaliation. Perhaps it was anger that not only sprouted her rebellious site, but also her libido. Then again, perhaps that was an excuse she told herself. At any rate, it started with a simple hello.

# Chapter Eighteen

"Haven't I seen you at one of these things before?" His voice was gentle, velvety with a beautiful accent that immediately grabbed her attention – Australian, wasn't it? She was so intoxicated by his voice - and maybe a bit from the alcohol - that Natasha was almost too nervous to turn around in her seat. What if the enticing voice came from some old, creepy man? After all, wasn't the room filled with a lot of geezers who looked as though they had mothballs built right into their suits?

A relaxed smile eased across her lips as she reluctantly glanced up, her eyes apprehensively crawling up his face. She was pleasantly surprised to see a handsome, caramel skinned man looking down at her. He had a one sided grin on his lips, kind of like a young, hot Elvis. His eyes appeared to increase in warmth immediately after they made contact with her own, almost as if relieved to see her reaction. His black hair was in an unusual style, sort of resembling someone who just got off a motorcycle without wearing a helmet; but that was fine, she kind of liked it.

Suddenly shy, he seemed reluctant to sit in the vacant place beside her, until she encouraged him to do so.

He wore a standard white shirt and black tie with matching pants. It took her a minute to recognize that he was actually a waiter at the event, not a guest. Not that she cared, but it struck her funny and she instantly started to laugh.

"Wait, aren't you working here?" She pointed at a nearby bar, where a bunch of the geezers and their much younger 'girlfriends' stood around, knocking back drinks. "You aren't going to get in trouble for sitting down on the job, are you?"

"I don't think I technically work here anymore," He searched her face, as if he wasn't certain of how she would take his comment. At the same time, he turned toward her and laid his arm on the back of the chair, his hand almost touching her back. His eyes were huge, full of passion and curiosity. "I may or may not have just quit."

"Oh wow," Natasha turned more in his direction, her leg almost touching his. Glancing down, she saw that her dress was probably a tad short for this kind of event, but the dark turquoise material was too difficult to resist when she opened her closet earlier that day. It was somewhat formal in its presentation, with crocheted lace over a smooth, tight fitting bodice. Hadn't her mother scoffed at Natasha upon her arrival, insisting it was something 'a whore wore to a wedding' rather than appropriate for this affair? Her eyes turned back to the stranger's face and she smiled, raising an eyebrow.

"You don't sound too sure of your current employment status," Natasha said coyly, attempting to sound cool, but wasn't too certain she actually pulled it off. "Did you just, like, walk out…"

"I just, like, walked out," His accent continued to fascinate her and she studied his face carefully. It was flawless, clean-shaved, with a perfect nose and huge, innocent eyes – although, something behind them told her that he wasn't so innocent. "I had it with my boss talking to me like I was a fucking moron and I quit. I did remove my name tag though, and threw it in the garbage on my way through."

"So, do I have to start rummaging through the garbage to learn your name?" Natasha tilted her head downward; her eyes glancing up and she pursed her lips into the most adorable duck lip expression that she could manage, without looking like a drunk posing for a Facebook photo at 2 a.m. "Or do I have to guess?"

"Well, I can tell you mine if you can tell me yours," He raised his brow slightly, then leaned in a bit more, just enough to nudge his leg against her own, sending a spark through her thigh and to the most interesting places.

"Natasha," She reached out to shake hands and his fingertips gently eased across her palm, sending unexpected sensations through her torso, causing her to involuntarily shudder; something that didn't appear to go unnoticed by her new friend.

"Mateo," He answered and gave her hand a squeeze, then much to her disappointment, let it go to loosen his tie. "I don't normally dress this way, so it feels quite uncomfortable. Unfortunately, I have to wear long sleeves in order to cover my tattoos. Apparently they are equivalent to the anti-Christ in these circles."

Natasha giggled and took another drink of her wine. She felt a little tipsy; warmth swam through her body and she suddenly didn't care about her ignorant uncle, her disrespectful family or the many irrelevant, fake people at this party. Although she originally thought Vanessa had the right idea, claiming too ill to drop in, she was suddenly glad to have made the effort.

"Well, in these circles, people aren't progressive thinkers," Natasha insisted and nervously finished her drink.

"You seem pretty progressive to me," His eyes brushed over her nude legs, down to her shiny, high heel shoes that matched so perfectly with her dress; another reason why she had picked this outfit tonight. How often do you get the perfect shoes for a dress?

"I like to believe I am," She spoke confidently, noting that his pupils seemed to increase in size with her strong attitude, much more than the girl next-door act that she usually played. Sitting up a bit straighter, forcing her breasts out a tad more, Natasha smiled. "Definitely more forward thinking than most people here."

"Then why are you here?"

"That's what I'm starting to wonder," Natasha spoke honestly and laughed. "It was definitely a waste of my time."

"It doesn't have to be a complete waste of time, wouldn't you say?" His question had some suggestion hidden behind it, or was that her imagination? "You make your own luck. Create the moment you want.

What would make you happy right now? What would turn this evening around?"

"Is that why you quit?" She felt her throat suddenly become dry, while her body radiated in heat. "Because you did what made you happy in the moment?"

"It was a little more complicated than that, but yeah, I guess you could say that," Mateo seemed to ease a little closer to her. "Sometimes the secret is that you have to follow your instincts, rather than logic."

There was something about that statement that sparked her to do it. There was something in that moment, with the combining elements of the evening that only encouraged her on, coaxing her to hold his hand and lead him from the crowd. Once away from probing eyes, he proceeded to walk directly behind her, his hand slipping over her waist to squeeze her right side. His other hand gently touched her fingertips, easing her in a different direction from where she was headed.

"This way," He muttered. "There's more privacy."

Away from the washrooms that were frequented by the guests of the event, to a smaller, less elegant and poorly lit part of the hotel. It appeared to be facilities for employees, but at that moment, it didn't matter. She would've gone anywhere with Mateo.

"Watch your step," His accent seemed a lot deeper now that they were away from all the noise. Opening a plain door, he held her hand and he helped her up a short step just inside a small bathroom. "Crapped up renovations." He attempted to explain. "Fancy smanchy hotels don't tend to worry about staff quarters being trip-proof."

For some reason, this statement made Natasha drop her head back and laugh. She wanted to tell him how much she hated the class system, but didn't have a chance to say a thing before Mateo leaned in to ravage her neck. His tongue, his teeth, his lips, they took turns trailing up her neck, greedily trying to grasp every section, while his hands wasted no time roaming up her dress, squeezing her thighs, causing Natasha to gasp in pleasure, as his fingers stroked and explored the fold of skin between her legs. His hands eased to the front of her body, causing a moan to edge up from the back of her throat.

Her fingers boldly moved past Mateo's waist to unbuttoning his pants. She wasted no time slipping her hand into the front, fingers grasped the hot flesh and he let out a low moan and stopped caressing her long enough to pull up her dress and pull down her thong. With both hands sliding down her hips, his tongue slid inside Natasha's cleavage, one of his hands reaching into her bra and coaxing her nipple out. The other hand went back between her legs and shot up inside of her, causing Natasha to squirm.

If he wasn't going to do it, she would. Her hands pushed both his pants and underwear down, revealing his thick and very erect cock, she pulled his body close to her own until he was easing inside of her. Feeling as though she was on the edge, craving the sensations that would send the pleasurable relief she needed, she wrapped her arms around his neck and legs around his waist, as he pushed her body against the wall, pumping into her slowly, almost cautiously.

"Harder," She whispered and he quickly followed her instructions, as she squeezed everything she had to get this as intense as possible; her legs around him helped to send her over the edge, as pleasure ran through her body. Hearing him panting in her ear, speaking short words like 'oh God,' only managed to make her more stimulated, as if his accent helped to get her off.

"I can't come inside of you," He said suddenly, as he abruptly pulled out.

Natasha's wobbly legs returned to the ground and she nodded, her heart racing and she was panting. "Can I….could you, from behind?"

At that stage, she didn't care. Her body was encompassed in pleasure; he could stick his dick anywhere, if it got him off. She was willing to be negotiable. For some reason, she thought they had to change positions, so she walked away from the wall and faced the door. He didn't seem to disagree and soon, she felt him, still wet from being inside her, slip into her ass. His hand grasped her crotch and he started to make a few loud grunts, his hot breath on the back of her neck and much to Natasha's surprise, the sensation of the anal stimulation was quite pleasurable. She felt her legs become weak, as intense sensations made her loudly gasp as she felt her entire body moving and she didn't care because the desire was so strong, so powerful and gratifying that nothing else matter.

Her body lurched forward just as Mateo let out a loud gasp and she felt herself tripping, his hard body smashed into her own.

Opening her eyes, Mateo was now standing, leaning over her, his shirt undone, his pants not fully zippered, and blood on his sleeve.

"You're bleeding," She muttered and instinctively reached for her forehead and pulled her hand back. Blood dripped from her fingers. "*I'm* bleeding."

It took her another moment to realize that several other people were in the room, standing just inside the door, staring at her in shock. Her skirt was still over her waist, no panties and her right tit hung out.

There was no dignified way to explain this away.

# Chapter Nineteen

The beauty of a good night's sleep is that it helps to process the many thoughts that polluted the mind throughout the day. Whether it be an indiscretion of the past, an unpleasant confrontation with somebody you wish would go away or the crude restaurant that serves up food in a trough; life had a way of sorting out in our dreams, allowing our brains to start off fresh the next morning.

That was exactly what Natasha experienced on her second day in Hennessey. She woke up feeling refreshed as sunlight floated through the window, gently reaching across the room, shedding light on a peculiar ornament on the spare room dresser. It took her a minute to realize that it was an upright pig wearing a pair of denim overalls with a piece of straw in his mouth. It had a creepy *Animal Farm* vibe.

And then again, hadn't the last day given her that same, weird vibe? It was like a little shock that continued to electrocute since arriving. One bizarre event followed another; as if she had somehow descended into her own version of *Alice in Wonderful* and it was quickly spiraling out of control. If someone were to tell her that this was a dream or she had accidentally taken a hallucinogen, she would've believed it.

"Can't wait to see what today brings," Natasha muttered to herself as she sat up in the bed, glancing at a nearby clock. It was 6:30 on her vacation and she awoke long before she would've, had she been home. It must've been the strange bed, she decided, but before she could convince herself to go back to sleep, she heard voices coming from downstairs. Was that Chase? Did he spend the night?

Rubbing her eyes, she yawned and immediately had a thought run through her mind; it was way too early for this shit. Was her aunt fucking him on the couch again? There was a silence and then another voice.

*That sounds exactly like Vanessa.*

Grinning to herself, she once again wondered about her hallucinogen theory of moments earlier, since it was unlikely her sister would arrive this quickly. Grabbing her phone, she dismissed the message from Clifford, her mother and her idiot friend from Vancouver, and sent a quick text to her sister.

*Wow, I miss you so much that I woke up and thought I heard your voice. Talk about sisterly dedication. Ha ha...*

Placing her phone down, she slowly rose from her bed, but as soon as her feet touched the ground, her phone vibrated against the nightstand.

*That's cause I'm downstairs.*

What? Vanessa was there? She was already in Flora's house? Was that even possible?

It suddenly didn't matter that she wore an old T-shirt and pair of shorts that she changed into after her day clothes proved uncomfortable to sleep in, or that her hair was going in several different directions, or that her bare face probably had fragments of yesterday's makeup; she had to go see her sister.

Well, after she peed.

As it turned out, her ears hadn't deceived her. In the kitchen, she found a slightly disheveled Vanessa sitting at the table, savoring a cup of coffee with an already dressed and preened aunt and of course, Chase, who apparently was a step up from a piece of furniture in the house. However, he was a piece of furniture that was about to break Clifford's balls the night before, so she surely wasn't in a position to complain, especially when he wore tight T-shirts that showed off his rippling muscles.

"Hi," She spoke self-consciously as she entered the room, attempting to run her fingers through the strands of knotted curls and act cute, like a three year old who wandered in the room first thing in the morning. "I guess I slept in or something?"

"Not at all, my dear, I'm an early bird and look who I found when I went out to water the garden this morning," She pointed in Vanessa's direction, as Natasha's sister attempted a tired grin. Regardless of being a bit frazzled in appearance, she still looked pretty together and reminded Natasha of a television character who just had a roll in the hay and yet, barely a hair out of place. "Apparently she believed it would be a better idea to sleep in a Jeep than to come inside."

"I didn't want to wake anyone," Vanessa said in response, a quiet, evasive voice that bordered on shy. Although she had met 'Aunt Flow' as a kid, they hadn't actually been in the same room for years. "It was pretty late when I got here and I didn't want to come banging on the door."

"You could've text me," Natasha suggested, but automatically knew to expect that all too familiar 'Oh, really?' expression on her sister's face. It wasn't as if she would've woken up had Vanessa sent a million text messages. "Yeah, never mind." She dismissed her original thought and glanced toward the coffee pot that hissed at her from the nearby cupboard.

"Help yourself to coffee, hon," Her aunt gestured across the room. "There's plenty there."

Up until this point, Chase remained secondary in her thoughts. It was as she started across the room, that Natasha was suddenly self-conscious about her naked legs in her little shorts and her thin top that barely covered her cheep, bright pink bra. It hadn't occurred to her when she packed that her aunt would have a testosterone filled ornament in the house.

Ignoring the eyes that she felt staring through her, Natasha proceeded to carefully pour a cup of coffee (still managing to spill some on the counter) while the others silently watched from the table. It was awkward. She was relieved when Flora started to speak again.

"You couldn't have slept well Vanessa, maybe you should go upstairs and take a nap or have a shower? I hope you brought a change of clothes?" She suddenly sounded more motherly than their own mother and Natasha couldn't help but to grin, wondering what thoughts were running through her sister's head.

"I might do that in a bit, actually, thank you." Her sister sounded as she always did with strangers, meek and mild, totally unpretentious and respectful. "I have a bag in the Jeep. Thanks for your concern."

"That's a long drive from Vancouver," Chase suddenly broke his silence, as Natasha poured some cream into her coffee and taste tested it before putting in a dash of sugar. She drank a few sips with her back to the others, as a small grin developed on her face, almost wanting to laugh hysterically at how proper Vanessa could be, while thinking the most viscous thoughts.

"Yes, Chase, it *is* a long drive." She replied.

"How many hours?"

"You know, I wasn't paying attention," Vanessa spoke hurriedly and only to those who knew her well, could there be a sense of irritation picked up.

"I bet," He spoke matter of fact and Natasha made sure to have a poker face as she turned around and sipped her coffee for another moment, taking it all in.

She felt a bit sorry for Chase. There was an insecure side to him that she wouldn't have expected, it was in his boyish mannerisms, as if he didn't quite fit into his own body. A man-child, was that even a thing?

"Well, you missed some excitement here last night," Her aunt spoke up and Natasha took that as her cue to join the others at the table. "We had a little issue after coming back from the pub."

"Oh, you went to a *pub*," Vanessa spoke matter of fact, her voice lifting with the final word as she met eyes with Natasha, who quickly looked away as she sat down between her two family members and across from a wide-eyed Chase. "I see."

"Just for food, honey, no boozing for us," Her aunt was quick to emphasize as a grin spread across her face. "Which is probably a good thing, all things considered."

"Clifford was here," Natasha finally spoke. "Waiting for me."

"Clifford?" Vanessa spat out the words, suddenly breaking free of her original cascade of wholesomeness, back to her true self. "The pu- Clifford was *here*? In Alberta?" She waited to watch Natasha nodding. "At this house? Clifford? The weirdo who-

"Yes, he was here," Natasha replied and then took a long drink of coffee. It was going down quite well and she was surprised how calm she felt, all things considered. Her sister was anything but, however.

"Well, I..I don't understand. How did he know you were here?"

"Mom."

"WHAT? Are you fucking kidding me?" Vanessa suddenly halted, as if just realizing what she said and with a look of terror in her expression, she glanced at their aunt who merely giggled at this reaction. "I'm sorry, but is this a joke?"

"No, it's very real. We got back and Clifford was here, waiting for me," Natasha went on to explain. "I'm not sure of the details, but he found out that I was here and showed up."

"Wow, that's crazy!" Vanessa said, shaking her head, glancing at everyone's reaction. "I can't believe it."

"That's okay, I think Chase may have scared the daylights out of him." Flora gestured toward her neighbor, who seemed to hold his breath in and push his chest out and Natasha had to quickly grab her coffee cup to hide her laugh. "I don't think he will be bothering her again."

"Well, there was a text on my phone this morning," Natasha said and moved forward in my chair. "I don't think he will come back here."

"For now," Vanessa replied. "This man is relentless." Her words were directed at both their aunt and Chase. "I think he's got something wrong with him."

"Anyway," Natasha felt anxious and rushed past the topic. "I don't want to talk about Clifford anymore, please." She put her hand up in surrender.

"I don't blame you," Aunt Flora said, gently patting Natasha's arm. "Unpleasant people aren't worth your time. I'm just excited to have both my nieces here with me. I hope you plan to stay for awhile."

The young women exchanged looks and something in Vanessa's eyes told Natasha, that she considered this more a rescue mission than anything else.

"Well, we'll see." Natasha said and winked at her sister, who brought back her poker face and nodded.

"Yes, we shall see."

# Chapter Twenty

＊茶茶朱＊

"I think you're crazy for driving here from Vancouver," Natasha dryly commented, as she leaned in toward the mirror that sat elegantly over the slightly beaten up dresser in the spare room. Applying her eyeliner, she could see her sister rise from the bed, rubbing her eyes and yawning. It was just before noon as the aroma of cooking bacon drifted upstairs, a 'late brunch' Flora prepared for the three of them.

"You know I like long drives," Vanessa slowly shuffled around and stiffly placed her feet on the ground. Natasha had long teased her sister for moving like a senior citizen in the morning. The truth was that she hated getting out of bed and her body retaliated every step of the way.

"That's a really long drive, isn't it like ten hours?" Natasha said and sat her eyeliner down and grabbed mascara from her makeup bag. Her eyes examined the reflection of her sister, as she stood and stretched her arms out in both directions. She was wearing a conservative skirt and blouse, as if she was about to go to work rather than drive to some random, hick town. "Why are you dressed like that? Why wouldn't you wear something more comfortable for the drive here?"

"Cause I left after going into the office."

"You were at the office yesterday?"

"Yeah, we had a meeting," Vanessa explained as she sat down on the side of the bed. "It was kind of a last minute thing, anyway," she hurried along, "I just packed a few things and jumped in the car."

"Did you bother to tell your husband where you were going?" Natasha asked, her hands moving mechanically over her eyelashes and she stopped to turn toward her sister.

"Of course I did," Vanessa said with a quick laugh. "He understood."

"You have a very understanding husband."

"That's why I married him." She curtly replied and stood up again. "I got to get my bag from the car. Maybe I should take a quick shower and change."

"So what do you think of...the gang?" Natasha said while pointing at the floor, indicating their aunt and Chase, who were downstairs working on some kind of repairs.

"Crotch pet is pretty interesting, although harmless and I adore Flow!"

"Crotch pet??" Natasha burst into laughter.

"Yeah, for some reason, I kept wanting to pet his crotch," Vanessa said while wrinkling up her nose. "I don't know why, but I wanted to touch it. Isn't that odd?"

"It seems to be a thing." Natasha continued to laugh as her sister headed toward the door with a mischievous grin on her face.

Twenty minutes later, the three of them were back at the kitchen table. Natasha wasn't used to eating such regular meals, particularly when she was working. Already, she could see her belly pop out, bloated from the nonstop food and coffee. Then again, it was a huge spread; eggs, a plate of bacon, toast, pancakes, home fries, strawberries, cut up melon and pineapple. It was tempting, but Natasha saw how she could quickly overeat if she was in this environment all the time.

Aunt Flora was dressed in her usual attire of jeans and a T-shirt, while Vanessa was barely dressed down from her office wear from earlier that day, now wearing a casual skirt and fitted T-shirt. Unlike Natasha, Vanessa had always been a lot more ladylike in her appearance and mannerisms. It wasn't that she delivered the most proper thoughts or words, but she was much better at sniffing out the situation and knowing when not to do or say inappropriate things.

Natasha felt slightly self-conscious, wearing what Vanessa referred to as her 'hippy clothes', a long flowing dress with a weird, eccentric pattern that was almost hypnotic to look at and yet, it caused people to look away as if it was too 'busy'. Her mother often remarked on how she didn't 'dress' like a professional, but what difference did it make?

Vanessa and Flora chatted on and she could barely get a word in edgewise. The entire conversation made it clear that the two clicked and although she shouldn't have been, Natasha found herself getting a little jealous. It seemed sort of ridiculous, but she tried to convince herself that it wasn't a big deal.

"Right Nat?" Vanessa was suddenly directing a question to her, just as Natasha was bringing a forkful of eggs toward her lips. A sudden move and the entire thing plopped back down on her plate, startling her for a moment.

"Ah, what?"

"See what I mean," Vanessa and Flora were suddenly joined together in laughter, while Natasha felt morbidly sober in comparison. What the hell were they talking about?

"What?" She finally asked.

"You! You always do this!" Vanessa said while giving her arm a quick tap and she continued to laugh as if a series of clowns were doing various yoga poses around them. "You zone out and don't hear a thing. You totally missed the last ten minutes of our conversation, I'm sure of it."

"I, well, I-

"Anyway, I was telling Aunt Flora that we hate our names."

Suddenly back on board, Natasha began to vigorously nod. "Oh yeah, we hate our names."

"They sound like something out of a bad 80s teen movie," Vanessa went on to explain that as children, they begged their mother to alter them. "Like why not a normal name like 'Jennifer' or "Natalie' – nope, we had to be "Natasha' and "Vanessa' as if we were the kind of girls who finished each sentence as if it were a question."

"Natasha and Vanessa." Natasha jumped in with her valley girl impersonation, waving her hands in the air as if about to put on a performance. Quickly, she fell back out of character and rolled her eyes. "It's pathetic."

"That's why we call each other Nat and Van, so we don't feel like hitting ourselves as much as other people must when they hear our names." Vanessa said enthusiastically, almost as she had regained her energy from her nap earlier that morning.

"I don't think anyone dislikes your name as much as you do," Flora insisted and waved her hand dismissively. "It's just a name, no one thinks that much about it."

"I disagree." Vanessa shook her head and dug into her home fries. "I think people hear both our names and think 'morons'."

Natasha vigorously nodded.

"I think you girls put more thought into this than anyone else. Besides," She continued, now focusing on her coffee. "Anyone who judges you based on your name, is kind of silly, wouldn't you say?"

"Vancouver is a judgmental city." Vanessa insisted.

"I think it is because we come from a judgmental family, that we think that at all," Natasha said and then quickly backtracked. "Present company excluded."

"I didn't even take it you meant me." Her aunt insisted, shaking her head and then taking a drink of coffee. "Your mom was judgmental growing up. I think she took more after our father than mom."

"I don't even remember our grandparents." Vanessa commented. "I remember their funerals, that is about it."

"Well, they died fairly young." Flora said as she stood up from her chair and crossed the floor to the coffee pot. Bringing it back to the table, she refilled all three of their cups without even asking, something that didn't phase any of them. "Your mom didn't have the best relationship with our parents, so I guess she decided to pretend they didn't exist. That's why she rarely comes back here or talks about anything having to do with Hennessey. She moved on and left the past behind her."

"Why? I don't understand." Vanessa said and held her cup up in the same way as their aunt, almost as if mimicking her.

"Your mom is not exactly a country girl at heart," Flora said with a shrug. "And that's fine, it's not her. Vancouver is a more appropriate place for Cynthia and that's what makes her happy."

"I wouldn't exactly describe mom as being 'happy'." Vanessa said and frowned. "I don't remember mom ever being happy, do you Nat?"

Thinking for a moment, she made a face. "She smiles sometimes?"

"See, that's what I mean," Vanessa spoke directly toward their aunt. "She doesn't seem happy, just going through the motions."

"Maybe she's not," Flora shrugged. "At the end of the day, it's only up to her to make that change."

"I think she thought marrying dad would make her happy, but I'm sure he cheats on her," Vanessa continued to bond with their aunt, gently touching her arm and leaning in closer. "Like, every chance he gets."

"Well, we don't know that for sure," Natasha attempted to remind her, but to no avail.

"I think you're a bit naïve, Nat," Her words stunned Natasha and she fell silent as the two went on to discuss Cynthia Parsons. Her aunt seemed to be of the opinion that it was none of their business, while the investigator in Vanessa felt it was necessary to unveil the truth.

Meanwhile, Natasha felt her mind drifting as she looked out the window and into the neighbor's yard. Chase was cutting the lawn. He was shirtless, his muscles bulging as he worked, Nike shorts flowing gently over his hips, his thighs-

"Remember that, Nat?"

Nodding, she pretended to listen. She felt that these words were simply meant to be a small gesture to make her feel as if she were still a part of this conversation. She continued to nibble the last of her food, drink her coffee and watch the neighbor, as he worked.

Then out came his wife. She moved with the same grace as an elephant would, as it strolled across the dessert. Her expression was painful to look at, almost as if it would hurt too much to smile. She approached Chase, who calmly stopped the lawn mower and listened to her words, his face that of an obedient child. After he nodded in agreement, she turned around and waddled back to the house.

What did he see in this girl? There just had to be a story there.

# Chapter Twenty-One

Vanessa and Aunt Flora continued their newfound love affair that afternoon, when the two decided to explore some local towns – the shops, the coffee shops – whatever else small town Canada had to offer. Natasha opted out of the trip, insisting that she needed some time to unwind, maybe sit down with a good book or take a nap. She certainly wasn't prepared to accept that she was kind of jealous of their bond, as she watched them chat about their upcoming adventures.

It wasn't that she felt threatened that her sister and aunt seemed to click so quickly – like *immediately* after they started talking - but the feeling of being the outsider looking in. Although her relationship with Flora was pleasant, she certainly hadn't developed a solid bond with her and was convinced that was normal, since the two of them barely knew one another.

But then along comes Vanessa, proving this theory wrong in a mere few hours. The two of them talked nonstop and seemed to practically finish each other's sentences, interacting how a female parent and daughter would on television, but that wasn't *realistic*.

Oh wait; was it realistic? For her entire life, Natasha hadn't considered that having a strong connection with your mother was anything more than idealistic. Sure, she knew there was some kind of connection, but not like the one you see on television. It was prettied up and glamorous, just as were the many perfect women that floated across the screen, with their flawless hair and makeup, trim figure and perky breasts. She had always assumed the intense connection between mothers and daughters on television was merely another exaggerated work of fiction; the kind of thing that made viewers smile and nostalgic for a childhood that they never had in the first place.

It was no secret that Vanessa and Natasha weren't close to their mom. Cynthia Parsons simply was not a kid person. For all the efforts she made to adopt Vanessa and then have a biological child, she had never shown either of the girls much attention while they were growing up. They were essentially brought up by a series of Filipino and Spanish women with broken English that rarely stuck around for long.

*Were they illegal immigrants that dad snuck in?*

The women were always quite young, usually in their late teens and early twenties, attractive and-

*Oh fuck! Vanessa is right! I am naïve. Very naïve.*

The realization hit her harder than Natasha expected. She hadn't said a word to Vanessa as the idea sunk in. She sat across the room, quietly peering at a book about the town history, while Vanessa and Flora made last minute pleas for her to join them for the day.

"It'll be fun, come on!" Vanessa coaxed as they were on their way out the door.

"We can wait for you," Flora insisted, her eyes sympathetic, as she gently patted Vanessa's arm and they shared a maternal-like smile. "It's not a big deal."

"No, no, please, you guys go along and have fun. Everything has been so crazy that I just want to relax, read a book and do nothing." She was well aware that a fake smile braced her lips and hoped it wasn't as transparent as it felt. Vanessa looked skeptical, but then shrugged.

"Okay, if you're sure?" Vanessa said with a relaxed smile.

"Yes, please, I'm positive." Natasha insisted and again, wondered if insincerity rang through, casually flipping her hand in the air and forcing a smile to stay put on her face. "Trust me, I think I just need to relax."

"Okay." Vanessa said and nodded enthusiastically and the two women walked out the door.

Immediately, Natasha felt a weight fall from her shoulders, the act was finally over. She could return to this miserable stupor that she had been doing her best to hide since arriving. Getting away to the country was anything but stress-free and relaxing. From the intellectually challenged girl on the plane stealing her iPod, to the arrival of Clifford at her door and having to make a huge scene in order to get him the hell out of dodge; it was more draining than if she had just stayed the fuck home!

Now her sister was off with their aunt; the two were suddenly the best of friends, practically holding hands as they skipped out to the truck, past Chase, who waved a sorrowful good-bye.

And what was the deal on this neighbor anyway? Hot guy, who clearly didn't fit in this town full of frumpy, unattractive men, with the wife that looked like she was hit in the face with a hot frying pan and had never fully recuperated. It was starting to feel like a huge joke rather than the actual events of her life.

*It's only been a fucking day! I feel like Alice in wonderland after she's fallen into some alternate universe, where plaid and hunting boots appear to be equivalent to high fashion and the most mismatched people are hooking up.*

Natasha took a deep breath and suddenly felt sad. Tears welled in her eyes as she recognized that it was nothing about Hennessey that was making her upset, it was a distraction from what was really going on right now. Since the accident, Natasha was forced to take a closer look at her life and she didn't like what she saw. Nothing was what it seemed. How many lies can you tell yourself and how long could you choose to believe them?

For instance, she had put her father on a pedestal – as if he could do no wrong and happened to marry a cold, miserable woman – when perhaps the sad truth is that he helped to create that reality himself. If he was an amoral husband who cheated, then perhaps their mother had no choice but to turn into the bitter wife sitting at home.

*But she did have a choice. She didn't have to stay.*

Her mind suddenly fell back in time and a conversation she recently caught. It was her mother having a chat with a friend on the phone, raving about a vacation and arriving home to have the latest renovations to their West Vancouver home completed. She enjoyed living a lifestyle that gave her social status within the community. Had she chosen that as being more important than possibly 'slumming it' on her own, strapped with two children?

It made Natasha more depressed than she expected, as she worked through the many examples over the years that proved her theory on both her parents – her mother, the social status whore and her dad who, it appeared, was simply a whore. It was unreal and on top of everything that had occurred in the last few weeks, caused Natasha to feel like she was losing grip. Her world was suddenly much less stable than it ever had been and yet, it was just a change in perception that was shaking up her reality.

Then again, was it? Hadn't her life become peculiar since Natasha hit her head? Was everyone right that she had changed since the accident? Was it her that wasn't thinking normally now?

Shaking from another flood of tears, she felt her body slide from the chair and onto the floor, as if it would create some stability. It was as if the world around her was moving in two different directions and she wasn't able to see it clearly; instead it was one, confusing blur. And it started the night she hit her head. Got knocked out, while fucking some random stranger in the bathroom at her uncle's political event.

This one thought seemed to calm her, settle the combating ocean that was coursing through her, as if the storm had suddenly passed. She had finally lived in the moment that night. Hadn't it been the first impromptu and dangerous thing she had ever done? Hadn't her life always been planned until that minute? Had that one decision thrown everything else completely off course?

Taking a deep breath, she got up from the floor and headed to the kitchen. Pouring a glass of water, she resolved that she needed a breath of fresh air. Barefoot, she slowly worked her way across the smooth hardwood floors and wandered out of the kitchen door. She found the deck that embraced the front of Flora's home to be so inviting. It was modest, slightly cluttered with a bench and a few wooden chairs, but at the same time, it created a feeling of warmth and intimacy. She eased into the nearest chair and sat down.

In contrast, Gerald and Cynthia's patio had a more sterile and unfeeling vibe that discouraged their girls from using it. Natasha remembered one specific time when she spilled nail polish on the beautifully landscaped stones that had been imported from somewhere; her mother's switch went from calm and her usual miserable scowl to hysterical wrath within seconds of watching the dark blue liquid drops on the sacred stones.

For that reason, the girls usually avoided the patio after that point. It was ironic when the family had a party a few weeks later, and drunken uncle Bob spilled red wine in almost the exact, same place that Natasha had scrubbed with everything from nail polish remover to bleach to get out the horrid stains. Cynthia certainly didn't scream that he was a classless imbecile when he made his mistake. The ironic part was that the stain was still there and her parents often laughed over the 'night Bob got a bit tipsy' and left his 'permanent signature' in the stones. Apparently nail polish is the signature of morons.

Refocusing and forcing these dismal memories from her mind, Natasha put her feet up on the opposing deck and sipped her water. Everything was calm. No cars went by, no kids were screaming from the neighbor's house, no distracting, half-naked men cutting their lawn. It was as if the universe gave her some alone time and she treasured it. She didn't want to deal with anything, other than her own thoughts. Even the text messages that have been sitting on her phone upstairs – they could wait.

Her thoughts were interrupted by the sound of a door opening. Turning her head, she saw Chase walk out of his house and their eyes automatically met. He gave her a cheerful wave and she noticed that he now wore a shirt again; different shorts and his virtuousness smile threw her off guard. He seemed somewhat hesitant for a moment, as if he wasn't sure what to do and then he timidly walked down his own step and toward Natasha.

# Chapter Twenty-Two

❦

There was something about Chase that struck her curiosity. He was a man of many contradictions. There was a naivety about him, his eyes filled with a sense of innocence and yet, he was having an affair with her aunt. He dressed in apparel that indicated an urban area, but lived in a rural area. He was in phenomenal shape, well groomed and tanned but yet, seemed somewhat insecure. There was a glow from him when he smiled, generally a happy-go-lucky personality and yet, he was tied to a woman who looked as if she never smiled.

*What the fuck am I missing here?*

But as he made his way up the step to her aunt's deck, he timidly pointed toward the chair beside her and paused for her reaction.

"Would it be okay-?

"Oh, of course, please join me," She removed her legs from the opposing rail, feeling that it was probably not appropriate to be so casual now that she wasn't alone. Sliding to the next chair, she pointed to her former seat. "I thought I would sit out and enjoy the day. It's so peaceful here."

"That it is," He agreed. "Sometimes a little too peaceful." He let out a short laugh that seemed to imply much more than he was willing to share. Was he here against his will? Not to suggest he was captured within town limits, but there was definitely a touch of frustration in his voice.

"Yeah, I can understand how that would be," Natasha nodded and looked toward the quiet country road, almost as if expecting Audrey to pull up next door with all the kids in tow, glaring in their direction. However, all remained peaceful.

The sun's rays grew stronger as they beat down on Natasha's face and she felt a sense of relaxation flow through her body. She wasn't certain how to continue this conversation with Chase, until she remembered the previous night.

"I wanted to thank you again-

"So where is-

Their words seemed to collide and both abruptly stopped speaking and laughed.

"What were you saying?" Natasha asked, turning in his direction.

Chase was staring at his hands; his broad shoulders slumped forward as if he wasn't sure of how to act around her. "I was just asking where your sister and Flora were?"

"Oh, I don't know," Natasha said and rolled her eyes. "They went to check out some shops in some other town? Maybe? I'm not sure."

"Mento?"

"Yeah, I think so," A smile crept on her face. "You mean, like Mentos? The candy?"

"Actually, I think they're technically breath mints," A soft grin crossed his face, as he threw her an awkward glance and slowly started to sit taller in his chair. "And yes, it's spelled the same way. Minus the 'S' of course."

"Um..I see," Natasha said with a serious expression on her face. "So what kind of things does one do in *Mento*."

Sitting back in his chair, staring off into the distance as if looking for the proper answer he finally gave his thoughtful reply. "Not much, actually." A smile lit up his face and he made brief eye contact with her. "It's a wild town at night, but during the day it's pretty boring. Not much different than Hennessey, but we like to think we are a little classier."

"So there's a little sibling rivalry between the sister towns?" She teased.

"Technically, we aren't sister towns, but-

"I didn't mean it literally," Natasha teased. "It was a joke."

"Okay, fair enough," He said and started to loosen up, as if he was slowly growing more comfortable with her. "And yes, there is some rivalry. We kind of look down at them, here in Hennessey."

"Why?"

"Well, they do a lot of stupid stuff," He said and pointed toward his left, as if in the general direction of the town. "They're kind of barbaric. Like, a lot of them come here trying to pick fights with people, especially on the weekend. There's a lot of crime over there, people breaking into each other's homes, that kind of thing."

"Sounds like petty crime," Natasha commented, automatically picturing a socially defunct town. "A little scary maybe?"

"Well, yes and no," Chase replied and turned toward her, his voice respectful and serious. "Actually, it's getting really bad. There's a lot of rape and incest, problems with drugs and alcohol too. Audrey used to see a lot of terrible things when she worked at the youth center there. That's part of the reason why she changed jobs, it was getting really bad."

"That's terrible," Natasha said, suddenly believing that these small communities were perhaps not so quiet after all. It sounded as if it was full of people that felt the rules didn't apply to them. "Like the wild west?"

"Kinda, actually," Chase said with some hesitation. "There's definitely a lot of people in Mento that believe that they don't have to abide by the laws. The sad part is that they often get away with it because of the lack of police presence in the community."

"That's kind of scary, actually."

"It is," Chase replied with a slow, apprehensive nod. "I mean it's not all bad. Not everyone from Mento is terrible, it's just that there's a lot of poverty and drugs."

"Wow, I'm a little surprised that Flora's taking Vanessa there."

"It's okay during the day. People like the ones I described aren't out until nighttime." He reassured her. "Like I said, not everyone from Mento is bad. Audrey is from there, actually."

"Oh, so how did you two meet?" Natasha asked casually, but she was dying to know how these two mismatched people possibly hooked up. It didn't make sense. Was she once attractive? Kind? Was Natasha missing something?

"We met in high school."

"High school sweethearts?" Natasha teased.

"Not really," He spoke earnestly. "I had just got dumped by a girl who I thought was the one. It was just before my graduation and it was kind of a shock. I guess she was dating someone else behind my back and well, I was pretty heart broken."

"Anyway, someone set me up with Audrey and," He shrugged, his eyes shifting away. "Here I am."

"So, was it love at first sight?" Natasha teased, prompting him to continue talking about this confusing love affair.

"Honestly," He said and looked into his eyes, she noted sadness cross over his face. "No, not at all. I didn't actually think we would see each other again."

"So what happened?"

"She got pregnant."

"Pregnant?"

"Yeah, like that night."

"On your first date?" Natasha was stunned. It shouldn't have surprised her; but it kind of did. "Really?"

"Yeah," Chase shrugged. "I was feeling pretty down about my ex and she really made me feel good about myself, saying lots of nice things and things kind of…happened."

"And she got pregnant?" Natasha nodded and felt like it was all finally coming together now. He was stuck, that's what he was actually trying to say.

"Yes, it was a bit of a surprise." He nodded and avoided her eyes again.

*For you, maybe.*

"Anyway, I wanted to do the right thing, and here I am."

"You must've had some feelings though," Natasha tried to coax him to continue speaking on the topic. "I don't think you're here against your will."

"No, I mean, we...work and I do love her, maybe not in the way that I thought I'd love the person I was going to spend the rest of my life with." He replied his cheeks turned a deep pink. "I guess love comes in many forms, that's what I've learned from all of this and we have great kids. A great life."

His body language said anything but, as his face grew grim. It was clear that Chase wanted to convince himself of that fact, but perhaps it was like a square peg fitting into a round slot. She didn't want to pry any further on the issue, deciding that it now fits together.

*Audrey the saint played on his insecurities and jumped his dick as fast as possible; I assume without using any form of birth control. It's the oldest trick in the book. Bitch.*

She felt sorry for him. It was clear that Chase wanted to see the best in people and probably neglected the mounting evidence that she had trapped him. Then again, how could he live with himself if he did know this reality? Maybe it was a protective thing, a way to deflect the truth. No one wanted to think that they had been played.

Deciding it was time to change the topic as the facts floating around them, she racked her brain.

"Thanks again for last night," Natasha spoke sincerely, feeling that he was probably just a good guy trying to help out. "I appreciated your help with Clifford. He was relentless."

"So it was like an ex-boyfriend or something?" Chase said and turned slightly in his chair, giving her his full attention. "He seemed kind of a weasel."

Natasha laughed softly. "He's more of an 'or something'." She ran a hand through her hair and nervously bit her lip. The topic made her uneasy, even though, something told her that Chase might possibly be the lone person who would understand. "Sometimes, we get ourselves in a trap that we can't get out of and it's not something you can really explain to anyone, so it's easier to not bother. That's where I'm at right now. It's not a simple circumstance."

"I can certainly relate." Chase replied, a short laugh followed his words while the man-child awkwardly leaned forward and studied his hands, as if in them, he would find the answers. "Once you crossed certain lines, there is no turning back."

Natasha felt her heart sinking abruptly, almost as if lurched into her chest and nausea formed around it. He knew all too well.

# Chapter Twenty-Three

The biggest surprise was that she actually liked Chase. Had she allowed her assumptions to guide her, Natasha never would've given him the time of day. Had she encountered him in Vancouver, she probably would've assumed he was some moronic, egotistic asshole, with no real substance and nothing profound to say; the kind of man that spend most of his time at the gym or at home, shining up his car or his dick. Not exactly someone she would get to know.

Maybe she was being unfair. It wasn't right to judge someone she barely knew and yet, she did it all the time. The girls walking through the mall, laughing in their dainty little size 0 dresses, looking as if they hadn't a care in the world. How many times had she reached the assumption that they were merely someone's princesses and was never required to work hard for anything in their lives? Was that really fair?

It wasn't confined to people she met in her daily life, but situations that came with them. Hadn't she assumed that Chases' wife was an opportunistic cow who got pregnant on purpose? Was it fair to make that kind of harsh judgment about someone she had never even spoke to, barely saw more than across the yard?

As it turns out, there are some things you can make an immediate and accurate assessment on and other things, you could not. This is what she found out after an extended conversation with Chase. He was unguarded and as he grew more comfortable with her, began to open up more and more, confessing that he wasn't certain that he was on the right path in his life.

"It's not that I regret my family," He hastened to say; perhaps, Natasha considered, rushed a bit too much. They both now sat with outstretched legs, using the railing across from them as a footstool, like old friends that weren't interested in trying to impress one another. "I feel like I could do a lot more, but I'm not sure what. I've always sort of done what I thought I should do, never thought that maybe there was something more for me out there."

"What changed that?"

"When I lost my job at the gym," He spoke matter of fact, as the afternoon sunlight caught a glint of vulnerability in his brown eyes and he twitched his nose, his long eyelashes flickered quickly, as if the sun were much too bright and so he looked away. "It was a real eye opener for me. I knew it was going to happen. I mean, I don't know if you noticed, but people aren't exactly concerned with fitness around here."

Natasha recalled all the overweight people she had noticed since arriving in Hennessey and managed to suppress her laughter, if even for a second. Following her lead, he grinned and simply nodded.

"So," he went on, as if the unspoken words were powerfully implied, "I kind of expected it, but it was still a shock and it wasn't so much the fact that I didn't have a job, as kind of wondering what to do now?"

"And?" His depth intrigued Natasha. It never occurred to her that he was somebody who was on a journey of self-discovery. She was so used to people mindlessly moving forward, never thinking about what they really wanted out of life, that this was a pleasant surprise.

"And I don't know." His voice was full of defeatism. Taking a drink of the beer she had brought to him earlier, he avoided her eyes. "That must seem pretty stupid to someone like you."

"Me? Why would you say that?" Natasha started to laugh and wiggled around in her chair. She had to pee, but didn't want to stop this conversation for fear that it would lose its current vibe. "Why someone like *me*?"

"Well, you know, someone who has their life together," Chase said, a hint of bashfulness in his voice. "You're a doctor, you probably live somewhere nice, lots of friends. You're sister and aunt are cool and you look like someone who takes pride in her appearance. You know... together."

Natasha's response was a sardonic smile and an exaggerated eyebrow raise.

"No?" Chase asked, tilting his head and curiosity filled his eyes. "I don't see anything that suggests otherwise."

"Well, there are things that would," Natasha muttered and began to laugh.

*If only he knew!*

"Okay, so like what?" He dropped his feet from the railing across from them and turned more in her direction. Appearing completely engaged, there was no denying that he was intrigued to hear her story.

*Oh what the hell?*

"Well, to begin with, the only family I either talk to or get along with *is* Vanessa and Flora. Most of my relatives are snobs, who care more about their social status than anything else." She hesitated, noting the surprise in Chases' expression and wondered briefly if she should go on. She did.

"My sister is my only real friend. My family tries to control me. I wanted to be a doctor to help poor people, people who were at a disadvantage, but my family managed to convince me to work in some snooty clinic instead." She hesitated for a moment. "Not that everyday people don't deserve health care too, it's just that I don't feel like what I'm doing matters."

"That bothers you?"

"That bothers me a lot. I didn't become a doctor for the title or prestige." She hesitated and bit her lip, thinking about the people that appeared at the door of a small, drop in clinic in the most down and out part of Vancouver. It was a portion of their training that required them to help people who were often neglected, most forgotten members of society. It differed from other clinics because no appointment was needed and patients weren't required to travel outside of their local area, perhaps to a place that was awkward for someone who already felt disregarded by society. "I just wanted to help people."

"That's good," Chase encouraged. "I think you should be proud of that fact."

"I am," Natasha said, suddenly feeling vulnerable, as a powerful moment overtook her and she felt herself blinking back the tears. "I um…I did something insane, Chase."

"What do you mean?" His voice was little more than a whisper and she realized that he was merely echoing her own tone. "What did you do?"

Sighing out loud, she thought back to the night of her uncle's political fundraiser. Other than her sister, Natasha had never spoke of that night with anyone.

"My uncle, he's a politician," She slowly started. "A self-serving politician. He doesn't care about people. He only cares about moving up the political ladder, making lots of money and basically we had a difference of opinion. He wants to have all the homeless people in Vancouver moved out of sight, rather than trying to help them. He doesn't want to increase funding for mental health or create more low-income housing or…I don't know, putting funds into homeless shelters. If he had his way, a dump truck would come along and swoop them all up and take them far away."

"He obviously doesn't say that though." Chase questioned, but it was clear that he got the picture.

"No, I mean…he doesn't say that, but you have to kind of read between the lines." Natasha explained. "He talks about 'cleaning up the streets' in very vague terms, but is less vocal about his intentions on closing a safe drug injection site and we need to keep that place open. It provides clean needles for addicts, first aid if it's needed and counseling and support. It's not there to promote drug use, like he kind of implies."

"Of course, he's careful how he words it, but he's putting his ideas out there and hoping to get funds from people who support his short sighted views. He doesn't understand the nature of poverty and drug use and he's not willing to listen."

"Your uncle sounds like an ass." Chase cautiously responded, as if he wasn't sure whether or not to share his opinion.

"He *is* an asshole," Natasha confirmed and nodded, briefly considering that maybe she didn't have to get further into the story. "Anyway, I decided to try and reason with him. I went to one of his political fundraisers and talk to him. I mean, I'm a doctor, I like to think that demands some respect in his eyes, but he brushed me off as if I were some silly hippie…"

Her voice trailed off and she glanced down at her current outfit. "I mean, I wasn't dressed like this at the party," She laughed and Chase joined her with a knowing smile. "But I explained myself well and he wouldn't listen. He didn't care."

"So what happened?"

"I sat down. I tried to digest his reaction and was trying to think of what to do next or how I could shake things up and then I had a few drinks?"

"Ah ohh.." Chase grimaced. "Sounds like you did something you regret."

"You could say that." Natasha took a deep breath and turned away from Chase a bit, almost in an attempt of self-protection. "I fucked a guy in the bathroom."

Noting the look of shock and reluctant amusement in his eyes, she continued. "And while doing so, I stumbled and fell into a wall," she pointed at the scar on her forehead. "That's how I got this and it was a huge scene because I was literally discovered in the bathroom with my dress up and panties down."

Chase opened his mouth, as if he wanted to say something and struggled with a smile, as if not sure how to react.

*Why stop now?*

"The guy was scared, he thought I was dead because I was unconscious and there was a lot of blood. He ran for help without making sure I looked…presentable and well, half the party was in the room when I regained consciousness a few minutes later."

"I…I don't know what to say…"

"You can laugh, Chase, it *is* kind of funny."

He did. In fact, he laughed so hard that tears were forming in his eyes and after watching for a second, she couldn't help but join him. For a minute, she didn't want to think of the repercussions of her actions, how they changed the course of her life; she just wanted to laugh.

That was when her aunt and sister arrived home.

# Chapter Twenty-Four

"Looks like we are missing a good time here," Aunt Flora commented as she came up the walkway, with Vanessa in tow. Both were carrying bags and while Natasha's sister had a peculiar, yet humored expression on her face, Flora appeared to be planting a smile on her face to cover something else. Perhaps Natasha was misreading it, but she could've sworn her aunt looked pissed off.

*Is she seriously jealous that I'm talking to her boy toy?*

"Oh, Nat was just telling me a story about ah...Vancouver," He paused and shared a smile with her, something that seemed to increase the frustration in Flora's face. This time she didn't attempt to hide it. Meanwhile, Vanessa now appeared irritated too, probably because Chase referred to her as 'Nat', something that no one else did, other than her sister.

This appeared to go over Chases' head. His unpretentious and sweet disposition contributed to a pleasant and relaxing afternoon.

At any rate, something told Natasha that she should go in the house, even if the idea had little appeal. Vanessa and Flora's arrival had stolen some of the magic of the afternoon, even if Chase didn't appear to sense any of the tension. It was just as she was putting the brakes on their conversation, that she noticed his eyes bug out and the joy fade from his face.

Audrey was getting home. Three car seats could be seen in the minivan, while at least one child joyfully bounced around. Natasha suddenly realized how cumbersome it would be to travel with three little children.

While Natasha had sympathy for Audrey's situation, the thoughtful feelings weren't mutual, as a cold gaze was shot from next door. Natasha noted that Chase seemed to overlook a lot of subtle clues, but he certainly didn't appear to miss this one. Abruptly jumping up, his entire charisma shut down and slumped into the ground, as if it melted off him and ran away.

*That bitch looks mean.*

"Chase, I need your *help* over here," She immediately yelled, after stepping out of the vehicle and glaring in Natasha's direction.

Without saying another word, he sat his bottle down and practically leapt from the deck and ran next door. Halfway there, he stopped for a brief moment to give a quick wave to Natasha, before heading home. Unfortunately, his choice in timing wasn't the best, because his wife just happened to look up at that very second. She scowled at him.

*Maybe she's not glaring. Maybe that's her usual expression. It certainly is terrifying though.*

She realized that this was probably a sign to go in the house, something that she wasn't looking forward to doing.

Picking up both her and Chases' bottles, she wandered inside, biting her lower lip at the same time. Feeling tension crawling up her back, it was quickly erased when she inhaled the scent of chicken.

Flora looked up from one of the bags, her expression still not overly friendly and pointed toward the oven. "I bought an already cooked chicken, just threw it in the oven to heat it up. Should be ready in a few minutes." She returned her attention to the bag and still appeared pissed off. Behind her, Vanessa's brown eyes were the size of a kiwi, as she pointed to her iPhone, as if to indicate there was something she wanted to tell Natasha, but wasn't able to say it.

Giving a quick nod, Natasha rushed to the counter and carefully sat down the two bottles, unsure of where her aunt put the empties. "I will be right back if you need help with anything, just running to the bathroom."

Flora didn't acknowledge her and Natasha wasted no time escaping upstairs and into the bathroom. She was dying to find out what her sister had to say, but not as much as she was dying to pee.

Once finished, she washed her hands then flew into the bedroom and grabbed her phone.

Noting that she also had texts from both her mother and Clifford – both of which she ignored – she found the latest message from Vanessa. Looks like there were a few.

*We need to get the fuck out of here.*

That was the most recent one. Going back to where the unread messages began, she started to read.

*Did you notice that our aunt is a bit crazy?*

And finally…

*Okay, I said something to piss her off. After we eat we need to make an excuse to leave.*

Weird. It wasn't in Vanessa's nature to say something that pissed people off; it was more like something *she* would do. What the hell had she said?

*What the fuck did you say?*

Followed by…

*Sure, we can leave tonight. That's fine.*

Dropping her phone on the bed, she glanced around the room and realized that her 'getaway' wasn't turning out quite as she had planned. It didn't cut down her stress level, but it certainly gave her some interesting thoughts to chew on. At least she had her stuff together, so they would be able to make a quick escape when dinner was finished.

She was hesitant to return downstairs and as Natasha suspected, the tension could've been cut with a knife. Neither her sister nor aunt was talking. What the hell had Vanessa said to create this situation? She was going to find out, but clearly it was a long story and not something that could've been texted.

Natasha started to set the table, noting that Vanessa's head was down, staring at her phone.

*What the fuck is going on?*

Although she felt like she should start a conversation, Natasha wasn't sure how to do so delicately, without ruffling any feathers.

"Well, you guys had a nice day for you..ah, drive," Natasha stuttered along, not sure what else was a safe topic. Vanessa looked up briefly and raised one eyebrow, while continuing to text. Her aunt ignored her comment.

She finished setting the table in silence, while Flora made a Caesar salad and Vanessa remained aloof. Wanting to check her phone, assuming that Vanessa sent her another text, she pulled the device out of the pocket to see no new messages. Glancing at her sister, who was now looking up, her expression blank. Natasha wasn't sure what to think.

Flora brought the salad bowl over and set it on the table. Vanessa pushed her chair in. Flora grabbed her oven mitts and opened the door to get the chicken. Vanessa glanced at the opposite side of the room, almost like a child that was forced to join the family for dinner.

"Can I do anything, Flora?" Natasha decided to ignore the discomfort she felt and just get through this shit. The sooner they ate, the sooner they could pack up and leave. She hoped her sister was okay to drive. Then again, maybe they could go somewhere and stay for the night.

"You can grab me a plate to put this chicken on," Her comment was dry, but not as unfriendly as Natasha expected. She obediently found and brought the plate to Flora, who was cutting up the chicken and putting the portions on it.

"Smells delicious."

"Yes, the shop in Mento make nice chickens," Flora commented flatly and she avoided eye contact with Natasha. The small lines around her lips seemed to deepen, as if she was pushing them to their breaking point. Aggressively, she cut the chicken, as if she were angry at it too.

*Well, this is going to be fucking lovely.*

Gathering up a tub of macaroni that was sitting on the counter, she took it to the table and noted that her sister had already helped herself to the salad and started to eat. When Natasha gestured toward the plastic container, her sister shook her head. Natasha placed it next to her own plate and took her seat. She glanced up at Flora as she walked across the floor to join them. Her face was drained of any joy that had been there only hours earlier.

Dinner was awkward, yet delicious. Natasha even made some comments on the meal in hopes that someone else would talk, but that didn't happen. Vanessa focused on her food and didn't look at either of them. Natasha attempted to not allow this to bother her, enjoying both the salad and chicken. No one ate the macaroni salad.

The meal was soon finished, the dishes put in the dishwasher and that was when Vanessa spoke for the first time.

"We have to leave," Her comment was short, abrupt and she didn't go into further details. She glanced toward Natasha. "At least, *I* have to leave."

"That's fine, I can go too," Natasha immediately decided, knowing that the tension would most likely continue after Vanessa departed. "I didn't get a return ticket, so this will give me a drive home and I can drive too. It makes sense."

Flora merely nodded and didn't comment. The girls packed up and left.

# Chapter Twenty-Five

❧❦❧

"What the fuck is going on?" Natasha wasted no time, prompting the question that had been on her mind since Vanessa and Flora arrived home from shopping.

Their departure had been awkward; no hugs, a few pleasantries and they were out the door. Had Natasha any idea what was going on, she would at least know how to react, but she hadn't a clue. Was she supposed to be mad at Flora or was Vanessa being overly sensitive about something? It wasn't as if that was something that happened often, but it was possible.

"And furthermore, are you okay to drive?" Natasha thought out loud and shuffled uncomfortably in her seat. The last thing she wanted to was to get behind the wheel and navigate. Although the girls were currently using GPS, it gave Natasha little comfort. "Maybe we can stop at a motel, I'll look online-

"Good luck trying to find an Internet connection in this God forsaken place," Vanessa replied, as she anxiously ran a hand through her hair. She appeared tired and emotionally frazzled. It was a side of Vanessa that she seldom saw. "I'm surprised these fucking hillbillies even are aware that the Internet exists."

"Hey, wait, that's my line," Natasha attempted to shed some humor in the moment, but she was the only one laughing. It was odd that she was so giddy after her conversation with Chase. It was too bad that they weren't able to say good-bye; perhaps she would find him on Facebook or-

".....day ever, followed by the worst week of my life," Vanessa sighed loudly and appeared to be holding back her tears. She took a deep breath, like she wanted to force everything down and sucked in both her lips, as if to keep from saying anything more. Natasha waited for her to go on, but she didn't.

"I'm sorry to hear that," She quietly commented, unsure how else to react in this situation. Natasha wasn't used to seeing her sister cry and felt lost for words. Should she ask what was wrong or just wait and listen? "I hadn't realized that anything was going on. I guess I'm so wrapped up in myself lately, that it never occurs to me that maybe someone else has a problem."

"No, no, that's not it," Vanessa assured her as she pulled on her sunglasses, as if applying them as a mask to hide behind. Then again, perhaps it was because the sun was starting to dip down in the skies and suddenly got hellishly bright. Either way, it unsettled Natasha that she could no longer see her sister's eyes.

"Well, I'm pretty self-involved lately and-

"I think Stephen is having an affair," Her words were blunt and dry. Suddenly everything felt heavy in the Jeep, but a quick glance in Vanessa's direction made Natasha feel weightless, as if this had been a secret that was tying her down for a long time and it no longer carried the same implications. "I'm actually sure of it."

"What?" Natasha said, practically choking on the words. "That's impossible, he's totally devoted to you and always has been...I mean, come on! I think you're worrying about nothing."

"I'm not, Nat," Her words were quiet, almost a whisper and followed by silence. Natasha felt it was inappropriate to say anything, but simply considered the possibility.

"I don't understand," Natasha said in a calm voice, looking away at the vast collection of trees on each side of the road. She felt as though it would take days before they got to civilization again. There had to be somewhere that they could stop and talk about this, but knowing Vanessa, she would feel more comfortable driving while upset.

*That's why she decided to take this road trip. She had to get away as much as she needed to get me out of Hennessey.*

"I haven't been telling you everything, that's why," Vanessa said and briefly glanced in her direction, then her eyes returned to the road ahead. "I don't believe in talking out of marriage, so I kept it to myself. I thought I was being crazy. That maybe we had been together for so long that it was natural to worry about something like this, but the signs are all there."

"What do you mean?"

"We've had the same fights again and again, he was spending less and less time at home," Vanessa started with an unstable argument, which didn't necessarily suggest much more than perhaps some unresolved issues. "Then I saw some text messages on his phone, found some emails on his Facebook from the same lady. She's a coworker at the school She's young, pretty, *white*."

*Oh. Not this again.*

Vanessa had an underlining belief that men preferred women from their own race. Black men preferred black women. Asians men preferred Asian women. White men, like her husband, had a preference for white women. It didn't matter that there was proof of the contrary all over Vancouver. If anything, Natasha actually thought the opposite to be the case, but there was no convincing her sister.

Of course, this was before Vanessa's engagement to Stephen, perhaps even shortly after their marriage started, but the matter had disappeared over time and until that moment.

"That doesn't mean anything-

"They're very flirty messages," Vanessa spoke calmly, all things considered. "Some have been suggestive."

"But that doesn't mean he feels the same."

"I found some messages before going to Hennessey, that suggest that it does go both ways." Vanessa spoke with confidence, secure that her theory had been proven and Natasha couldn't help but believe that she found some satisfaction in being right. "He's having an affair."

"Did you discuss this with him?"

"No, I just packed up and left. It seemed like the most logical thing to do at the time." Vanessa spoke in a rational voice. "I left him a note. He wasn't home."

"I'm sorry," Natasha spoke from the heart and noted that her sister wasn't replying. "I wish there was something I could do or say."

"There isn't anything."

"So, is that why you were upset today?" Vanessa asked, calmly trying to put it all together. "Or did something else happen?"

"I was attempting to keep my mind off everything this weekend," Vanessa admitted, her eyes locked on the road. She showed no emotion, at least, not that Natasha could see. "Trying to pretend nothing was wrong. And when I was with aunt Flow earlier today, it worked for a while. We were chattering about this and that, having fun out shopping and then suddenly it hit me, this is the same woman who is having an affair with a married man. She's the 'other woman' in someone else's life."

"I guess she sensed something was wrong," Vanessa confessed, briefly stopping to check the GPS and then continued. "And asked me. Of course, I didn't want to tell her what I knew about her, so I simply said that I thought my husband might be having an affair."

"You told her before me," Natasha said with accusation ringing through her voice. She spoke before thinking and immediately regretted it. "I'm sorry, I didn't have a right to say that. I'm..ah...I'm sorry."

"I wasn't planning on telling anyone yet," Vanessa replied, not appearing to be frustrated with Natasha's outbreak of emotions. "Believe me, that was the last person I planned to say anything to, but I think a part of me wanted to challenge her, to see how she would react."

"I don't know what I wanted from her," Vanessa shook her head and checked the GPS again. "Maybe to admit her mistake, I don't know why I brought it up."

"So what did she say?" Natasha asked, wondering what created all the tension she had witnessed earlier that day.

"That sometimes people take each other for granted in a relationship and that's why things start to fall apart."

"Well, that could be-

"That sometimes women lie about whom they really are before they marry and then the man feels he is married to a stranger."

"I don't think that-

"That sometimes people grow apart."

"Well, that seems possible," She agreed, unable to deny that may have been the case with her sister. If she had kept this secret, how many other things did Natasha not know?

Not that it was any of her business. Vanessa was probably right to keep things locked safely between her and Stephen, but at the same time, today's confession was somewhat of a Pandora's box.

"Those things didn't bother me," Vanessa admitted as they drove on, suddenly entering another small town. People wandered along the sidewalks, while others seemed to hang out at some kind of parking lot. "She's right, that probably played a part."

"But then I admitted my fear that maybe he preferred a white woman."

"Which is ridiculous." Natasha injected, shaking her head. "If anything, it's probably the other way-

"She agreed with me."

"What?" Natasha was slightly stunned. "She agreed with you?"

"She said it was completely natural that a man would prefer a woman of 'their own kind' and that sometimes people liked to 'experiment' with a different colors because they were curious."

"WHAT?" Natasha yelped out the words, almost jumping from her seat, but fortunately, the tight grasp of her seatbelt held her back. "Are you fucking kidding me? She actually said that?"

"Yes."

"In those words?"

"Yup."

"Oh my fucking God," Natasha said as her heart raced in fury. She felt her face grow warm as an angry tear escaped her eye. She quickly wiped it away. "I can't believe she would say something like that."

"Well, she is mom's sister, after all." Vanessa replied, seeming to be much calmer, as if the confession was removing layers of tension from her body.

"What did you say?"

"I was too stunned to say anything," Vanessa admitted. "I guess a part of me always relied on people like you to say that I was wrong, so I was a little shocked. Then I kind of got angry. Then, I kind of said some stuff."

"What stuff?"

"I told her that you had a picture of her fucking the neighbor on your phone and asked her how his wife would feel about seeing that."

*Oh. That.*

# Chapter Twenty-Six

❧❀❧

Feeling edgy and frustrated at the same time, Natasha reached for the radio and started to turn the dial. A depressing country song came on; she made a face while beside her Vanessa let out a frustrated groan.

"I can't handle that shit right now, Nat." She brought her left hand to her forehead and grimaced, suddenly looking completely depleted of energy. It was difficult to tell if she was crying, as huge, black sunglasses covered half her face.

"I can't handle this music anytime." Natasha muttered in response and somehow felt as though her sister wasn't even listening. She continued to go through the stations – either finding terrible reception, draining monotone voices or more country music. Finally, she decided to turn the radio off all together.

Quietly sitting back, she couldn't help but notice that her sister was driving rather fast. Having just passed a sign with a picture of a bear, moose or some sort of wildlife animal on it, she nervously considered that those signs were probably up for a legitimate reason. Recognizing that her sister was upset, she anxiously wondered if it was a good idea allowing her to drive. But what could she say?

"Van, you look exhausted," Natasha spoke in a comforting voice, similar to the tone she would use in her office, when dealing with a patient who was in a highly emotional state. "Maybe I should drive for a while, you barely had time to sleep last night and I-

"Please, I want to get there alive," Vanessa spoke in such a biting tone that it took Natasha aback for a moment, before she countered.

"Well, I'm as likely to get us there alive as you are right now," Natasha pointed to a sign - and what she thought was a silhouette of a moose - but as it turns out, was indicating slippery when wet. Fortunately, her sister wasn't paying attention to her flaying hands. "You're driving fast and you're in a mood, I think we need to try to find somewhere to stop for a while and calm down."

"I'm perfectly calm, Nat and I'd appreciate it if you wouldn't criticize my driving. If anything, I'm a better driver than you and I'm sick and tired of people suggesting that I can't drive cause I'm Asian." Vanessa said, her voice a mixture of emotions and electricity that was unlike the sister Natasha knew. Vanessa had always been the calm one, the person who kept it together no matter what: until now.

Natasha felt her own anxiety shoot up into the realm of anger, ready to attack, she was surprised when it quickly fell flat and instead, she started to cry. At first, she attempted to hide her tears from Vanessa, but that didn't last long.

"I can't take this!" She began to wail excitedly, feeling her body shaking beneath the seat belt and suddenly felt trapped, her instincts were to remove it, jump out of the car and run away. However, instead she simply pulled it away from her body and wiggled beneath it, as tears dripped off her chin, sliding down her arm.

Sharply pulling over to the shoulder of the road - fortunately no cars were either in front or behind them - Vanessa turned on her signal and put the Jeep into park. Removing her sunglasses, she exchanged somber looks with her sister, unfastened her seatbelt and reached out to give her a hug. Continuing to cry, Natasha inhaled the soft, familiar scent that helped to soothe her all weekend and smiled.

"You stole some of Aunt Flow's perfume." She muttered in Vanessa's ear as she slowly released her and look into her sister's serious face.

"Yeah, it's nice," Vanessa spoke in a matter of fact voice and reached into her purse, pulling out half of a bottle of the beloved Marc Jacobs potion. "Do you want some?"

"You stole *the bottle*?" Natasha asked, her mouth fell open in shock. Suddenly stone cold sober, she couldn't believe it, as Vanessa took the elegant bottle out of the box and sprayed a little her way. Wrinkling her nose, inhaling the luxurious scent, she let out an appreciative groan. "That *is* nice."

"It is."

"You *stole* it?" Natasha returned to her original question and moved back into her seat, although turned slightly toward her sister. "I can't believe you did that."

"It seems too nice for *her*," Vanessa attempted to justify and shrugged, putting the bottle back into her bag, which was probably less valuable than the perfume. "I was pissed and I don't know, I guess you're rubbing off on me."

"I don't steal stuff, what are you talking about, I.." Natasha thought for a moment. "Do I?"

"You always steal! What are you talking about?" Vanessa said and returned to her driver position, pulling on her seatbelt. "You've been stealing for years! Everything from *every* hotel you've ever been to. I think you'd steal the beds if you thought you could get one in your purse."

"I do *not* and the stuff I *do* take is there as a complimentary gift," Natasha insisted and sat forward in her seat, glancing out the window.

"I've seen you steal samples from your office, samples at makeup parties, samples from grocery stores…"

"They're samples! They're meant to be taken."

"Not by the handful."

"No one's ever said anything."

"You wait till they aren't looking!"

"I…I don't see your point." Natasha stumbled through her words and watched as her sister pulled back on the road. "And besides, I never lifted an entire bottle of perfume from someone's dresser."

"It was in the bathroom and it was going to be ruined in there with all the heat from the shower," Vanessa said in attempts to justify her actions. "People who don't know that shouldn't be allowed to have perfume."

"It's like $100 a bottle, Van! I'm sure she doesn't exactly buy it often."

"Maybe her boy toy bought it for her." Vanessa replied, suddenly sounding like herself again, humor ringing through her voice.

"I doubt it since he doesn't even have a job." Natasha countered and shook her head. "I can't believe you *told* her about the pictures." She commented as she watched the never-ending fields from the Jeep.

"I didn't mean to," Vanessa admitted and some emotion returned to her voice. "She was implying that maybe Stephen would prefer a white woman since he's white and I got mad and said it didn't give him an excuse to cheat." Vanessa said and sighed loudly, only hesitating for a moment before finishing her story. "But she wasn't interested in hearing what I had to say and suggested that it was completely fifty-fifty and while I acknowledged that I may have had a role in it, I certainly don't think I encouraged him to run out and cheat."

"*If* he cheated," Natasha felt the need to inject this comment, reminding her sister that nothing was proven at this point. "You don't know that he was cheating, Van. It could be a huge mix up."

"Nat, this isn't a half hour sitcom, a woman knows when her husband is either cheating or wants to," Vanessa spoke patiently; perhaps a bit condescending, Natasha noted but didn't say anything. "Anyway, I told her that she didn't understand, it was complicated."

"And?"

"And she pointed out that she was married before and knew what it was like to have a relationship drift apart, blah blah blah and all the time, I can't stop picturing that photo you sent to me of her riding the cowboy next door."

"Ah oh..."

"So anyway, she said that some people 'did better' by staying single and then she started to talk about you-

"*Me?*"

"Yes, she talked about how 'that city boy' came to the house and how upset you were, how it was clear your 'kind' are better off single too."

"*My kind?*"

139

"High strung," Vanessa calmly replied. "I believe the words she used were 'high strung'. She said that men don't like that kind of woman and something about how you would probably earn more, so it would emasculate most men...."

"What? Are you fucking serious?" Natasha squeaked, feeling her earlier emotions hit a boiling point and turn to full fledge anger. Suddenly, she wanted to go back to Hennessey and tell her aunt off. "Lots of women are doctors and they are married and-

"I know, I know," Vanessa insisted and gently touched Natasha with her hand, to show her support. "She's got some crazy, pretty limited ideas."

"Is that when you showed her the picture?" Natasha asked, feeling a surge of rebellion.

"Not quite, I insisted she was wrong, of course, but she wouldn't have any of it." Vanessa said, a wry smile on her lips, she continued her story. "She claimed that 'young girls' these days don't understand what men want and need and that's why we can't hold onto them. That was around the same time that we started to talk about mixed race relationships too, so I was already on my last nerve."

Natasha opened her mouth to reply, but her throat was suddenly so dry, that the words wouldn't come out.

"So, I pointed out that maybe she was more capable of figuring out what men want and need," Vanessa evenly commented and grinned. "That's when I showed her the picture, in the middle of the small town grocery store, with her neighbors around us."

Natasha started to laugh.

"I'm not saying they all saw the photo, but a few of them definitely heard our conversation." Vanessa spoke proudly. "So that's why she was a little tense over dinner."

Putting it together, Natasha shook her head. "I can't believe you even stayed that long. If I had pulled that stunt, I would've left as soon as I got home."

"I was planning to but when we got there and you were snuggled up to the community stud-

"We weren't 'snuggled up', what are you talking about?" Natasha interrupted and sat up a little straighter, as if it were to somehow represent her character. "We were just talking."

"Well, yes, but you looked pretty comfortable with one another." Her sister smirked. "I thought she was jealous so I thought it might be better to stay and rub it in a little more, so that's why I stayed till after we ate."

"It was awkward."

"It was necessary."

"I'm not sure about that," Natasha muttered and glanced down at her nails and saw her sister giving her a humored glance.

"So, how was it?"

"What? Talking to Chase?"

"Yeah, talking." Vanessa let out a sarcastic laugh. "Yeah, I want to know what you thought of the hot guys talking skills."

"But...that's all we did, we talked.."

"Yeah, right, I could tell that more was going on there." Vanessa laughed as if they were in on the joke together. "You clearly fucked him while we were gone, it was so obvious."

"No." Natasha suddenly felt like a five year old who was being accused of taking the last cookie in the bag, then replacing it in the cupboard. "I'm serious, nothing happened."

"Please, your hair is mushed up, so is your makeup, your bra strap is fucked up..."

Natasha glanced down to see her bra strap had clearly unfastened and fell down her sleeve as it occasionally did, but that didn't mean anything.

"Oh, that bra strap always does that, I got it at the misfit section of the store." Natasha replied, pulled it up and attempted to reattach it to the front cup of her bra. "It randomly detaches."

"The misfit section of the store?" Vanessa started to laugh. "Granted, that seems totally appropriate for you, I don't believe there is a 'misfit' section of the store."

"You know," She said while struggling to hook the bra strap into the delicate little notch in the front of her bra. "Where they have clothing that is defective."

"I think it's the defect section, not the misfit one and why are you buying stuff there," Vanessa said as she glanced in her rearview mirror and frowned. "You're a doctor for fuck sakes, can't you afford a regular price bra?"

"I like a bargain." Natasha replied defensively. "And I didn't have sex with Chase."

"I don't believe you."

"I *didn't.*"

Vanessa shook her head with a sardonic smile and didn't reply.

# Chapter Twenty-Seven

Natasha pretended to be sleeping because she didn't want to have a conversation with her sister: at least, not at that moment.

She was attempting to process everything that had taken place that weekend, but more importantly, the fact that no one ever seemed to listen to her. It was as if she were a five year old who yammering about make-believe worlds and phantom friends. It sometimes felt like her words were meaningless; the tales spun by a psychiatric patient who was delusional, not to be taken seriously.

Clifford showed up despite the fact she had been clear that she needed time. Even after the face-off in Flora's front yard, he continued to text her throughout the weekend. He insisted they have 'one more talk' that was 'extremely important.'

Then there was her mother, who believed she was fucked up and apparently, so did her aunt. Had the two shared notes on the subject? Even worse: were they still sharing notes? After spending two days with Flora, she already had written her off as high strung, hard to deal with and unlovable, in one, quick swoop.

Then again, it was almost as if her sister agreed. Sure, she defended Natasha when their aunt attempted to put her down that day, but when it came to the situation with Chase she drew a fast assumption. At first, it looked as though her sister was teasing her over the matter of the hot neighbor, but somewhere along the line, Natasha could sense that she assumed it was true. Why wasn't her word that nothing had happened enough on its own?

Somewhere during her life, Natasha had grown used to people disrespecting her. It was bad enough that her family did this to her, but she also saw proof of the same thing at her work. Sometimes it was coworkers and other times, it was patients, but it was not uncommon to have somebody give her that dismissive look that she pretended not to see. It made her feel powerless and out of control; it made her feel weak.

But how could she change it? How did you make people respect you? When Natasha first entered college, she believed it was because she looked young for her age. Then after a few remarks about her waif-like figure, she wondered if it was because she looked too small and childlike to be taken seriously. Then another comment on her 'cuteness' made her fear that she would have to hack off her hair, stop wearing makeup and look like a hag to be seen as a reliable source. Not that she would even consider doing any of those things.

It was frustrating, especially when looking around her workplace at *men* who appeared young, fit, attractive and for some reason, it was almost as if their credibility was higher for all the same reasons that went against Natasha. It infuriated her, but whom could she complain to about the matter? It wasn't her coworkers at fault; it was the perception that was created by society.

Quickly forgetting her fake sleep state, Natasha jolted and watched her sister do the same. Ignoring this reaction, she asked the question that was burning on her lips.

"Do you think women are taken less seriously in their chosen professions when they're attractive or young?"

Taken aback by the question, Vanessa merely shrugged. "Where is *that* coming from?"

"I was just thinking about work and well, actually *life* in general and how no one takes me seriously and I wondered if it's because I look young or cute...or whatever, that I'm not taken seriously."

"I think in your case, it's not because of your appearance – although, yes, I generally think that women are judged more harshly when they look good," She quickly added, waving her hand in the air. "I see it all the time."

"So you *don't* think that's why people don't respect me."

"I wouldn't say that *no one* respects you, Nat." She quickly clarified. "I just think that maybe you lack enough confidence and people read that and react accordingly."

"Great! How the hell do I get confidence at this stage in the game?" Natasha shrunk in her seat, knowing that her sister was absolutely correct. She didn't walk into any room - whether it is work, Uncle Arnold's political events or her parent's place – feeling like she deserved to be there. It was almost like she had to prove that she belonged in the room at all. Sometimes she even felt like her patients had to be shown an enlarged version of her certificate, stating that she was actually a doctor. "You have to believe in yourself more," Vanessa attempted to explain, fumbling through words, as if not sure what to say. "I think it's an ongoing thing. It's not a thing where once you have it, you got it for life. It fluctuates, at least it does for me."

"It does?" Natasha sat up straight and eyed her sister from across the vehicle. "But you always seem so confident, no matter what the situation. You never act self-conscious or scared."

"I just hide it well, Nat." She spoke softly, sadly, even, and shot her a sympathetic smile. "Trust me, I often don't feel too confident. I didn't feel confident this weekend, with everything going on with Stephen, but I just faked it, acted as if all was well. I think you'd be surprised if you only knew how often that happens."

Natasha nodded as she considered these words. "You're probably right. I guess I just have to learn how to fake it till I make it."

"You just have to believe in yourself more and stand up to people who try to undermine you. Stand up to the Cliffords of the world, tell them to fuck off."

"That seems so harsh," Natasha decided as she played with the strap of her hippie purse. "Why can't everyone just get along and be cool with what other people want to do? You know? Even with Flora, is it any of my business what she does with Chase?"

"No, but that shit's just funny," Vanessa began to laugh. "Unfortunately, your idea of the world and everyone else's is different and as much as it would be better if we all got along, it just doesn't happen that way. People are locked in their own little power struggles and ideas about how life is supposed to be, rather than just allowing people room to breathe."

"Do you ever feel like that about your life?"

"Sometimes," Vanessa admitted. "Like right now, I hate my job. I want out. I want to explore the world and write about it, but my boss wouldn't allow me to do that and keep my job. Stephen encourages me to do it, but maybe that clears me out of the way so he can cheat."

"You don't know that," Natasha once again reminded her. "I think you're reading it wrong."

"I think you are saying what you think I want to hear." Vanessa countered and their eyes met. Natasha looked away.

"Maybe you're right." She admitted and laid her head back looking at the roof of the Jeep. "Maybe that's what I feel like I should be saying to make you feel better. I guess I just don't want you to jump to conclusion."

"I'm not," Vanessa insisted. "It's only been after a lot of thought on my part."

The two women fell silent. They drove on and signs of life reappeared, as they entered some small town that looked about as hick as the one they just left. People were wandering in and out of a grocery store, which sat next to a well-known pharmacy and after a little more driving, more in the downtown section, they discovered some restaurants and small shops.

"Hey, want to stop and get a drink or coffee…something?" Natasha suggested. "I feel like I need to move my legs and wiggle my toes a bit. This place looks…interesting."

She observed a group of women — some dressed up in heals and skirts, others wearing jeans and trendy tops - entering one particular establishment that appeared to be a nightclub. The doorman was a tall, husky man who managed to capture Natasha's attention.

"Hey, let's go in there."

"A nightclub?" Vanessa made a face. "In a small town like this, I don't think so.."

"Come on!" Natasha insisted and noted that her sister was slowing down and looking for a parking place. "Just for a drink."

Sighing loudly, she didn't reply, but instead, drove the Jeep on the side of the street and put it into park.

"This better not be a bad idea and we can't stay long," Vanessa reminded her. "I want to get the hell home and it's a long drive."

"I promise, I'll have one drink, you can have a beer? A coffee? Whatever," Natasha insisted. "Maybe I can test my aggressive skills and show my new, confident, aggressive side."

"Assertive," Vanessa corrected her. "You want to show you're *assertiveness.*"

"Yeah, whatever," Natasha started to climb out of the Jeep. "Let's go."

# Chapter Twenty-Eight

❦

"This is revolting," Vanessa quickly summed up her surroundings, after the two women entered the dingy little bar. The room had a sticky, scented, aroma that filled Natasha's lungs and automatically caused her stomach to lurch. Glancing around the dimly lit establishment, she quickly located the washrooms just in case her she had to make an abrupt trip. This, combined with the blaring country music, was too much.

Reaching out to tap her sister's arm, hoping that she could ease her back out the door, she was met instead by damp material. Turning back, she quickly pulled her hand away after seeing it instead placed on a huge man's back. He must've been 700 lbs. His entire body was thicker than both Vanessa and her own put together. Turning, he threw her a skeptical, offended glare and Natasha jumped back.

"Sorry!" Her voice rose to an almost unrecognizable squeak, as fear crawled through her spine. This man didn't just look unpleasant behind his big, burly beard, but he also smelled the part and Natasha quickly realized that it was him, not the bar that had almost caused her to vomit moments earlier. She suddenly felt the need to wash her hands and hurried off to the ladies' room.

Through her purse, she felt her phone vibrate. Pulling it out, she immediately saw the message was from Vanessa.

*Where the fuck did you go?*

Glancing around the small, yet empty washroom, she quickly replied.

*Bathroom*

Just as Natasha started to scour away the stench and possible germ-Fest that resided on the creepy, dirty guy from outside, Vanessa came rushing through the door.

"Jesus Christ, Nat!" She shouted over the deafening sounds of a fiddle solo that somehow seemed much louder in the bathroom, than in had in the bar. Skeptically tapping the hand-drying device with her elbow, she felt a whoosh of warm air hit her hands just as she noticed two girls entering the bathroom behind Vanessa. The first of the two, an overweight woman wearing a blue tank top with ample cleavage hanging out, glared at the well-dressed Cambodian woman standing in the center of the room, while her sidekick meekly followed behind. Both went into a stall.

Trying to ignore the fact that her sister was clearly furious, Natasha nodded toward the door. Something told her it would be beneficial to get the hell out of the bathroom – maybe even the bar – before the blue top lady left the stall. For some reason, however, Vanessa wasn't having it.

"What the fuck!" Vanessa snapped and moved closer to Natasha, her voice growing louder. "You left me out there with a bunch of hicks who probably never saw a brown girl in person before and ran off to the bathroom? Seriously?"

"I'm sorry!" Natasha muttered, her eyes grew in size, as if to indicate for her sister to shut up. She abruptly grabbed her arm and pulled her toward the exit. "Let's get out of here."

"Wait! What?" Vanessa replied, suddenly stopping outside the washroom door. "No no no! We're not going anywhere! You wanted to come to this bar and we're having a drink before we leave. See, this is why people think you're flighty-

"I am *not* flighty" Natasha insisted, as she felt her face burning up, her heart thumping like a jackhammer, as queasiness moved in.

*This place gives me the fucking creeps. Why can't Vanessa pick up on that? The people here are making my skin crawl.*

"Yes, you are! One minute you want to come in here, now you want to leave." Vanessa snapped, completely unaware of the attention the two of them gathered from the locals. There was little doubt that they weren't from that area and were being thoroughly inspected from every corner of the room. "No, we're *staying*."

"But you just said...you know, about being the only brown person here." Natasha muttered uncomfortably, her eyes scanning around the two of them, as if on the lookout for the person who would come attack them at any moment. "We don't have to stay."

"I don't care if I'm the only brown person here or who's ever stepped foot in this town," Vanessa quickly corrected her. "If they have a problem with me, that's too fucking bad."

With that, she spun round and marched to the bar – which had a huge Confederate flag hanging over it - leaving Natasha standing alone, when the two girls from the bathroom walked past her. The blue-topped, huge tit lady gave her an unfriendly glare as she went past, almost like an animal in heat that didn't want to share the only other male in the room.

Not that there was a lack of men in the room – well, she guessed they were men anyway - since a great deal of the women were almost as husky and masculine looking in appearance. On the other side of things, many of the males were so overweight that they actually had breasts jutting out of their extra large T-shirts, so there was that element too.

Quickly catching up to her sister, she noticed that the bartender was probably one of the few friendly faces in the room. She was young, probably barely legal drinking age herself and had her black hair pulled back into a messy ponytail. Her eyes shone from a nearby light and she smiled at Natasha as she approached, then hurried off to grab two bottles of beer. Quickly opening them, she slapped them on the bar.

"Do you girls want some glasses?" She smiled and glanced between the sisters. Vanessa quickly answered 'no' and paid for both.

Natasha wanted to express her discomfort again, but had a feeling that Vanessa wouldn't listen. Leading them both through the modest crowd, Vanessa headed toward the back of the room. Directly across from them was a small dance floor, where a few women stiffly moved to a random, country song. A quick glance toward the DJ, she was surprised that he was actually a young, attractive man. Not surprisingly, there was a pack of women that were hanging close to him, like wolves on a potential carcass.

Hesitant to even sit down on the chair, Natasha took a sip of her beer. She quietly looked at her sister, but wasn't sure of what to say.

"I'm sorry," Natasha spoke with some reluctance in her voice. "I didn't mean to seem flighty, Van. It's just that this place kind of gives me the creeps."

Vanessa seemed to drop her guard and gave a quick nod. "It kind of gives me the creeps too." She made a face and glanced around. "Let's finish our drinks and leave."

Feeling some relief, Natasha almost started to relax when she saw two older men approach them. One was tall and lanky, wearing a blue plaid jacket with a black T-shirt underneath. His jeans looked like they were purchased from the $5 bin at Wal-Mart and his long, messy curls would've been endearing, had he been a rock star in the 90s; they didn't have the same feel when pouring out the sides of a John Deere cap.

Behind him was an overweight guy, besides wearing a baseball cap, with long stringy hair hanging out the sides (and probably bald underneath; at least, that was Natasha's assumption) he wore glasses over his beady, dark eyes and his long beard certainly didn't add to his appearance. He wore a hunting jacket and boots, as if he just finished up a long day of shooting Bambi, following by a manly pissing contest.

"Hey ladies, you clearly aren't from around here," The plaid jacket guy remarked and showed no hesitation to sit across from them, while his meek friend gave a shy smile before doing the same. "You look like city girls. What brings you to our quiet little town?"

Natasha was gob smacked by the ease in which they sat down, as if old friends, catching up after many years. She opened her mouth to say something, but it was Vanessa that spoke first.

"What was your first clue?" Her question was meant to make a point more than it was encouraging conversation, but yet they continued to talk.

"Well, let's see, you don't dress like most of the women that live here," The plaid wearing guy gestured to the women behind him, a couple of which were giving him a strange look from nearby. "You're all *citified*, like someone you would see on TV."

"Citified?" Vanessa repeated and only someone who knew her well would recognize that she was doing so in a mocking tone. "You don't say?"

"Yeah, it's okay though. You city folks don't know any better." He spoke matter-of –fact and Natasha felt herself pulling back her chair, continually sipping on her beer. "It's just the way you are."

"Interesting." Vanessa continued to play the game, while Natasha ignored the creepy stare from overweight, hunting jacket guy – who didn't appear to blink – as he observed her face in quiet contemplation. "I'd never considered such a thing."

"Yeah, my sister went off to the city and she became like that and we just loved her anyway." He bit his bottom lip and tilted his head in curiosity. "Are you one of those refugee, they talk about in the news?"

"What?" Vanessa made a face and Natasha almost spit out her mouthful of beer; not sure if she should laugh or be offended by the odd question directed at her sister. "What are you talking about?"

"Like one of those people from a foreign country," He pointed toward the door as if a troop of brown, black and yellow people were about to come flying through the entrance. "On a boat, like one of those there Syrians, can't even speak any English?"

"I obviously speak English," Vanessa made a face and glared at him. "In fact, I probably speak better English than you" She snapped.

He opened his mouth to reply, but didn't say a word. With a hesitant smile on his face, the plaid wearing weirdo rose from the seat, while his partner in crime did the same. They walked away.

Exchanging looks, the sister's broke out in laughter.

# Chapter Twenty-Nine

❦

"This bar is like a *My Name is Earl* meets the *Trailer Park Boys*," Vanessa observed as she polished off her bottle of beer, before shoving it aside. Her eyes skimmed the room as if it was her own, private freak show. She sat up extra straight, defensiveness surrounded her and it was very clear that nothing was going to get the best of Natasha's sister that night.

"I believe both those shows would be rightfully insulted by your comment," She felt the need to defend the programs, thinking of them as harmless and light, as opposed to the dark, heavy feeling that she was saturating the entire room. There was something very sinister hovering over them; it wasn't just a matter of being ignorant hicks, but a group of people who weren't necessarily to be trusted.

"Maybe we should leave," Natasha casually commented, making sure to not challenge her to stay longer. Relaxing her body, she waved a hand around. "Who wants to be at this dive anymore. We really should get going-

"You know what really gets me?" Vanessa asked, as if she hadn't heard a word that Natasha just said. Her dark eyes narrowed and there was a slight wrinkled underneath one of them, as she leaned in closer to Natasha. The scent of beer was on her breath. "What gets me is that they keep looking down their noses at me, as if they're somehow superior cause they're white and that really pisses me off. Especially, when most of these people are probably inbred with a grade 5 education."

"Really?" Natasha said, her voice lifting higher than she had intended. "I mean, I think they're looking at us weird cause we aren't from here."

"Nah, they're looking at *you* weird," She quickly corrected Natasha. "They're looking at *me* as if I'm inferior."

Glancing at the crowd, Natasha didn't see it, but maybe it was something that only Vanessa could sense in a room such as this one. Then again, weren't *they* just as bad for judging these people? Weren't they unfairly generalizing?

Not that she would dare share this theory with Vanessa: she would shit a brick.

"I...I don't know..." Natasha wondered how she could end this train of thought and get her sister out of the door.

"I *do* and you know what," Vanessa asked, her face continuing to scrunch up in frustration. It made her look old. Not that Natasha would ever tell her that information either. "I think they need to see that *we* belong here too."

"Hey, I don't know about that," Natasha corrected her, putting one hand up in defense. "I don't think I *want* to belong here."

"Well, we don't belong," She said, her face returning to its usual, beautiful form. "I misspoke, I mean, we have every right to be here too. They aren't better than us."

Giving the room a quick glance over, noticing that one old man had his pants hanging down so far that the crack of his ass was displaying – and not in a hip hop, fashionable way either – she somehow couldn't see how they would consider themselves better than anyone. If anything, it was more likely their defense mechanism when dealing with people who clearly didn't hate themselves.

Then again, was Vanessa right? Even if she were, Natasha wasn't about to encourage that they stay a moment longer.

"I think we should get going," She rose from her chair, hoping that Vanessa could be coaxed out of the bar – and then it happened.

Through the speakers, a song came on that connected them. It was the first non-country song since their arrival and judging by all the women's reactions – as they rushed to the dance floor – they weren't the only ones who appreciated it. Somehow, it didn't actually fit into the scene, but then again, they didn't either.

"It's our song!" Vanessa said in a loud voice that attracted attention from a group of guys nearby, as she excitedly stood up from the seat. Her face lit up for the first time since arriving in the bar, if not the entire weekend.

This was their song and they loved it. The Nicki Minaj hit that always made them smile, no matter what the circumstance. It was as if it came along at just the right time to break up the tension. Without thinking, without giving it a second thought, the two women rushed to the dance floor and launched into their usual lip syncing performance of 'Super Bass'

This tradition started years earlier at a family wedding reception and managed to embarrass their mother, as well as the man Natasha had been seeing at the time, even though it was pretty innocent in nature. In fact, most people would laugh when the two young women dramatically went through the motions of performing 'their' song. It was harmless fun.

Of course, it was customary to begin a lively dance immediately when the chorus started; and that was how Vanessa and Natasha found themselves on the dance floor at a small town bar. It didn't bother them that everyone was looking at them weird – at least, not at first – they weren't about to break tradition for anyone. In fact, it wasn't until almost the end of the song that Natasha realized that her supposedly 'terrible' dancing was causing people to back away, almost in fear of her moves.

"What?" Natasha asked as she slowed down and looked into her sister's face, which carried a combination of humor and skepticism. "What the hell? Why are you looking at me like that?"

"Nat, you dance like Elmo with a vibrator shoved up his ass," Vanessa said and burst into laughter. "It's terrible."

"I'm *not* a terrible dancer," Natasha countered and took note of the accumulation of strange looks she was getting from all around her. One woman in particular was rolling her eyes, while another was conspicuously whispering something to another young lady, as she watched. "I dance with a lot of *expression,* that's all."

"That's one way to put it," Vanessa teased as the song came to an anti-climatic close. Natasha made a duck lip face that came across more as a pouting, and she followed her sister's lead off the dance floor. Gesturing toward the door, she asked, "Wanna leave?"

"More than anything!" Natasha said and rushed ahead, gently touching Vanessa's arm, as she ushered her toward the door. "Please, let's get out of here!"

But it was before making it past that bar, that the same two guys who had dropped by their table a little earlier decided to make another appearance. The 'talker' of the two, protruded from the bar and blocked them both from their otherwise clear path to the exit. He had a friendly smile on his face, as if Vanessa hadn't insulted him a little earlier that night.

"Well, there's my girls," He commented with a shit-eating grin on his face. His eyes glowed under a nearby light, a slight figment of intoxication was hinted, as he continued to chat up the two 'citified' women. "Looks like you were having some fun out there on the dance floor."

"Yes, we were," Vanessa answered dismissively, while trying to get around the stranger. It was just then that his friend joined him and sheer girth of the two, managed to totally block the way. "Now we're leaving."

"Hey, what's the rush? The night is just starting." His eyebrow rose and it suddenly occurred to Natasha that he was very intoxicated. Slightly worried that this brought out the animal in an otherwise harmless moron, she felt her body ease back slightly; her eyes skimmed the room in order to figure out an exit strategy She had a bad feeling that this conversation wouldn't go as smoothly as the last.

"The rush is that we have somewhere to be," Vanessa answered, standing slightly taller than she had a few minutes earlier. Her eyes challenged him and something told Natasha that she wasn't about to back down. "And that somewhere isn't here."

"Oh, I bet you girls got somewhere you gotta be all right," A moronic grin crossed his face and he glanced back in Natasha's direction, his eyes scanned down her body with ease and back up to her face. "Well, I just bet."

Grimacing, Vanessa shook her head and rolled her eyes. "Whatever man, we're leaving." She stepped forward and he put his hand out, as if to proclaim peace.

"Now don't run off and git mad at me, I'm just sayin' that I don't blame you," He continued to have a mocking tone that was making both the women confused. "I would have somewhere I'd rather be too, if I had this little darling on my arm."

He gestured to Natasha, who suddenly felt her eyes widen in horror. He thought they were a couple!

*Good grief! This guy is watching way too much fucking lesbian porn and thinks that we're together.*

Vanessa, however, appeared to be confused by this statement.

"What are you talking about?" She asked, her face cringed in bewilderment. "This is my sister."

"Your *sister*?" He asked and exchanged looks with his buddy, before he began to laugh in an exaggerated form that only managed to piss off the two women. "Is that what you pussy lickers call it now?"

Alarmed by her own thoughts, Natasha almost missed her sister's response to this remark. "I said *sister*. What the fuck is wrong with you?"

"Yeah, this little white girl is your *sister*," He said as he moved in closer to Vanessa, as if to challenge such a possibility. "You mean to tell me that your daddy's jumped a fence to some Mexican town?"

"*What??*" Vanessa replied abruptly, automatically causing the stranger to step back. "First of all, I'm *not* Mexican, I'm Cambodian for fuck sakes! If you ever left this fucking hick town, you might know the difference between the two."

"Hey, I-" His hands were up in defense, as he continued to back off.

"And second of all," Vanessa continued. "I'm not a lesbian! This *is* my *sister*."

"Yeah, sister, asshole," Natasha suddenly found her voice again, even though impromptu thoughts of violence were dancing through her head. "You know, the person *you fuck* when your cousin isn't around?"

With that, she grabbed Vanessa's arm and abruptly pulled her toward the exit and out the door.

# Chapter Thirty

❦

"You know what I was thinking?" Vanessa's voice rang out from the other side of the dimly lit room, interrupting the silence that they had shared since arriving at the motel.

The adrenaline surge from the bar had quickly worn off and provided them with exhaustion, forcing Natasha to search on her phone for a place to stay for the night. She was relieved when her sister complied, for fear that Vanessa would've otherwise taken a firm stand on driving all night.

"What?" Natasha finally replied. Lying in her uncomfortable bed, where she breathed in the stale air that was connected with a room only cleaned on the most basic level: fresh sheets, a quick vacuum where the eyes could see and a shiny bathroom. She felt as though germs were floating about, while viruses sat dormant in the sheets. If she somehow caught syphilis from this gross room, it wouldn't have surprised her.

"Maybe we're judgmental assholes," Vanessa replied in a soft, childlike voice that indicated no sign of confidence. Natasha didn't take these particular words too seriously, but rather focused on the tone of her sister's tone. There was something behind it that was seldom exposed; a vulnerable side that maybe she just felt safe exposing in the dark. She briefly wondered if her relationship with Stephen was the same.

"We aren't judgmental assholes," Natasha quickly corrected her, barely doing more than batting an eyelash. It was almost as if she didn't move, she wouldn't shake up the germs in the room and expose herself to some obscure disease. "We're just normal people who call them as we see them."

"I don't know about that, Nat." Her voice regained some of its usual confidence, as the sheets could be heard ruffling and she sat up in bed. "We were quick to judge all those people too."

"What people?" Natasha was exhausted and grew frustrated with this conversation.

"Aunt Flow, Chase, the hicks in the bar." She stalled for a moment and continued. "See, I just answered my own question. I assumed they were all white trash at the bar."

"That's cause they *were* white trash at that bar," Natasha muttered, tightly squeezing her eyes closed. "And in case you are forgetting, *they* judged us too. Flora thinks I'm a ditz, she thinks your husband would appreciate you more if you were white, the people at the bar assumed we weren't sisters cause you aren't white, that we were lesbians and *you* are Mexican." She shook her head and started to giggle. "How much more judgment do you need to feel justified in judging *them*."

"But two wrongs don't make a right." Vanessa argued.

"So, they don't?" Natasha reluctantly replied.

Vanessa fell silent and her phone suddenly lit up and vibrated. Grabbing it from the nightstand, the glow of light reflected on her face as she studied the screen.

Vanessa rose from the bed and started to pull on a jacket, grabbing her purse.

"Where are you going?" Natasha asked as she sat up in bed.

"For a walk," Vanessa answered flatly. "I need some fresh air."

"Well, at least let me go with you." Natasha started to rise. "This is a creepy motel with a bunch of sketchy people staying here, you shouldn't be out roaming around by yourself."

"Why not?" Vanessa let out a little laugh. "I don't plan to be gone for long, I'm going for some fresh air and then I'll be right back. I have my phone with me if I need anything. Plus, you're tired, go to sleep."

"You should go to sleep too, we have a lot of driving ahead of us tomorrow." Natasha insisted. "Let me at least come with you."

"No, you stay here," Vanessa headed toward the door. "I want to be alone."

"But-

"It's fine, Nat," Her voice was sterner this time, as she headed toward the door. "Please, get some sleep and I'll be back shortly. I saw a candy machine out there, maybe I'll get a snack or something." Her voice was light now, as if there was nothing to worry about. "Stay put. I will text if I need you."

"Are you sure?"

"Yeah, I'm positive." She continued to sound upbeat. "Maybe I will call Stephen for a minute and check in."

"It's midnight."

"He won't mind."

Natasha wasn't so sure, but decided that there was no use arguing with her sister. She was strong willed once a decision was made, it was better to let it go.

"Okay, but be careful."

Once alone in the dark, she slid back under the covers and started to think about Vanessa's question. Were people judging them only because they were judging others? It was a concept she discovered years earlier in a spirituality book, but she simply ignored it. Now, it was hard to deny that perhaps her sister was right.

It was ironic, she considered, that in Vancouver she didn't judge poor people, but wanted to help them. In small town Alberta, it was a whole other story. She contemplated this fact through a cloudy mind, as she fell into a deep sleep. It was only when she woke up to the sunlight shining through her window that Natasha turned to ask Vanessa-

*Where the fuck is Vanessa?*

Her sister's bed was empty; the sheets still pulled back as they had been the night before when she left to get some fresh air. The room was empty. Glancing toward the tiny bathroom, Natasha quickly realized that Vanessa wasn't in there either.

Jumping into her sandals beside the bed, she grabbed her phone and sent a text.

*Where the fuck are you?*

Nothing.

*Get back to me as soon as you see this message.*

Rushing to the door, Natasha pulled it open, expecting to see her sister's bludgeoned body in front of the door, but there was nothing. The sunlight beamed down on the many doors as if they were the gateway to heaven itself, but there was no sign of her sister. Cautiously walking outside, she decided to look around. Maybe Vanessa was in the Jeep. Maybe she went for an early morning coffee?

Back inside the motel room, she pulled on her clothes from the previous night, grabbed her phone and hurried out the door. There was no one around. Glancing at her watch, she realized it was 6 AM and most people would probably still be sleeping. In the parking lot, there was a huge truck used to ship products, a medium sized camper and a few random cars. Vanessa's Jeep sat quietly in the middle, but upon glancing through the windows, Natasha quickly realized her sister wasn't in it.

Peeking at her phone once more, she felt panic shoot through her when realizing she had no new texts. Rushing back toward the motel, she paused and glanced at the line up of closed doors. She briefly wondered if she should tap on each one to see if anyone had seen her sister, but immediately dismissed the idea. No one would appreciate a stranger pounding at the door at 6 AM to ask about a missing person.

Should she call the police? Wait – wasn't there a rule about waiting 24 hours?

*She could be dead by then! Some psycho probably grabbed Vanessa and forced her away at gunpoint. Should I call Stephen? Did they talk last night? Maybe I can backtrack through the timeline and figure out approximately what time she went missing, so that I can tell the police when they ask.*

Natasha felt as though her mind were spinning out of control. Pain shot through her chest and she forced herself to breathe slowly, realizing that she was having a panic attack. Rushing back to the motel, she flew into her room and sat on the bed. Closing her eyes, Natasha took long, relaxed breaths and ignored the cold sweat that took over her body, the fear that ran through her heart.

Did Vanessa go for an early morning walk? Maybe she didn't hear her phone? That would make sense. Maybe, Natasha decided, she was being irrational. Her sister was too smart to do anything stupid, her senses too alert to get in trouble. She had always been the rational one of the two. It was absurd to think that this time was different.

Glancing at her phone, Natasha considered calling Stephen, but she didn't want to alarm him yet. She'd wait until seven and see what happened. If Vanessa didn't respond by that time, then she would figure out a plan of action. Until then, Natasha would calmly go through her usual morning routine; take a quick shower, change, put on a bit of makeup and see what happened. It was just after she put on a fresh 'hippie' outfit that the door swung open and Vanessa walked in.

Raising an eyebrow, Natasha opened her mouth but didn't know what to say.

# Chapter Thirty-One

※⊱♥⊰※

"Where the *fuck* were you?" Natasha finally said with much more anger than she had intended. The truth be known, it was interlaced with the fear that her sister had been kidnapped, murdered or both – and yet, here she was, traipsing into their dingy motel room, looking like she had recently showered, her hair dripping over the same clothes she wore to bed the previous night.

*The fucking clothing she wore before she went for a 'walk' and-*

"What do you mean?" Vanessa asked calmly, her eyes a pool of innocence, as if she had just exited the bathroom door, rather than tiptoeing into the motel room that they shared. Tilting her head, she studied her sister's expression. "I was just outside."

"No you weren't *just* outside," Natasha continued to show her fangs, countering the statement that a stranger would've quickly believed without a question, even though the evidence showed otherwise. "I was just outside, walking around the motel, in the parking lot and searching for your brown ass and you definitely, absolutely were *not* out there."

"Why were you looking for me?" Vanessa calmly asked as she gently closed the door. "You could've just text me, I had my phone on." Her hand slid into her pocket and pulled out her iPhone. Glancing at the device, her face fell somewhat.

"Oh," She let out a tiny, elegant laugh. "I guess you did. I'm sorry, Nat, I guess I-"

"Don't fucking start with me, Van. I'm not doing this again."
Natasha's remark was sharp and to the point. Normally, she would've
felt some guilt for being harsh with her sister – but not this time. This
time was different, because regardless of her earlier denial, she knew
precisely what was going on.

"I..I think you misunderstood, Nat, I-

"No! I didn't misunderstand anything, Vanessa." She said her sister's
name sharply, making what was usually a confident young woman to
suddenly look quite fragile. It was rare that either young woman referred
to each other by their 'real' name and when they did, it was generally
a bad sign.

Vanessa crossed the room and sat on the edge of her bed. "At least
let me explain before you jump to conclusion."

"Go ahead," Natasha refused to drop her defenses. Crossing her
arms over her chest, securing a pounding heart beneath them, a part of
her wanted to scream; but an even bigger part of Natasha was furious.
"I'm listening."

"There's nothing to tell," Vanessa said, their eyes met and a small
smile edged her lips. "I got up long before you, took a shower and went
for a walk."

"I've been running around this fucking property for almost an hour
and you're trying to tell me, that in that time your hair is *still* dripping
wet." Natasha said, gesturing toward the wet drops on her shoulders
and back of her t-shirt. "Try again."

"You know what?" Vanessa suddenly grew defensive and jumped
up from the bed, distancing herself from Natasha. "I don't owe you an
explanation. I'm fine, that's all you need to know."

Natasha pursed her lips, shook her head and frown lines grew beside
her eyes. She felt tears behind them, but refused to let them escape. "I'm
not doing this again."

"It's not like college," Vanessa said, attempting to plead her case.
"I'm not going to take irresponsible risks, so you don't have to worry
about my safety."

"You don't get it, do you?" Natasha heard her voice screech and
suddenly realized that a stray tear had fallen down her cheek. Wiping

it away quickly, she saw her sister, step forward and Natasha responded by stepping back. "You don't get it. It's not just about your safety, it's an indication of a bigger problem."

"Now you sound like my counselor." Vanessa shook her head and rolled her eyes. "I'm not 17 and being crazy, I'm an adult woman and I'm being smart, I don't see what the big deal is...anything is fine in moderation."

"Not in your case," Natasha turned away and grabbed her suitcase, searching through it for a distraction. She couldn't look in her sister's eyes. "You know, the perfume thing should've been a sign, cause you used to do that *too*."

"I only stole Aunt Flow's perfume cause of what she said to me, not because I'm a klepto." Vanessa spoke with confidence once again, standing a little taller as if she had risen from the accusations and was home free. "There's a difference, you know."

"I don't know, actually." Natasha said in a small voice.

"I'm fine, Nat." Vanessa insisted and headed toward her own suitcase, abruptly grabbing it from the floor and heaving it onto the bed. "You're worrying over nothing, I assure you of that."

Natasha didn't reply.

The two gathered their stuff in silence. It wasn't until they paid for their room and got in the Jeep, that they spoke again.

"Did you want to stop anywhere for breakfast?" Vanessa asked mildly, as if nothing unusual had taken place that morning. Not that it surprised Natasha, because her sister had a way of jumping back to the center position at a moment's notice, as if nothing out of the ordinary had taken place.

"No." Natasha stubbornly responded. "I want to get the hell home. The last few days have been insane."

"No coffee? Seriously?" Vanessa countered. "You think I'm going to drive for hours in a car with you without your coffee? I don't think so."

"I want to get home," Natasha insisted. "As fast as possible."

"Well, maybe *you* don't want a coffee, but *I* do." Vanessa spoke with a calmness that was almost more infuriating than had she responded with anger. "There must be somewhere in this dead end town that has fucking coffee."

"Oh yeah, hick towns are big Starbuck fans." Natasha snapped. She shook her head and looked out the window as they drove away from the motel.

"Well, there has to be *somewhere*." Vanessa insisted and ignored the attitude she was getting in response. "These shit towns usually run on coffee and alcohol, don't they?"

Natasha smiled in spite of herself. Then she felt it. That undeniable lurching in her stomach, before it growled in hunger. No matter what, she refused to admit that she was starving and chose to cross her arms in front of her stomach and applying pressure, in hopes it would smother the loud growl that was waiting. It didn't work.

Vanessa shot her a humored look. "Not hungry, are you?"

"I just want to go home," Natasha continued to insist. "I'll eat when I'm there."

"Look, I'm hungry," She said as she gestured toward Natasha's stomach. "You're obviously hungry. We have a long drive home. Let's stop and get some food and then we'll head back on the road."

"I think-

"That you can't stand looking at me for that long?" Vanessa attempted to finish the sentence. She remained composed, unaffected by this turn of events. "That's fine, we don't have to talk. Just grab some food, eat quickly and go."

"Ok." Natasha's voice was small, childlike in response, feeling some guilt over the accurate explanation that her sister gave because it was true. She didn't want to deal with this right now.

They found a busy, family-style restaurant that seemed to be geared toward truckers and random travellers. Maps, tourist information and other pamphlets could be found just inside the door, alongside a large bulletin board full of several notices about everything from local bars to house cleaning services and real estate agents. Neither girl was interested in the information, but merely getting to their table, ordering food and moving on.

The waitress was young, probably fresh out of high school and with a smile, quickly took their orders and rushed away. The sister's didn't speak again until after she brought them each a cup of coffee. In fact, it wasn't until after Natasha took her first sip and closed her eyes for a brief moment of recognition, that Vanessa spoke.

"So, are we going to talk about this or what?" She continued to display her poise, leaning forward in the booth. All around them were various people – everything from seniors with children to truckers quietly sitting in the corner, eating a hearty breakfast – everyone minding their own business, relatively normal compared to the people in Hennessey.

"I would rather not."

"Why not? You seemed to want to a few minutes ago."

"You know why not."

"It makes you uncomfortable?" Vanessa asked and took a drink of her coffee. Wrinkling her nose, she put the cup down, picked up another sugar packet and added it. Her spoon, gently stirred the contents inside the off-white cup, as her eyes turned back to Natasha. "That's it, right? It makes you uncomfortable?"

"It doesn't exactly make me bubble with joy." Natasha whispered and glanced around. "This was a big problem with you before and you know why."

"But I'm older, more experienced with life," Vanessa insisted. "It's gonna be fine. I just have to be careful and discreet."

"I can't believe that you're doing this and yet, if it were the other way around, you certainly wouldn't be happy, would you?" Natasha countered and sat back in her seat. Crossing her arms again, she couldn't help being perturbed. "You know what I'm talking about, Van."

A light seemed to shine in her sister's eyes and Natasha immediately regretted using her nickname, because it somehow indicated her approval, as if it were okay? Did it give her a pass? Was she making too big of a deal of it? *Was* it any of her business?

"Let's go back a bit for a minute." Vanessa suggested. "Let's go back to the first time, when I was in school and then look at me now. I'm not going to let it rule my life this time. It's something to spice things up from time to time. It won't hurt anyone."

Natasha raised an eyebrow. "Really? You think Stephen won't care?

"Stephen won't care," Vanessa insisted. "Because he's doing exactly the same thing."

# Chapter Thirty-Two

It wasn't until after the waitress dropped off their food that Natasha felt heavy; her arms, her legs, her entire body felt like rocks, as if she was wedged in a place she didn't belong. It was as if Natasha had somehow got off course in her planned life path and now didn't know how to get back on. Perhaps this had been the case for months, but suddenly it felt very real.

Tears were lurking in the back of her eyes and a chill from the air conditioning hit her face, while across the table, Vanessa dove into her food and finally looked up at Natasha, with a bewildered expression.

"Why aren't you eating?" She inquired as one, perfectly manicured eyebrow rose, her dark eyes shot a look of kindness with an unmistakable flicker of boldness behind them. "You were starving a minute ago."

"I don't feel well." Natasha replied, not even sure if this was true. In reality, she felt nothing, as if a huge rock had landed on her body and she wasn't able to do a thing: laugh, cry, eat or think.

"Are you going to be sick?"

"No," Natasha looked toward the nearby window. The sunlight was shining in beautifully, while an older couple stiffly walked toward the restaurant and she felt the heaviness start to lift, but a lump formed in her throat at the same time. She had to look away.

She could hear the distinctive sound of 'Money for Nothing' flowing through the room, but in such a subdued tone that Natasha almost missed it all together. It was one of those songs her father used to have flowing through the car speakers; on the rare occasion he drove his daughters to school. Forget about ever asking to listen to the Spice Girls: it wasn't going to happen. Natasha would argue, but Vanessa would sit in the back seat, snapping her gum and staring out the window.

"I'll be fine." Natasha finally concluded her thought and reluctantly took another drink of coffee, easing into the food a little at a time. Vanessa almost devoured her breakfast.

*I guess she worked up a fucking appetite this morning.*

Natasha felt she was finally coming alive after a few drinks of coffee and a slice of bacon. She enjoyed a leisurely breakfast, ignoring the fact that her sister was already finished. The waitress had already fluttered around with more coffee and Vanessa sat back with an air of confidence, enjoying every last drop. She was a different woman from even a few days ago, Natasha noted, but remained silent.

"So, what started it this time?" She decided to be direct and hear the story while she nibbled on a piece of toast that was drowning in butter, the salt mixed with a processed strawberry jam substance was undeniably, the most delicious thing in the world at that moment.

"I was pissed off at this girl at work," Vanessa said as she reached for her spoon and rolled it around on the plate. Natasha noticed how she avoided eye contact, as a familiar yet annoying 70s rock song now filled the room. It was one of those songs people sang karaoke to, but wouldn't actually listen to under any other circumstances.

"You were pissed off at a girl at work?" Natasha asked as she continued to chomp on her food, a combination of eggs and toast now, as if suddenly in a hurry to enjoy the breakfast she almost snubbed moments earlier. "I don't get it."

"I was pissed off at a girl from work, in comes her hot husband and I thought to myself, 'how does a bitch like that have such a gorgeous man on her arm' and then it occurred to me, that maybe I could have him too." Vanessa replied with certainty, as if her confidence only grew with each passing moment.

"So pretty much the same way it did last time?" Natasha asked before filling her fork again.

"Yeah," Vanessa answered, showing a moment's hesitation as if insecurity crept in. "Except replace high school with work."

Natasha nodded. Revenge sex had always been what instigated Vanessa the most; she loved the idea of being powerful in someone else's vulnerable moment, while hurting someone in the most intimate way possible. It had started off exactly the same way years earlier, while Vanessa was in her final year of school. It quickly became a problem: a big problem.

"It's not going to be like last time, though," Vanessa was insistent, as if she knew what her sister was thinking. Her voice, soft like a butterfly's wings, as if she were trying to seduce Natasha in a completely different way of viewing the situation. Vanessa was very manipulative when she became this whole other person.

"But why now?" Natasha attempted to put the fact together. "It's been years. *Years*, Vanessa…why now? I don't get it."

"Well, I'm not being totally truthful with you," Vanessa said with a small, innocent smile, her hands continued to roll the spoon around on the plate; she pursed her lips and shrugged. "I knew, for a fact that Steve is cheating on me. I was mad; I guess I wanted revenge on him too. I managed to keep loyal to him for all these years. I certainly had opportunities. I had temptation. I was growing bored in our relationship and I guess he was too."

"I know he was cheating because he told me," Vanessa confessed, a brief moment of hurt crossed her eyes and she stopped playing with the spoon and placed her hands on the table, leaning forward. "I got your text after another huge fight with him and I left. I came here."

"Does he know where you are?"

"Does it matter?"

"How long has this been going on?"

"I don't know," Vanessa admitted. "And frankly, I don't care. It doesn't matter if it was once or 3000 times, it happened. We're done."

"Why didn't you tell me this before?" Natasha felt her demeanor soften toward her sister. "Why did you just tell me fragments of the story?"

"You had a lot going on here and I …I thought maybe it was better to not give you the full story yet," Vanessa said, pushing a strand of hair behind her ear. "I've been worried about you since your accident-

"Okay, don't do that," Natasha immediately cut her off. "This isn't about me, it's about you. It's about the same problem you had when we were teenagers and I had to hide it from our parents. It's about the thing that was controlling your life when you started college."

"But maybe it wasn't," Vanessa shrugged casually. "I think we were being a little too dramatic back in those days. I just happen to like sex. It doesn't make me an addict. I think that people jump on the addict bandwagon and use it for unpleasant behavior."

"I don't know about that," Natasha said as she finished her food, hesitating as the waitress brought over some more coffee. "Okay, let's step back a bit. So, it started when?"

"Well, I suspected that Steve was losing interest for the last year. He was doing suspicious things, like staying late after school, supposedly helping a student. He was completely ignoring me," She slowly dipped her spoon into the coffee and poured in some cream. "I was getting... antsy and well, he was ignoring my advances. I actually think he knew that this would push me to cheat first."

"So you cheated first?"

Vanessa nodded, her expression like that of a child who had been caught in a lie. "It started with the coworker's husband."

"Cause she pissed you off?" Natasha sipped at her coffee, her stomach now felt as though a brick had landed in it. "So you fucked her husband?"

"Yeah, there was this work function and well, I got him away from her and we went off into the woods and-

"The woods?"

"Yeah, it was this nature walk thing," She swung her hand dismissively. "Stupid motivation, teamwork, the culture, improving bullshit thing we did. Anyway, we hooked up a few times after that and I felt...alive again. And that's how it started."

"How many guys?"

"A lot." Vanessa replied. "I'm always looking for opportunity."

"Oh man," Natasha said as she closed her eyes, shaking her head. "Unbelievable."

"Really, it's no different than most men except, it's acceptable when it's a man." Vanessa pointed out. "If I was a man, this wouldn't be an issue. It would be a 'boys will be boys' thing."

"I'm not sure about that."

"Anyone I know?"

"Chase."

"*What??*"

"The night I got to Hennessey and slept in my car?" Vanessa said, tilting her head, her eyes giving Natasha an upward glance. "He was concerned when he noticed the Jeep, so he came over to see what was going on. He knew Clifford was bugging you the night before and thought maybe he was back, with a different vehicle. I got in pretty late and the lights were off. He probably thought I was your...stalker."

"When? What time did you get in?"

"Around 4? I think?" Vanessa said thoughtfully. "He came over and I recognized him from the picture and well, it kind of got me thinking. I mean, he was pretty handsome and nice body, it had been a long drive, and I was kind of feeling...

"I get the idea," Natasha put up a hand to stop her from going on. She knew her sister would talk pretty openly about her sex life, if she were given the chance. "So, you did Chase?"

"Yeah," Vanessa replied. "I did."

"Did Flora find out?"

"Oh no, when we had a fight, it was for the reasons I told you. I didn't lie." Vanessa replied. "She has no idea."

"And this morning?"

"I was out all night." She confessed. "This guy, I saw him outside earlier, when you were in the bathroom. I wandered out and we agreed to meet later."

"A stranger?"

"Yeah," Vanessa spoke in a small voice. "I would rather it that way."

A popular 90s song came on just as the restaurant began to empty out. Natasha stared in her coffee cup, unsure of what to say or what to think, for that matter. It was her sister's life.

*But last time...*

# Chapter Thirty-Three

At first, Natasha was calm. She took in her sister's words and let them whirl around her brain, as if they were an elaborate ride at a carnival. Although she participated in their conversation, her side was minimal and to an outsider, it probably seemed to be two young women discussing the latest fashion trends or celebrity gossip. No one would've guessed that the beautiful lady with the caramel complexion was confessing that she had reentered the world of sex addiction.

"You aren't saying anything," Vanessa commented, her original confidence seemed to deflate, if only slightly. She leaned her arms on the table, studying Natasha's face.

Defeated, Natasha shook her head and leaned back in the booth. "I don't know, Vanessa. What do you want me to say? Seriously? What am I supposed to say about this?"

Their waitress approached with a pot of coffee and both shook their heads no. Wishing them a good day, she left their bill and scurried off.

"We may as well get going," Natasha suggested, grabbing her purse and sliding out of the booth; it took a minute for her to realize that her sister wasn't doing the same. "Vanessa, we gotta go."

"I think we need to talk about this some more," Vanessa spoke evenly, although she looked to be almost in tears. "I can tell you're mad."

"I'm not mad," Natasha replied and sat her purse back down. "I'm just disappointed."

"I'm fine," Vanessa assured her. "It won't be like last time, I promise."

"I hope not."

"I'm serious," Vanessa insisted and bit her bottom lip, as she often did when in a jam. "It's probably a phase and who knows, maybe we will get back together."

"You really think there's a chance of staying together if you're out humping every guy that walks by?" Natasha spoke in a low tone, making sure that no one could hear them, now that the restaurant was quieter. She could see the hurt in her sister's eyes, but yet felt compelled to continue. "I don't understand, Vanessa."

Natasha picked up her bag and grabbed the bill. Vanessa quietly followed and didn't say another word until they were back in her Jeep. The keys were almost in the ignition, when she stopped and shifted her attention to Natasha.

"It's not going to be like last time. You don't understand why I do it," Vanessa insisted. "It's not just the challenge or to get revenge, it's more for me. It's about...feeling alive again."

Natasha silently listened. There was something in her voice, vulnerability or perhaps a sense of fear that alerted her attention. It was a fragment of desperation begging to be heard.

"My life has been consistent for years. I've been married forever. Our lives are routine. Work is pretty much the same, even though it's freelance. It's always the same stories, the same slant, like I'm being told what to say in my articles. I'm essentially fed the story I'm supposed to tell. It's not fun anymore. None of it's fun." She paused for a moment and looked out the window. "I felt like I was dead. Like, I was going through the motions."

"Did you talk to Stephen about this?" Natasha asked with a voice that was as smooth as butter, no longer carrying the frustration and judgment she felt in the restaurant. "Maybe it's something you could've worked out."

"I tried to talk to him," Vanessa spoke in little more than a whisper, her fingers moving over the steering wheel. A strand of her long, smooth hair stuck to her chin and she quickly flipped it away. Taking a deep breath, her eyes scanned the nearby highway. "But he didn't seem to get it. He *likes* the predictable, comfortable life and hates surprises. He couldn't understand why it was slowly killing me."

Natasha felt as though she should insert a comment, an opinion, a flicker of wisdom, but nothing was coming to her at that moment.

"I remember one night, I was excited that we actually had plans to go out," Vanessa said, rubbing her eyes, she suddenly let out a yawn. "We were heading out to a nice restaurant. I finished my work early so I could get ready, put on a new dress that I had been dying to wear and…he came home and said he was *tired*," Vanessa's face hardened, her eyes expressionless.

*She doesn't love him anymore.*

"I wasn't asking for the moon, I just wanted to go for dinner." Vanessa spoke calmly, but her eyes searched Natasha's face for reassurance. "I tried to negotiate. I tried to tell him we wouldn't be late, that it would be fun or we could do something he liked on the weekend. I even pulled up their menu online and tried to tempt him with food, but Stephen wasn't interested. He wanted to stay home, sit in front of the television and watch some stupid reality show."

"Ewww," Natasha couldn't help but make a face. "I see your point. But maybe he had a bad day at work? Maybe he was exhausted."

"But that's the problem, Nat, he's *always* exhausted," Vanessa said as she turned in her seat. "Too exhausted to cook dinner. Too exhausted to clean. Too exhausted to go out. Too exhausted to fuck. Too exhausted to take the *fucking* garbage out."

"Wow."

"Exactly."

"I wasn't aware that it was that bad." Natasha confessed. "Why didn't you ever tell me?"

"Because its marriage. I thought that it was better to keep problems between the two of us. I didn't believe in sharing any part of my marriage with anyone but Stephen." Vanessa said and turned a little more in Natasha's direction. "And he thought that since I worked from home most of the time, that I was around the house, so I could drop whatever I was doing and unload the dishwasher or whatever. People think that just because you're working from home, that you aren't *really* working, that you're doing a dab of work here and there, then you troll Facebook the rest of the time."

"Isn't that *what* you do?" Natasha teased and immediately had a bottle of vitamins thrown at her. "Hey!"

A smile swept over Vanessa's lips and Natasha felt herself doing the same.

"Anyway," Vanessa continued, "maybe that's no excuse for cheating, but that's why I did it. I was tired of feeling dead and I was even more tired living with a corpse who took me for granted."

"But you always made it sound like everything was great," Natasha commented, but quickly knew the answer. "Never mind, I think I understand."

"Do you?" Vanessa asked, her eyebrows raised, a pleading look that indicated that she was concerned that Natasha's words had no real meaning. "Do you understand?"

"I understand why you felt the need to react or why you were frustrated," Natasha insisted and turned toward her sister. "But why not just leave him? Why not go to counseling? Why cheat?"

"I didn't plan it," Vanessa confessed. "I was angry with Stephen and I don't know, I didn't know how to get through to him to resolve anything. I felt like maybe he didn't want to fix anything." She paused. "Then one day I went to work and the same coworker that pissed me off for years, really hit a nerve during one of our staff meetings. It doesn't matter what about, but in the end, I was kind of obsessed with it. I couldn't stop thinking about why she seemed to attack me in front of the boss, why she hated me."

"I thought about what kind of person she must be, to belittle others and decided that she was probably as miserable in her life as me, but rather than feel sympathy for her, I felt powerful because I could see into her world." Vanessa said, while inspecting her nail polish and returning her attention to Natasha. "Then one day, this gorgeous man walked in the door and we immediately made eye contact. Like, intense eye contact. Of course, she comes flying out of nowhere and it became clear he was her husband or whatever, she made a huge scene, making sure everyone knew that he made this effort to come see her. It reminded me of high school, when people flaunt their boyfriend's in your face, as if it means they are somebody because someone loves them," She quipped and Natasha let out a sharp laugh.

"That doesn't stop in high school, unfortunately."

"No, well, true," Vanessa seemed to lose her train of thought, but quickly got back on track. "He kind of looked at me that day, as if he was begging me to save him. His eyes were on me, as she was hugging him. It was kind of pathetic and well, you know the rest of the story."

"So you screwed him on this work thing? No one noticed?" Natasha said in disbelief.

"There was a lot of people and their spouses, mine wasn't there of course," Vanessa said bitterly. "Which pissed me off that he bailed on me once again. He stayed home to 'chill out' and play video games, so I left the apartment already full of piss and vinegar. Then I met the others and of course, their spouses were with them and the girl from my work was prancing around, being the center of attention, while her man lagged behind and well, we started to talk and fell even further behind the group…."

"I think I see where this is going." Natasha said, hoping her sister would get the hint that she didn't need more details.

"It happened fast….really fast. It was exciting. I felt alive and I couldn't go back," She shook her head. "I needed that excitement again. If Stephen wanted to rot in the chair in front of the television, that was his choice, but it wasn't mine."

Natasha nodded in understanding.

"So…"

"So I kept doing it." Vanessa admitted. "And every time, I feel like I'm slowly coming to life again."

# Chapter Thirty-Four

✦❀✦❀✦❀✦

There was a certain naivety about Natasha that was endearing and charming, yet completely frustrating at times. She was an intelligent woman – a doctor, who was top of her class – but reading people, wasn't her strong point. She didn't necessarily see the best in everyone, but it was as though she had tunnel vision and missed a lot of things along the way. It was like her mind was in the clouds, drifting away and only occasionally fluttered back down to earth to find out what was going on.

Not to be mistaken. Once Natasha clued into someone's deception or sinister actions, they were history. Fieriness would blast through her heart and everyone who was nearby would know exactly how she felt. It was a shock to those who witnessed it because her usual, laid back and calm manner made this change in behavior completely unexpected. Unfortunately, it came across like she was slightly unhinged and that could be problematic.

That was why their family used the accident to explain Natasha's sometimes-rash behavior. In fact, it had always been there, had they cared to notice. And really, it wasn't so rash, but merely a reaction to what was going on around her. Why was everyone supposed to be calm all the time? On television, we love characters that spring into action, attacking others either verbally or physically, yet in real life, we want everyone to be relaxed, composed and showing almost no emotion at any time. And yet, we consider this to be sane? How could that be? That wasn't being human.

It took many years for Vanessa to come to this realization. Being the minority in a Caucasian family does that to a girl. While the little white girl can act as she likes, there seem to be different rules for the little brown girl. Vanessa assumed this had to do with her color, since their mother made references to it whenever angry with her oldest daughter. It wasn't often, but it was enough. A little girl only had to be told once that she could easily be sent right back to where she came from, to understand that there was some regret involved in the original decision.

Her father would laugh as if it was a joke, merely quipping, 'Sure Cynthia, you jump on a plane to Cambodia and take her back to that God forsaken village." Shaking his head, he wouldn't even look Vanessa in the eye, as tears burned her lids. She knew what that meant. She knew exactly what they were saying.

It was probably a disappointment to have used so much time and money to adopt this little immigrant girl, only to get pregnant shortly after. It wasn't like they could save their receipts and take her back; it probably surprised her mother that it wasn't the same with a child from the third world country, as a dress from a boutique. Vanessa was a symbol. She was the little girl they 'saved' from such deplorable conditions, the living, breathing proof that they were good people who did their part in the world. It's like the good deed of the lifetime.

Fearing that they would do as they threatened, Vanessa had been good. She was quiet. Diligently, she worked along on school projects, colored in coloring books, drawing pictures and composed stories about what her world looked like; it was the only way she could express what was going on in her heart.

Her stories started off innocently enough. They were usually about a little brown girl that was the slave in her family or the child that lived in the doghouse with the family pet. Later, her stories were full of rebellion. She wrote about the teenage girl who climbed out her window, ran away with the cute, white boy down the street and lived happily ever after.

Not that she had much luck in that area. She was tiny for her age. Flat chested, shapeless; boys didn't even know she existed during most of her adolescence. It was as though she didn't exist at all. Plain, boring, hardly in the same league as the others in her class, she hung back and quietly did her work, secretly fantasizing about that day things would change.

Her younger sister adoringly tagged along behind her, never questioning why they looked so different, as if she hadn't even noticed. The only time their obvious physical differences were brought up was when Natasha asked Vanessa why she was tanned year round. When Vanessa gently explained that it was because she was a different color, it was almost as if it suddenly hit Natasha for the first time.

"Oh," She said, tilting her head to the side.

"You know, like the girl in your class that your friends with?" Vanessa attempted to explain to her little sister, who was around seven at the time. The two were walking toward their mother's car after school, holding hands as Vanessa lead her to the Lexus on the other side of the parking lot. "I think you said her name is Ary? She's Cambodian too."

"Oh," Natasha replied, her forehead wrinkled. "But she talks different from you."

"Her family just moved here," Vanessa attempted to explain. "She's ESL; English second language. She's still learning."

"But you can speak English like me."

"I came here when I was a baby, that's why, Nat."

It was never brought up again. And with Natasha, it wasn't an issue. Only her parents made everything feel weird, as if she was a stray that showed up at the door and they kindly invited her in, allowing her to stay and now she was indebted.

Her frustration grew over the years and turned into anger. No one can be submissive forever and the day came where that latch broke open all the way. It happened when Vanessa was seventeen. She had been seeing a Chinese boy who treated her very tenderly and lovingly, but she didn't feel the same. He wanted to marry her, introduced her to his family and insisted that they wait to have sexual relations. He felt it was the proper and respectful thing to do because of the religious beliefs of his family.

Vanessa liked the boy, but she didn't love him. The truth was that he was merely the first guy who had ever paid attention to her and that's the only reason she agreed to go out with him at all. She felt as though he realized what it was like to be of a different ethnicity; there was a sense of understanding between them. But getting married was a whole other matter.

It was after meeting his family, spending time at their house, that she saw her future in his parents. The mother was quite overbearing, appearing to run the entire household, while the father was miserable in his own way. They chain smoked, argued, but appeared compliant in public. It was when her boyfriend suggested that they could marry and spend many years together – as his parents had – that Vanessa started to back away and fast.

She felt like a caged animal that was dying to get out, and it occurred to her that marrying this boy would be going from one form of entrapment to another. She rebelled against the idea of marrying at all and quickly broke it off with him, breaking his heart at the same time.

Guilt drove her. Desire to rebel drove her even further. It was then that she began to casually date, preferring boys that had no inclinations of relationships or marriage. She wanted to be set loose from her cage to explore.

The first boy was Ray. He was one of the kids dragged to her parent's annual Christmas party, bored as she was, the two hid in the basement and drank a bottle of wine. She couldn't recall exactly how it happened, but they had clumsy sex on an old couch pushed in a corner for the kids to use, since they were barely allowed on the 'good' furniture in the living room.

It wasn't great. It was just okay. Ray suggested that they try again and it became a little better each time, but still, kind of boring. That was until one day, when she knew both her parents were home and above them in the kitchen. The idea of maybe getting caught made her very aroused, which quickly turned into intense pleasure as she rode the rich white boy in the basement, while her parent's argued upstairs.

She actually felt herself come as her father called her mother 'an uptight bitch', while Ray squeezed her ass with one hand and covered her mouth with the other.

It became a bit of an addiction at that point; fucking someone in the same house as her parents, just under their nose, was the biggest turn on of all. Sneaking guys into her room at night was a challenge, but she managed it. She grew tired of Ray and moved on to others – not necessarily white and usually not rich – but guys she met randomly; on the bus, at the mall, in class. It became a game, a challenge. She wanted to collect their names in a little black book, try every position and be the girl who guys wanted, lusted after, like the beautiful celebrities that men wanted. She wanted to be *that* girl.

It didn't happen that way. Most of the sex was terrible, clumsy or unfulfilling. She started to be more careful when choosing her partners, in her first year of college. It was easier at that point because there were lots of single men, wanting to get laid as much as she did. Her numbers grew, as did her lust. It did become a bit of an addiction, a challenge, making it difficult to concentrate on anything else. It was her obsession, sitting in class, she would fantasize about the teacher, the boy beside her... sometimes even the girl, but that was something she was too frightened to try.

Then her secret caught up to her. Quite surprisingly, it wasn't from the rumor mill - although there was some of that going on at the time - luckily she didn't look the part of a 'nymph', so no one believed it. It was actually when Vanessa's marks started to drop dramatically, that she talked to the only person she could confide. She talked to Natasha.

Her sister was stunned by the confession. She hadn't even heard of sex addiction at the time and originally thought it was a joke, until looking it up online.

"You have to get help," She insisted, after Googling the topic. "This looks like it could be serious, Van. Maybe you should look into counseling."

She did. It helped. Until it didn't.

# Chapter Thirty-Five

If it had been anyone but her sister, she wouldn't have believed it. Sex addition; could that actually be *a thing*? It sounded ridiculous. It was a little difficult to believe that someone's twat could take over their lives and in truth, it was something Natasha had a hard time understanding the first time around, let alone now that she was older. As a doctor, she should know addiction came in many forms. As a sister, it wasn't so easy to accept.

The first time round was difficult enough. Somehow, Natasha managed to get her sister into counseling; paid for by their parents, with the belief that their daughter had been very 'anxious' in college. Shortly after, she met Stephen and things went back to normal. Well, assuming they were ever normal. Natasha often wondered if Vanessa was telling her everything. There were holes in the story she already told her. She even secretly wondered if their father had done something to Vanessa as a child and she wasn't telling. He did seem to have a thing for young, brown women.

Vanessa seemed to think that her addiction stemmed from her need to feel alive. Back in the day, the counselor said it was a means of taking control; a power that stemmed from anger. It was weird thinking of her sister as being angry, when she always appeared to be so in control. Then again, Natasha now wondered if that was really the biggest sign of all.

She sort of blamed her parents for this one. The research she did indicated that sex addicts often come from families where the parents are cold and unfeeling. Wasn't that their parents in a nutshell? Then how come the same thing hadn't happened to Natasha?

Then again, she once had sex with a complete stranger in the bathroom during a political fundraiser, so perhaps it hadn't completely skipped her. But it was only that one time. Her drug of choice tended to be a few drinks – a glass or two of wine, a shot of whisky, a cold beer – that sometimes led to negative behavior, but still, no signs of addiction for her.

Then again, her parents had treated Vanessa a little bit differently. They seemed to have special expectations for their adopted child and for a long time, Natasha thought it was simply because she was the oldest.

"Well the good news is that we are almost back in British Columbia," Vanessa said, breaking the silence that had enveloped the Jeep since they left the diner. Both lost in their own thoughts, it was almost a rude awakening for Natasha to return to the present moment. Blinking rapidly, she witnessed the signs indicating that they were about to enter their home province.

"Thank God!" Natasha said and relaxed in her seat. "I've had about enough of cowboys and rednecks."

"Not everyone in Alberta is a cowboy and redneck," Vanessa reminded her, humor in her voice. "You can't put an entire province in the same category."

"Yeah, well, we stumbled upon the worst of the worst."

"Nah," Vanessa said as she wrinkled her nose and reached for her sunglasses. "I'm sure there are much worse places in Alberta, we just haven't discovered them *yet*."

"Let's leave the 'yet' out of it, if you don't mind" Natasha whimpered and shrunk down in her seat. She noticed the sun was suddenly brighter; her hand reached inside the woven bag that appeared as if it had better days, finding a pair of heart-shaped sunglasses. "Oh, I forgot I had these in here! Awesome."

"You know, I think this was a good experience for us." Vanessa spoke with confidence. "I think it was good to get away to bond and connect."

"Yes, it was," Natasha's voice was soft and she shared a quick smile with her sister. "Although, I kind of have to pee, so if you can find a service station soon, it would be awesome."

"Yeah, I need to get some gas."

"I still think you're nuts to drive all this way. We could've jumped on a plane and been home already," Natasha commented, waving her hand in the air, glancing at the car next to them and back again. "Not that this isn't fun at times, but you can only sit in a car so long before you start to go stir crazy."

"I think that ship's already left the dock for you," Vanessa teased.

"I'm not the one with a sex addiction."

"Touché" Vanessa giggled. "However, I think we all have our secrets, don't we?"

"Secrets?" Natasha asked, her head falling back in laughter. "Van, a secret is like, I have an STI or I stole money from some old lady, while selling Avon. Not, 'I have a sex addiction and nailed the married guy who lives next to Aunt Flow' I mean, come on, I think that's a whole other category, don't you?"

Vanessa couldn't help but laughing with her and nodded. "Yeah, you kind of got a point there." Then after a moments hesitation, she asked, "So, did you have an STI and steal money from an old lady?"

"No!" Natasha insisted with a horrified expression on her face. "I'm just saying there are different levels of secrecy. I don't know if your secrets are quite the same as most people's. It's kind of big."

"I don't know," Vanessa replied, shaking her head. "I'm not so sure. I actually think the opposite, I think most people have some dark secrets hidden away, that they aren't telling anyone."

"Maybe."

"Don't you have any, Nat?" She asked, as she slowed down behind the car in front of her. "Come on, what about that night you banged the guy in the bathroom. That can't be so different from what I've done."

"Yeah, but I did it *once* with one guy…or maybe another guy too," She hurried along. "But the point is that we aren't in the same category. I'm single."

"There was *another* guy?" Vanessa probed, giving her sister a sideways glance. "That same night? At uncle Kramer's party, you mean?"

"No, there was another guy, another night, since the accident," Vanessa slowly began and shook her head. "I was with Clifford and he was pissing me off and I don't know what happened, I found myself making eyes at the guy at the next table and the next thing I knew, we were in the bathroom hooking up."

"No conversation involved? You were suddenly in the bathroom, screwing this guy?" Vanessa asked, as a hearty giggle erupted from her throat. "Wow, you're not kidding! You definitely are in a different category from me. I usually at least have some kind of conversation with the guy first. What did you do, point at him, point at the bathroom and go at it?"

"Well..I guess, yeah, come to think of it," Natasha replied over her sister's gleeful laughter on the other side of the Jeep. "You know, I never thought about it, but when you put it like that…"

"When I put it *like that*, as if there are any other ways to put it. He was at the next table and you kind of signal to him that you wanted to fuck him?" Vanessa teased and playfully hit Natasha's arm. "I might have a sex addiction, but you got this down to a science, Nat."

"I wouldn't say that exactly," She grinned. "It was only once. It's not like I do this all the time."

"So was it good?"

"Are you somehow getting turned on by this, cause I'm not encouraging your disruptive behavior," Natasha replied in an elegant manner that only made Vanessa laugh twice as hard. "It was fantastic, but that's beside the point."

"So, you hooked up with this random guy, while you were on a date with the Pussy?" Vanessa clarified and her laughter began to ease off, if only slightly. "That's crazy. Do you think maybe that's a sign?"

"There was something he wanted to talk to me about and I guess, I didn't want to deal with it," Natasha gestured around the vehicle, as if it somehow explained everything. "I think it was a sign that I fucked up something in my head when I had my accident, because it was unlike me to do something like that."

"You are forgetting *how* you hit your head, right? You were banging some guy in the bathroom, right?" Vanessa remarked as she wiped a joyful tear from her eye without looking away from the road. "That happened *before* the accident."

"But that was different. I did that out of anger toward uncle Kramer and also because I was a little drunk. It kind of clouded my judgment," Natasha attempted to calmly sort it out. It felt good to try to make sense of this story out loud, for some reason it made more sense when the words were released to the world, rather than circling around in her brain. "Plus, he suggested it. He was touching my leg, it was a different circumstance completely."

"Fair enough."

"I mean that since the accident, my brain goes in very extreme or unusual places, for me." Natasha attempted to explain. "My thoughts are more extreme now. I feel less inclined to hide how I feel and just go with the flow."

"And if you see someone you want to fuck, you make it happen, even if you are with someone else and in the middle of a restaurant?" Vanessa couldn't help but tease.

"We didn't do it in the *middle* of the restaurant, let's be clear on that fact," Natasha corrected her, calmly taking in her words, not the least bit offended. "It was in the bathroom. It's not like we had an audience."

"*That* time," Vanessa made reference to the night she hit her head and Natasha couldn't hold back the laughter any longer.

"Okay, you got me there."

"So, overall, it doesn't sound that bad. Your thoughts aren't that crazy."

"Well, most of the time."

"Most of the time?"

"Sometimes they get a little crazy," Natasha quietly admitted. Without allowing herself to second-guess the next confession, she reminded herself that her sister had entrusted her with a huge secret. "Since the accident, I sometimes have some dark thoughts."

"Really?" Vanessa grew serious. "What do you mean? Like wanting to slap someone? Shove an old lady, that kind of thing?"

"Like attacking someone or dying," Natasha calmly replied and then suddenly, "Oh look, there's a gas station ahead, can we stop?"

# Chapter Thirty-Six

"So you think about dying or how you want to whack someone, is that what you're trying to tell me" Vanessa eased into the question as they turned into the gas station parking lot and pulled up to a tank. Putting the car in park, Natasha was surprised to catch a look of horror in her sister's eyes. She silently waited for an answer as her fingers slipped over the steering wheel.

"I didn't say that exactly," Natasha suddenly felt anxious about all the cars in the parking lot and signaled toward them. "Come on, we should hurry up, it seems really busy here." She paused for a brief moment and unfastened her seatbelt. "Come on, Van. Chop chop!!"

Vanessa finally broke eye contact and started to slowly follow her sister's instructions while at the same time, Natasha opened the Jeep door. "I'm going to pee, do you need anything in the store?"

"Ah," Vanessa thought for a moment. "Nah, it's okay. I've got to go in to pay for the gas, so-

"Oh, I can get that," Natasha insisted. "I don't mind. You're taking me home, after all."

"Well, someone had to get you out of there, but that's besides the point." Vanessa insisted a she got out of the Jeep. "You can get it next time."

Natasha shrugged and wandered into the gas station. It was large and felt oddly homey for a place you got gasoline and had a pee. Large,

190

comfortable chairs were in the corner, where people could apparently sit and unwind. A sign indicating that Wi-Fi was available was a nice touch; she glanced around to locate the bathroom. A symbol indicated that it was down a long hallway.

Strolling along, searching for the women's washroom, she was stunned to instead look directly into the open door of a Men's room. Some old fart, lacking in modesty, was taking a piss in full view of anyone who happened to pass by.

Abruptly turning her head, she pretended not to see, even though it clearly wasn't her fault for stumbling into such a sight.

*Why the fuck does he have the door wide opened? Fucking moron.*

*Oh shit, there's that dark voice. Fuck, I shouldn't have told Vanessa. She looked freaked out. What does she think, that we're going to go all Thelma and Louise or even worse, Natural Born Killers?*

She couldn't remember entering the bathroom or walking into a stall, but somehow she was there and sitting on the toilet. How often did that happen and should she be concerned that she had done so without being conscious of her actions?

Back to her original thoughts, she decided that maybe she should be careful about what she tells Vanessa. People didn't like to hear about craziness. They pretended that you could tell them anything, but truthfully, they didn't mean it. She would water down the story for her sister, if she inquired further. It was the only thing to do.

But it was only after washing her hands and looking for a snack that wasn't full of chemicals and sketchy ingredients, (she settled on 'fresh' fruit in the cooler) that she forgot her original concern regarding the confession. That was, until she got back in the Jeep and Vanessa was giving her a serious look.

"Sorry to take so long, but I was trying to find a snack, but couldn't find anything that wasn't full of-

"It's fine," Vanessa waved a hand in the air, looking slightly impatient; she shifted into drive and pulled out of the parking lot and back on the road. "I know about your weirdness when it comes to food, what I don't understand is your weird thoughts you mentioned earlier. The ones where you bash people's heads in."

*Fuck.*

"That was probably a bit of an exaggeration," Natasha commented airily, taking a drink from her bottle of water. "I mean that *sometimes* I think about physically hurting people who piss me off. I don't think that is completely unusual, who doesn't think of that from time to time?"

"It concerns me," Vanessa spoke articulately, as if she were talking to a child. "I mean, you do watch a lot of *Dexter,* maybe that says something?"

"Oh come on!" Natasha howled, waving her hands in the air. "Are you *kidding* me? Lots of people watch *Dexter* and they aren't exactly chopping people up and throwing them in the water. Give me a break!"

"I don't mean that you will follow his routine, I just mean, maybe it has enhanced these thoughts or encouraged them somehow?"

"Oh yeah, and the heavy metal I used to listen to is what encouraged my devil worshipping?" Natasha bit into her apple and rolled her eyes, hiccupping through her laughter. "Are you insane? I watch *Dexter* because I find him highly entertaining and he's also pretty handsome. Plus, when he fucks a girl on the show, it's pretty hot. I would think that if anyone could appreciate that fact, it would be you." Her eyes narrowed on her sister.

"Okay, point taken," Vanessa had a mixture of shame and apology in her voice. "God, it's not normal to fantasize about hurting someone."

"Unless they are tied up in bed?" Natasha quipped.

"Okay, I got it, Nat," Vanessa said, one hand in the air to indicate that she surrendered. "Point taken. I'm just worried about you."

"It's nothing," Natasha insisted, purposely making light of the situation. "It's only a fantasy that I've had a few times. Clifford brings it out the most, but sometimes it happens when I'm around strangers. I don't actually pick up an object to hit them with or anything like that, so I think I'm safe so far."

"So far?"

"Come on, if it ever comes to that, I will talk to someone."

"Maybe you should anyway."

"Glass houses, Van, glass houses."

Both fell silent for a while and Natasha continued to eat her apple, but she enjoyed it less with each bite. She finally rolled down the window and was about to throw it out when Vanessa yelled at her.

"What the hell are you doing?"

"Throwing out the apple."

"That's littering!"

"But it puts the apple back into nature to decompose. Maybe a squirrel will nibble on it or something."

"No! You are not littering. My luck, there's a cop hiding in the bushes and I will get a ticket."

Natasha groaned and rolled the apple core up in a Kleenex and set it on the dash.

"You're acting weird," She sulked. "I wish I had never mentioned the bashing people's heads in thing."

"It's a bit disturbing," Vanessa said with a shrug. "It makes me wonder what other sinister thoughts you have rolling around that brain of yours, if you think about hurting people. Plus, you're a doctor so that makes it even weirder. You're supposed to be helping fix people, not bashing their heads in."

"Okay, for the millionth time, I don't want to *literally* 'bash' anyone's head in. I merely stated that I sometimes fantasize about physically hurting people or at the very least, threatening to, I don't think it's exactly dangerous since I'm not doing it. Case closed."

"But who and what situations are you usually in?"

With a loud sigh, Natasha rolled her eyes. Growing frustrated and bored with this conversation, she considered how to assure her sister, so that it ended.

"It only happened a few times, mostly when I was with Clifford," She insisted casually. "He wouldn't listen to me and I was frustrated and I fantasized about grabbing a heavy object and hitting him repeatedly."

"Just with Clifford?"

"Maybe with Dad once and perhaps even a few strangers on the street or in stores that were super rude, but not like, everyday and everyone." Natasha bit her lower lip and considered her words carefully. "It's a flash through my mind, nothing more or less. I don't physically pick up something to do it." She let out a self-conscious laugh and realized that she was lying. She actually had picked up an object a few times, briefly brushing her fingers over it, grasping it tightly and hesitating while a flash of anger flowed through her.

"I feel like you aren't telling me something." Vanessa commented as a small drop of rain fell on the windshield. Followed by a sudden downpour. She turned the wipers on and continued to concentrate on the road. "I'm not judging you, Nat, I'm concerned. I'm worried. You hit your head hard, it could've affected your thinking and if that's the case, it's totally not your fault."

"I know."

"So?"

"I'm not being completely truthful with you," Natasha was hesitant to say the words, but felt her body relax once she did. "I dream about it a lot too. I have a lot of dreams where I am…maybe hurting people. But they're only dreams. They don't mean anything."

"Are you sure?"

"Yes, seriously Van, it's nothing." Natasha admitted and felt some relief from telling the truth, but continued to think it was a mistake to say anything. "Please don't make me wish I hadn't told you. I wanted to share that I also have secrets, but they're kind of weird. Fantasizing about attacking someone is probably unusual, but I'm willing to bet that it's not rare. It's not a problem."

*So far…*

# Chapter Thirty-Seven

❧✿❧

She reached for her phone and instantly dropped it back on her lap. Rolling her eyes and shaking her head, it only took a second for Vanessa to react.

"Oh no! Not The Pussy again!" Her voice was full of disgust and frustration, almost as if she were the one being harassed. "He needs to get a life."

"Although I do agree with your theory on Clifford, this time it isn't him," Natasha replied, momentarily closing her eyes, an unexpected glimmer of sunlight beamed through the window and centered on her face. "It's even worse. It's mom."

"Wonderful," Vanessa said with unmistakable sarcasm running through her voice. "What does the queen of mothers want?"

"Well, according to this text, she is summoning us to speak with her whenever we get back to Vancouver," Natasha said and slid the phone back into her purse. "I'm not replying. Anyway, the point is that she wants to meet with us to discuss 'what happened' in Hennessey."

"Oh Jesus."

"Exactly." Natasha said as she glanced out the window. "But nothing happened, as far as she knows. It's not like Flora knows anything about you and Chase and, other than that, she insulted you and I don't think I did anything, so I don't get it."

"She was pretty pissed when we left, so God knows what she told mom," Vanessa reminded her and cleared her throat. "There's that whole scene with Clifford, right? Maybe that's what she's referring to, do you think?"

Natasha sat in silence and went through the events that occurred while visiting her aunt. There wasn't much, just the visit from Clifford. Certainly, her mother couldn't be pissed off at her for that incident.

"You did steal that bottle of perfume," Natasha reminded her as she watched her sister suddenly grabbing her own iPhone. "What is it? Is she texting you now?"

"I don't know," Vanessa replied and wrinkled her nose. "Can you check, I'm not getting off the road if it's from her."

Reaching for her sister's phone, Natasha glanced at the screen. "Yup, it's the same message she sent me," She started to laugh. "Exact one, actually and ah-

"What?" Vanessa asked, suddenly looking both tired and frustrated. "Did she mention that argument me and Flow had?"

"No, it's ah…it's a picture of a dick," Natasha said, briefly managing to suppress her laughter. "Someone sent you a picture of his dick. Oh my God! Are you sexting?"

"*I'm* not sexting," Vanessa said and suddenly was pulling over to the roadside. "What? Who would send me that?"

"Oh shit, you don't want to see this one-

But it was too late; Vanessa had already put the Jeep in park and had grabbed the phone. Her eyes grew twice their normal size and her mouth hung open. "Oh my God. It's Stephen. He sent me a picture of…."

Suddenly reduced to tears, Vanessa moved her fingers up and down the screen, studying the various photos that had come to her phone, one by one. They were of her husband with another woman.

"I'm sorry, Van. I just saw the first one and didn't realize that…I mean, I wouldn't have told you like that, if I had known what was about to follow…" Natasha swallowed the lump in her throat, knowing that this was heartbreaking for her sister to see, even though their marriage had clearly been in difficulty. Regardless of what she had done, it couldn't be easy to view pictures that represented his infidelity. The knowledge would be difficult enough.

Quickly wiping a stray tear away, Vanessa shook her head. "It's okay, Nat. You had no idea and I would've seen it eventually anyway and I deserve it. With everything that's happened, he's hurt and angry and rightfully so and this was a way of letting me know."

"He didn't have to send pictures, Van," Natasha reminded her. "That's very immature and classless."

"I know," Vanessa replied as she scanned over them again. "The girl is white and younger, I should've known."

"Van, don't take it that way. Don't compare yourself, it's unhealthy," Natasha unbuckled her seatbelt and reached over to hug Vanessa, who appeared to be lost in a trance, staring at the images over and over. "You guys have got to talk and maybe, I don't know..."

"It's over," Vanessa replied softly as Natasha gave her another strong hug then moved away, back into her seat. "These pictures are a reminder of that and I deserve it. I've no right to get on a high horse. I mean, not exactly the best way to let me know that our marriage is finished, but I guess it shows his anger and hurt."

"Does he say anything or did he just send them?" Natasha asked. "I can't believe Stephen would do that! I mean the affair is hard enough to believe, but the pictures? Doesn't seem like him."

"He can be vengeful," Vanessa quietly replied. "He said that I'm not the only one having some fun this weekend."

"Did he know about the guys this weekend?" Natasha raised an eyebrow, slightly confused about the whole ordeal. It was as though she were missing details. "Is he tracking you or something?"

"I think he assumes that I went away to be with a guy this weekend. I didn't exactly give him an explanation." Vanessa calmly sat her phone down. "You know it's one thing to think your marriage is over, but quite another to have it actually happen. I guess in some sad way, I needed to see those photos."

"I don't think you needed to see them," Natasha grabbed the phone and slid her fingers up and down the screen, viewing what he sent. They included pictures of his penis, followed by some girl performing oral sex and another of him fucking her from behind. "It's almost as if he did this with the motive to send them to you. I mean, most people aren't in *the act* and suddenly decide, 'hey, I should grab my camera and capture this', know what I mean?"

"Oh yes, it was definitely revenge sex." Vanessa agreed, taking a deep breath, she wiped her face and signaled to return to the highway.

"Are you sure you're okay to drive?" Natasha asked. "I can if you want."

"No, I'm fine," Vanessa slowly eased back into traffic and wiped one last tear from her face. "I'd rather be driving right now, it calms me."

"Really? It has the opposite effect on me." Natasha commented, studying her sister's face. "I get too anxious and can't handle the other traffic."

Vanessa didn't reply, clearly deep in her own thoughts, Natasha decided to stay quiet. She simply wasn't sure what to say in this circumstance. Obviously, her sister was hardly the innocent victim in the affair, but she didn't deserve this treatment either. If the marriage was over, it was fine, but to take a collection of pictures to send her? That was unforgivable. It pissed her off. She felt anger flow through her veins, while her sister sat next to her, probably feeling remorseful and depressed.

"Do you think we have trouble with relationships because of our parents?" Natasha suddenly asked, thinking about the message from their mother. "I mean they hardly had a normal marriage."

"Well, let's see, dad cheated on mom and here I am," Vanessa dryly replied, her eyes staring ahead. "Mom probably had fantasies about bashing his head in on more than one occasion, so that's your fantasies. You date a lot of clingy guys. Probably cause you are so free and independent and that type they are drawn to. I guess that's a bit of dad too."

"I think I stay clear of serious relationships *because* I grew up seeing them fighting. Of course, as you know, I never thought dad was cheating until recently."

"I can't believe you never put that together before," Vanessa said with a fragment of humor in her voice. "He didn't hire all those young nannies to just look after us, he hired them to look after him too."

"I don't know about that, I-

"Trust me, Nat, I'm positive." Vanessa insisted. "I almost walked into it one time. I can't remember which girl it was, but she was from Mexico, I think. Thankfully, they didn't see me. I heard some weird noises when I passed the door and it was open ajar and well," She pointed to her phone. "There was a lot of that going on."

"Oh."

"Yeah, oh."

"Why didn't you tell me?"

"You were still pretty young. I was probably 12 or 13 at the time, so I had a better understanding, but you were too young and I didn't mention it to you after that."

"They only have that older lady cleaning the house now."

"I don't think it was just in the house. I think that was only convenient at the time," Vanessa insisted. "We all have our secrets."

"Our family is fucked up."

"In fairness," Vanessa started to sound more and more like herself again. "I think most families are a little fucked up. Not just ours."

"But we don't have to live with everyone else's family." Natasha reminded her. "Do you plan to tell them about Stephen?"

"Not unless Aunt Flow told mom," Vanessa seemed weary again. "Shit, why did I tell her anything?"

"Before me," Natasha reminded her. "You told her *before* me, don't forget that fact."

"I think it felt easier to tell a stranger." Vanessa considered. "I deeply regret it now."

Vanessa's phone beeped again and she purposely avoided looking at it. "Can you check that? I'm afraid to look."

"*I'm* afraid to look," Natasha teased and grabbed her phone. "I...oh..."

# Chapter Thirty-Eight

"You know what" Vanessa's voice was subdued and calm after hearing her phone beep again; she pursed her lips and stared ahead. Huge raindrops once again pounded against the windshield, as she continued to make progress on their return to Vancouver. Her eyes narrowed and she slowly reached for her bottle of water. "I don't want to know. If it's more pictures, delete them. I won't give him the satisfaction of upsetting me more than he already has today."

"It's not pictures this time," Natasha replied with some hesitation. "It's from someone named 'Bob'."

Turning to her sister, she automatically saw her expression change from composure to anxiety, as she once again pulled off the road. Silently, she reached for her phone and read the messages and started to reply.

"Is this for real? That has to be some kind of joke?" Natasha was slightly stunned by the words that were in the text message. "Are you *really* thinking of doing that?"

"I'm not sure, what do you *think* I'm thinking of doing?" Vanessa seemed to be testing her and Natasha took that to mean that she planned to lie. A cold chill ran through her soul as she suddenly realized that she didn't know her sister at all.

"The cam girl thing? What's that about, Van?" Natasha asked with a certain amount of caution in her voice. Feeling her heart race, it occurred to her that she wasn't necessarily ready for the answer she was about to be given. A part of her wanted Vanessa to lie: to not know the truth. The other side hoped that everything would ultimately come out - not the half-truths that she was beginning to see were plentiful when dealing with Vanessa.

"I have this friend…"

"Bob?" Natasha asked as she twisted slightly in her seat; not enough to appear accepting of what was about to be said, but to indicate that Vanessa had her full attention. There was a tension in the Jeep, a minor flux in what had already been a bit of an awkward day. "And?"

"He used to work for this cam girl thing in Seattle and it was pretty lucrative, so he decided to move home and start his own business." She appeared hesitant to continue. "Doing the same thing, only with slight adjustments…improvements."

Natasha merely nodded without replying.

"He asked if I would be interested in possibly working for him…on the site and I said, I might." Her explanation was matter-of-fact, with attempts to plead her case and yet, no shame in her voice. "Work is getting more and more demanding, my boss is an asshole and I thought that this would be something I could try on the side, see how it goes…"

"So, let me get this straight," Natasha was a bit taken back by the judgment in her own voice, yet she made no effort to stop it. "You're going to strip and play with yourself on camera for money?"

Vanessa nodded. She quickly looked away from Natasha and back toward the windshield, as the rain continued to pelt down. "I'm not ashamed of the fact that I like sex and if I can make money doing this kind of thing, why not? Maybe I'll try it and not like it, but it's easy money."

"Are you kidding? You're going to put your face out there, in public, where anyone could possibly see you? This is the porn business, Vanessa. It's not a cutesy little web show on YouTube, it's pornography."

"So? It's not like I'm being held hostage in some dirty little hotel room and forced to strip for money. I'll be working on my own terms, Bob takes a small cut and the rest is my money." She suddenly grew defensive of her decision. "Furthermore, I don't plan to go out looking like or being 'Vanessa', I plan to wear a wig, change my makeup, that kind of thing. We will mostly be featured in other countries, not Canada, so the likelihood of anyone knowing me is pretty small."

"Are you sure they can do that, isn't the World Wide Web, world wide?" Natasha questioned. "And furthermore, how much makeup do you plan to wear in order to not look like *you?* How does one do that, exactly?"

"It's complicated and to be honest, I'm still learning. It's not like I have all the answers yet, Nat. It's something I'm looking into."

"Something you're seriously looking into, is what you mean," Natasha was quick to correct her. "It's not like you're *kind of* considering it, it sounds like you've already made up your mind. That's scary. You don't know what kind of weirdo's are out there, Van."

"It doesn't matter, they can't find me." Vanessa assured her and glanced at Natasha. "Look, I trust my friend. We've known each other since college, we've been in contact consistently over the years and he's been open about the kind of work he does. He's learned a lot from his last job and he knows this business inside out. Actually, when I suggested joining his company, he was a little hesitant, but I managed to convince him that I could do it."

"I didn't know the porn industry was so particular." Natasha quipped and immediately regretted it; she wasn't trying to degrade her sister, but at the same time, she was stunned by yet *another* realization she had made about Vanessa that week.

"So, if this last few days hadn't happened, if I hadn't stumbled on this stuff about you, would you even have told me?" Natasha asked, feeling that she was finally going to the heart of the issue. "Would you've told me that you were breaking up with Stephen? That you were cheating on him? That your sex addiction appears to return in full force? That you're thinking of becoming a cam girl? I feel like I don't even know who the hell you are and I'm afraid about what else I don't know about!"

"That's it, I swear!'" Vanessa's voice rose and she ran a hand through her hair, frustration growing on her face and anxiety clenched her voice until she could barely speak. "I don't have to tell you every little detail of my life, Nat. It doesn't mean that I don't love you, but clearly I realize that this would make you uncomfortable. I would've told you about Stephen when things were more sorted out. I may've eventually told you about the webcam thing, I don't know," She stumbled through her words and appeared to be holding back her tears. "I don't think I'm a sex addict, I think I'm in touch with my body and I don't think its negatively affecting my life, that's what an addiction does, right?"

"I don't know anymore." Natasha answered honestly and took a deep breath. "I don't know, maybe you're right. Maybe I didn't have to know about all of this, but I thought we were close and that we shared everything."

"I don't' think *anyone* should share everything. Not even with their sister. I think people need a certain amount of privacy in their lives." Vanessa answered honestly, her tone slightly calmer. "It's not that I never would've told you, but it seemed a bit premature."

"I suppose," Natasha reluctantly agreed. "I see your point. I'm sorry, I shouldn't have jumped down your throat."

"You're right," Vanessa replied and signaled to turn back onto the highway. "You shouldn't have."

"I…I feel like I don't know you," Natasha attempted to explain and realized she was repeating herself.

"You know what you have to know," Vanessa said as she returned to the highway. "The point is I'm fine. I'm a little upset about this stunt Stephen pulled this morning. I'm upset that my marriage is ending. My life is kind of a mess right now, but I think we both feel that way lately. Things are up in the air with you too and maybe the fact that you can't count on my life having any stability is frightening to you. It's like we're both on shaky ground."

Natasha slowly nodded. "That's true. How do you know?"

"Because that's how I felt when you hit your head and suddenly started to talk about how you weren't even looking forward to going back to work, once you fully recovered."

"I could've gone back a week or two later," Natasha confessed. "I didn't want to, so I exaggerated my symptoms as an excuse. I needed a break before I jumped back in with both feet. And now my time is almost up."

"So what are you going to do?" Vanessa asked. "What are you going to do when you have to go back to your old life?"

Natasha was silent for a moment. Shrugging, she shook her head. "I don't think I have any choices about my future."

"You'll figure it out."

Biting her lip, Natasha looked out her window and didn't respond.

"You've had a lot of distractions." Vanessa offered. "Maybe you need to go home, hide in your apartment and stare out at the ocean and see what comes to you."

"I think you're right." She quietly replied.

# Chapter Thirty-Nine

❧❧❧❧❧

Nothing sounded more appealing than sitting in her tranquil apartment and staring out at the ocean. Curling up on the couch with a cup of tea, avoiding her phone and get centered; Natasha didn't want to think about anything that occurred since the accident. The past month was starting to feel like a bizarre dream, a circus ring of misfits and freaks dancing their way in and out of her life.

But it wasn't a dream. It was her life: possibly her nightmare.

The girls remained silent, as they got closer to Vancouver. As much as Natasha wanted to go directly home, she couldn't because they had been summoned to see their mother, a task that Vanessa insisted would be better to get over with quickly. Natasha thought it was sort of like ripping off a Band-Aid that was stuck with superglue.

"You know, Van, we could pretend we didn't get mom's message." Natasha thought out loud. The overcast skies lurked overhead with an ominous presence, depleting her energy and making her somewhat depressed. "Reception isn't great out in the boonies, maybe the text message never went through, cause I don't know about you, but the idea of-

Vanessa suddenly slammed on the breaks causing Natasha to bounce ahead, quickly pulled back by her seat belt. Reaching for the security of the dash, her eyes followed a baby deer running across the highway. He hesitated briefly in the other lane and glanced at the Jeep before running out of sight in a nearby forest. It happened so fast that Natasha automatically jumped into the adrenaline-filled moment and excitedly exclaimed, "Oh my God! It's freakin' Bambi!! Did you see it, Van? Wasn't it gorgeous? She looked right at us, and I-

"Are you kidding me? She could've killed us both, Nat," Vanessa snapped, apparently still in the shock after almost hitting the wild animal. Glancing in her mirrors, she started to drive again. "Thank God that no one else was on the road. If anyone was behind us, we could've been rear ended or fucking killed!"

"But we weren't, everything is okay." Natasha was suddenly elated, as if the deer had been a sign. The fact that no other traffic was around – which is a rarity on the highway – not to mention that they were safe, neither hitting the deer, or in an accident, was no small miracle. Glancing at her sister, it was clear that she didn't see things the same way.

Vanessa's face was twisted so tight that it almost seemed like it would explode. It wasn't clear if she was about to scream or cry, but nothing in her expression indicated that she understood the wonder of what just happened. Natasha thought it was probably better to say nothing and instead, sit comfortably in her own moment of bliss. Maybe, she decided, it was just for her.

After that, she watched carefully out of the windows for any more wildlife, but for the most part, it was limited to birds. Pensively staring at them, she wondered what it would be like to soar through the skies, just flowing through the gentle breeze and ignoring the world below. It must be wondrous, she decided, just flying freely, from tree to tree, watching the world below as if none of it mattered. She was envious and wished to do the same.

Vanessa got a couple text messages and almost as if in silent agreement, Natasha refused to look at them; not that she was asked. In fact, her sister was oddly quiet and Natasha had a difficult time reading her expression. She didn't look to be necessarily troubled, but at the same time, no signs of happiness appeared on her face. Maybe she was second-guessing some of her recent decisions? Then again, maybe she was second-guessing the fact that she shared details of her life with her sister.

Had she been asked about their road trip two weeks prior, Natasha would've assumed that it would've brought them closer together, enhancing their bond rather than pulling them apart. She felt distant from her sister as they drove through the province, inching their way back to Vancouver. Natasha wondered if they would talk after arriving home or would they slowly drift apart. Something was weird between them yet; she felt no desire to address it.

She was exhausted. This trip hadn't managed to rejuvenate her, but just throw her on a slightly altered path. Maybe it was better to be ignorant about her family; she didn't have to know about her father's disingenuous behavior, nor did she want to be aware of her sister's private life.

*Fuck! My dad is a cunning, manipulative cheater and my sister is a sex addict who fucks random strangers and wants to get in the porno industry; what the fuck am I going to learn about my mother?*

She momentarily felt sorry for Cynthia Parsons. After all, the woman was with a man who cheated on her, which either meant she was insanely naïve or she simply preferred to be blissfully ignorant.

*But does she seem that blissful?? She's miserable. She knows.*

Natasha had never considered her mother a victim of circumstance, but perhaps she was all along. In any event, these facts made her feel as if she was the least dysfunctional person in her family. It also made her want to distance herself from them, maybe it was their insanity that made her put a blind eye to their questionable behaviors? Hadn't there been clues?

Natasha closed her eyes, pretended to be sleeping and thought about her childhood. Her father had rarely been home. Her mother was always keeping busy, with what appeared to be, ridiculous time-wasting tasks that had no meaning. At the time, Natasha thought she was just foolish, moronic even, but now… maybe it was her way of coping.

It was true that they had a lot of young, attractive nannies. It was also true that her father was charming with them, their mother indifferent and even rude. It was true that they generally didn't stick around for too long. But had she seen or heard anything that indicated that he was sleeping with any of them?

As for Vanessa, had there been clues that she was a sex addict? Not really. Natasha wasn't allowed to go in the basement when Vanessa had boys over, she was ordered to stay in her room. Nothing she had seen or heard indicated that her sister was fucking half the neighborhood, until Van came to Natasha in tears during her first year of college. She confessed everything to her younger sister; the endless affairs, her slipping grades in college and briefly, a fear of pregnancy. It was bizarre; Natasha kind of wished she hadn't chosen her to share this with, but maybe someone outside the family?

It wasn't that she didn't love and support her sister, but Natasha wasn't comfortable knowing this kind of detail. Hardly a prude herself, it felt weird learning that the older sister she admired, wasn't the person that everyone thought.

*And now we are back to my fucking parents. Is anything real in my family?*

Perhaps, Natasha considered, that's what offended her the most. The lies. Her family presented one image, but behind closed doors, they were something entirely different. It was like being an amputee and covering up the missing limb with expensive clothing when you went out. Then again, it was easy to see why Vanessa felt comfortable hiding her true self for so long – and uncomfortable revealing it.

"Natasha!! Open your eyes!" Vanessa harshly demanded, her voice a combination of fear and anger. "We were almost killed back there! Can you keep your eyes opened for wildlife, instead of daydreaming about pink unicorns and talking daisies?"

"What?" Natasha replied in confusion and disbelief. "What are you talking about? I was thinking about-

"The same thing you always think about," Vanessa bitterly cut her off. "Bambi, the lovable deer that could've killed us both. If you had your way, we would be back there traipsing through the woods, looking for the deer so you could take it home."

"Don't be ridiculous," Natasha whined. "I'm not allowed to have animals in my building."

The laughter that followed was disgruntled, at best. Vanessa appeared to be fighting it, but was unable to deny her sister's gentle and light response to a hasty and hostile attack. It was pretty typical, Natasha didn't allow the world to be unkind to her, even when she would've been justified to fight back, it wasn't in her nature to do so; if that made her a 'hippie', then so be it.

"Nat, you're one of a kind." Vanessa giggled in spite of herself, her face fallen from the serious and stern expression of moments earlier, almost in tears from the unexpected joy that filled her presence. When she didn't respond, Vanessa continued to speak. "I just want to get back to Vancouver, get this conversation with our mom over with."

"I guess so," Natasha replied, deciding it was better to go with the current energy, rather than to get angry about the tension that filled the car only moments earlier. It wasn't worth it. "At least if we're together, we can stand up for one another."

"That's right." Vanessa shared a smile with her sister and considered that maybe that was the real lesson of the day. You didn't have to understand someone in order to love them; and you didn't have to agree with their decisions, just accept that we're all on our own journey.

# Chapter Forty

"How come we haven't turned the radio on in ages" Natasha asked as she leaned forward in her seat and began to play with the dials. An array of music flowed through the Jeep, ranging from heavy metal to country, with some classical thrown in the mix. Vanessa appeared to be dismissing her, fixated on the road, as if in wait of wildlife to jump out once again. "It's too quiet in here."

The sound of Stevie Nicks' voice piped through the Jeep and Natasha immediately began to sing along to 'Edge of Seventeen'. She didn't have to look at her sister to know that she was grimacing from the driver's side, but she didn't care. This trip was getting way too tense and she needed the music to lighten the mood.

The music was suddenly shut off.

"Oh please, for God sakes, Nat," Vanessa shook her head as they eased closer to Vancouver. "I'm so tired and you're giving me a headache. Come on!"

"You know, just cause you're in a shitty mood doesn't mean I have to be too." Natasha spoke in an even tone, with no malice intended, but never less, seemed to piss off her sister.

"Nat, I'm really tired. It's been a long trip and we have to go see mom and that's going to be more bullshit," Vanessa muttered as she played with the heat settings and sighed loudly, her eyes never leaving the road for a second. "Can we have some quiet time, please?"

Natasha didn't bother to answer. She didn't feel it was right to suffer through the final end of their road trip, but at the same time, she wasn't in the mood to argue. It was her sister's choice to be miserable, but it certainly wasn't her own. Glancing into the neighboring cars, studying the faces of the passengers and drivers, she questioned what it would be like to be someone else. She wondered about their troubles, their worries, where were they going today? What did their lives look like?

"I hope this meeting with mom is over fast. I want to get in, hear her out and leave," Vanessa continued, her nose was scrunched up, yet flaring out in the way it did when she was angry. Natasha felt frustration taking over the atmosphere of the Jeep and couldn't help but to be resentful. Why was it necessary for her to bring them both down? Why couldn't they have some music playing and enjoy the moment, rather than to fixate on an upcoming conversation.

"Let's not overthink it." Natasha calmly suggested, but could tell that it wasn't to be accepted. Her sister continued to make a face that showed deviance, an inability to accept reality as it stood. "Hey, the sooner we get back, the sooner you can start your porn career."

"It's not a porn career." Vanessa immediately snapped and Natasha recognized that it probably wasn't the time to bring that topic up; and yet, something forced her to continue.

"It is," Natasha countered as she recognized the outskirts of the city. "I mean, you can tell yourself it's only a little peep show or whatever, but it's porn. It's interactive porn, rather than making a movie or having someone take pictures of your twat."

"You know, this is why I wasn't going to tell you about it in the first place," Vanessa countered, followed by a loud sigh. "You don't understand. It's *not* the same. It's apples and oranges."

"Yeah, and they're both fruit, just a different kind of fruit." Natasha replied, forcing an even tone, when she really wanted to snap right back at her sister, but she refused to get carried away in the anxiety of the vehicle. "That's what I'm saying about the porn."

"Okay, whatever," Vanessa raised her voice once again, doing very little to hide her frustration. "I get it. You think I'm getting into a smutty industry. I get it! Can you at least do me a favor and not mention it to mom, when we go see her?"

"I have no intention of 'telling mom', if that's what you think," Natasha countered, feeling anger growing inside of her. "This isn't about me running to tell mom, as if to shame you or something, this is about you making a pretty dumb decision."

"Just cause you wouldn't do it, doesn't mean it's dumb." Vanessa voice raised a decibel higher, her hands gripping the steering wheel. "It's none of your business anyway. Like I said, I wouldn't have even told you if it weren't for the fact that you saw that message on my phone."

"So what else are you *not* telling me?" Natasha calmly asked, pulling herself out of the argument as much as she could. "That's what I'm wondering about now, what *else* are you *not* telling me?

"Nothing! We've already been through this!"

"Nothing?"

"No," Vanessa said as she grabbed her water and took a quick drink. *"Nothing."*

Natasha wasn't sure if she believed her and didn't comment. Maybe it was better if she let it go. She wasn't even sure how to process the information she had stumbled upon already that weekend.

"It's not the big deal that you think it is," Vanessa attempted to bring life back into the topic, but Natasha didn't reply. "In fact, it's putting on a show. You aren't even necessarily doing anything, just going through the motions, saying what you know they want to hear, bringing them...joy."

"That's one way of putting it," Natasha couldn't help but mutter.

"It's higher class customers, people who can afford to pay more money for something to break up their afternoon at the office or when they're feeling lonely." Vanessa attempted to explain, but Natasha wasn't listening. She knew her sister would go to great efforts to justify it — that's what people did when they were 'caught' doing something that they knew was sketchy — so she let her talk and pretended to listen.

The fact was that it wasn't so much *what* she wanted to do. It was all the question marks that followed. Was she *just* doing this cam girl thing? What if she already started? After all, Vanessa took pride in the fact that she often worked from home. She only occasionally went to the office, most of the time choosing to work at home. Natasha always accepted this as the truth, but who knew what the truth was anymore?

She noticed her sister glancing at her, as if to get a reaction and rather than encourage their discussion any further, she instead shrugged apathetically and looked away. There was no sense continuing with this conversation. It was time to get to their mother's, get that over with, and then go home. A nap sounded liked heaven at that point in the day!

"Can you text mom? Ask her if we can go over in a few minutes?" Vanessa woke her from the daydreams of a comfortable bed. Scrunching up her face, she reached for her iPhone and typed out the message. Hitting send, she waited for a reply.

"She said to come right over, that she has 'a little' time right now." Natasha replied. "How thoughtful of her to take time away from doing *nothing* to see us."

"Whatever, let's get this over with." Vanessa replied, running one hand over her eyes and yawning, causing Natasha to do the same. "I'm sure she wants to rant to us about Aunt Flow."

Natasha yawned a second time, rather than to reply. She didn't care at that point. She felt heaviness in her chest when thinking about the upcoming conversation, because it was usually negative and draining. She considered that other than her sister, her family rarely brought her any joy. It made her sad when she once again considered that perhaps she wouldn't even have that aspect of things any longer.

Vanessa had always been the one person that Natasha related to: who got the insanity of their family, the support her parents never extended. Sadness and disappointment flowed through her when she considered that there was an obvious wall developing after the last couple of days. There was a big part of her that felt like pushing the Jeep door open — right in the middle of traffic, hopping out and running away. She felt claustrophobic, confined, almost as if no air was reaching her lungs, as if her body was harnessed down rather than in a flimsy little seatbelt. Trapped, like an animal and being transported to somewhere else she didn't want to be either.

Anger built up as they edged closer to their parent's expensive home, in the 'rich' part of Vancouver, the place that others strived to live in, as if it somehow meant their existence was more valuable than most. It enraged Natasha as she viewed the line of perfectly manicured lawns, sparkling BMWs and Lexus, sitting in the driveway, as elegant neighbors roamed around the property, making sure everything was immaculate, so no one would see them as anything but perfect. The world they came from was a joke, a lie.

*And my life is a lie too.*

Smoothly pulling into their parent's driveway, Natasha thought she could see her mother's face, as it briefly glanced out the window. She felt anger rise up, bubbling insider her and she was ready for anything. This was it. She was finished with her family's bullshit. If there was anything to be said, this was her chance.

# Chapter Forty-One

❦

Natasha spent the bulk of her life being compliant. It had always been easier to go along to get along. Where or why she picked up this debasing habit, Natasha couldn't remember, but it appeared to serve her well for a number of years. She would flutter along like a butterfly, never really dealing with confrontation, whether it is with her family, Clifford, a patient at work, a coworker; the list went on and on. It was simpler to ease out of a situation, to move on to something else and leave any possible unpleasantness behind.

Those days were over. She had simply had it. Her family was deplorable, but chose instead to hide behind a sparkly, distracting mask, in order to conceal whom they really were – and who they really were, was nothing more than 'white trash', like the relatives that her mother often referred to over the years. They just hid it behind designer clothing and a professional demeanor. And it made her sick.

Natasha was originally so relieved to be back in Vancouver, that she almost did cartwheels. She wanted to leap out of the car and kiss the ground, she was so happy to be home, but it was as they drove into her parent's driveway that she felt a heaviness weighing down her stomach and quickly spread throughout the rest of her body. Even her arms felt denser, as if she couldn't raise them from her side, but instead struggle to not lean forward from the weight. This was what her family did to her. This was the reality she was only starting to face.

Vanessa walked beside her in silence, almost as if she were more annoyed than anything; as if the few days hadn't changed their relationship. In many ways, it made Natasha regret her trip to Alberta, but at the same time, she saw that it would come together in the end. There was a reason why she had to go through this, why she felt like a part of her was ripped open and now had to heal. It had to take place, even though she had been putting it off for way too long. Hadn't she always recognized that there would be a day when everything changed? When she would have to come back down to earth?

Reality hit her hard the moment her mother opened the door. The angry, minuscule lines surrounding her lips seemed more intense that day, very much a symbol of the many years she smoked; yet another secret that no one was supposed to know about, something hidden from her rich bitch friends whom she sat around drinking wine with on a Tuesday afternoon. Who did that?

Anger seemed to clench her entire face, as if it were held hostage by decades of fury and repression. It sat in every line on her face, each pore, every eyelash, it clasped on for life, almost as a barricade. Natasha looked at her mother's face, in her eyes and decided that she didn't want that to become her too. She didn't want to be old and angry. She didn't want to carry that misery around. She didn't want to become her mother.

"Come in girls," Cynthia's greeting was short, more of a demand than a suggestion. Vanessa immediately looked tense, while Natasha suddenly felt relaxed, almost casual, slightly rebellious in nature, she had no plans in allowing their mother to intimidate her. Vanessa could be the obedient child if she wanted, just as she had when they were kids, but Natasha was having none of it. The jig was up.

Neither said a thing, as their mother gently closed the door and silently led them into the living room. Natasha half expected to find her father waiting there, dressed in a suit and tie, as if he could barely take five minutes from his busy career to bother with a family meeting. But he wasn't around. The room was flawless as usual, not a spot of dust on the coffee table, the hardwood floors shined and the couch looked as though no one had ever sat on it.

*I'm surprised we're allowed to fucking sit on it now.*

Natasha sat down beside her sister on the couch, while their mother picked a large chair, almost as if she were the queen on her throne, about to address her subjects. Her tiny frame looked even more so in the huge chair, as she sat on the edge in a ladylike manner, careful to look the part of a well-breed woman, hardly one to just throw herself back comfortably; whatever would people think?

Natasha sighed loudly in frustration, something that didn't go unnoticed by her mother, who shot her a look that was anything but kind.

"Are we keeping you from something Natasha?" She asked the same question that she had when they were children. It was a question that brought tears to her eyes when she was five: but she wasn't five now.

"Yeah, actually, you're keeping me from the rest of my life," Natasha said with such defiance in her voice that both Vanessa and her mother sat up a little straighter. This wasn't the usual Natasha answer. The usual Natasha answer was a casual shrug and a mellow, 'No', with a hint of nervousness underneath it. Today was a new day.

"Well, I wouldn't want to keep you from your life," Her mother snapped back, her eyes narrowing even further. Beside her, she could almost feel Vanessa relax, as if she recognized that the heat wouldn't be on her this time around. "Especially when you two have been so busy making fools of yourself in Alberta. Do you not realize that your uncle is working hard, trying to get voted in and here you are both out there, running around like lunatics?"

"Oh yeah, right!" Natasha sat back on the couch as sarcasm ran through her voice. "Yeah, if uncle Arnold had his way, he would get a huge dump truck and fill it up with homeless and poor people then drop them down the road in Vernon. If anyone is making a fool of themselves, it's him."

"Natasha, you know that's not true," Her mother fumed, her face turning a light shade of red. "He wants to help those people. How can you say such a thing?"

"I say such a thing cause it's true," Natasha's voice unintentionally rose and she felt frozen to the couch. "Do you even know any of his policies? He hates poor people. He's out for the rich guys like dad, not for the people who need help."

"That's a pretty one-sided view of things, Natasha and you know it!" Cynthia snapped, her face scrunching up, as her nostrils seemed to grow in size. "I don't think you're listening to what he has to say, or you'd know it's not true. Not that it's going to matter anyway, after the stunt you pulled at his fundraising event, it seems highly unlikely that he will get voted in now."

"Oh, come on!" Natasha's voice raised yet again, both her hands jetted up in the air, to express her frustration. "Are you seriously going to try to say that my 'stunt', as you put it, is the only reason why he wouldn't get voted in? Do you think people in this city are stupid? He's a fucking moron."

"He's your uncle!"

"I DON'T FUCKING CARE!" Natasha was now screaming and jumped up from her seat. "If you're finished scolding us as if we were children, *I'm* going home *now*."

*I want to hit her. I want to physically hurt. I want to grab her by the throat and-*

"..accident, you've never the same since." Her mother was speaking, but Natasha could barely hear her over her own fury.

Taking a deep breath, recognizing that an adrenaline rush had taken over her body, causing her to become the incredible Hunk version of herself, she tried to calm her breathing. She was the only one standing, but she refused to sit back down. Glancing at Vanessa, she recognized the 10-year-old child that had taken over her body and now, it kind of made sense that she rebelled sexually, but it was still odd.

"I think you affected something in your brain when you hit your head," Her mother's eyes were accusing, her tone slightly patronizing. "You've never been the same since that accident. I'm thinking about calling your doctor and finding out if we can get you some psychiatric help."

"If anyone needs psychiatric help, it's you," Natasha heard the words fall from her lips, without even having planned to say it. She pulled her hippie purse a little closer to her body, her eyes darting toward the door.

She felt her phone vibrate and it occurred to her that she didn't have to stay, that it wouldn't be unreasonable to walk out the door, call a cab and go the fuck home.

*Finally!*

Vanessa had a fearful look in her eyes: almost as if she silently begged Natasha to stay, but it wasn't going to work. In fact, if there had ever been a time that she had no compassion, no concern or no sympathy for her sister, this was it. She could stay here and be pulled in by their controlling mother, but Natasha was done. She wasn't playing this game anymore.

Turning, she was followed by silence as she walked out of the living room, and then walked out of the house. A weight fell from her shoulders immediately and she felt as small and light as a child, almost to the point of vulnerability, as she called a cab. A smile lifted her lips and relief flooded her whole body, as if she had narrowly escaped getting hit by a car.

*I guess I kind of did.*

The sun touched her face and it gently beckoned her home. She felt as if a whole new world had opened up for her, ushering her in quickly before she could fall from this spell. It was beautiful and perfect.

The cab pulled up to the house about the same time that the door behind her flew open, her mother attempting to encourage Natasha to come back inside, but she shook her head no and ran down to the awaiting car. Climbing inside, she sighed a breath of relief.

"Tough day?" The Muslim man behind the wheel glanced in the rearview mirror, as they started to drive away. Her mother cautiously pulled herself back in the house and closed the door.

"Tough week!" Natasha exclaimed with a newfound confidence in her voice. "But it's over now. I can finally go home."

# Chapter Forty-Two

Natasha had never been so happy to be home. It felt like ages since she was in her peaceful apartment, looking out over the beautiful English Bay, while sitting on her plush couch; this was what she worked hard for, not a fancy car or expensive clothing and handbags. It was this view. Was she mad? Shouldn't the ocean belong to everyone? Shouldn't the view of something this extraordinary be a right, not a privilege?

*All the fat cats selling real estate probably wouldn't agree with me on that one.*

She pondered her thoughts, while enjoying a nice herbal tea, smiling to her herself and pushing negativity from her mind. Of course, that only worked for about an hour, until her buzzer abruptly rang, causing Natasha to jump.

*Back to the real fucking world: so who's this? Did Clifford put a fucking tracking device on me, so he could stalk me from the moment I arrived back in town? Is it my mother, here to give me shit for walking out on our conversation or dad, giving me shit for her? Why can't it just be a fucking Girl Guide selling cookies for a change?*

Of course, deep down, she knew who would be outside, waiting to get in. It was her sister.

"What's the magic word?" Natasha couldn't resist the urge to tease Vanessa, even though she anticipated her to be in a huff, just because she felt so jovial about being back in her regular stomping grounds again.

She felt like a grin was glued to her face and nothing much less than amputation of left arm could take it away.

"Nat, let me the *fuck* in!" Her sister fumed through the intercom. It briefly occurred to Natasha that she didn't have to follow her sister's instructions and actually, she didn't even have to answer the buzzer at all. That realization oddly gave her some comfort. She reluctantly allowed Vanessa into the building. A few minutes later, she was knocking at her door.

Natasha bounced across the room and let her in. Heaviness filled the air immediately, as her sister stood before her with a grimace on her face, her hair no longer in a neat ponytail but partially falling out and Natasha's suitcase in her hand. She looked as if she had just walked there from their parent's house; even her expensive shoes were dirty. A sliver of black eyeliner was running out the corner of her eye, barely noticeable but still, quite unlike Vanessa.

"Come in!" Natasha ignored the lack of merriment in her sister's face and pranced across the hardwood floor in her bare feet. It was rare for Natasha to ever wear shoes or socks unless it was necessary. It felt kind of weird to have anything on her feet. And well, when she thought about her ancestors...

"....there and I had to deal with her alone," Vanessa was practically yelling, as she dragged the suitcase in the door and slammed it behind her. She stopped in the middle of the floor, as if she were a pouting child that refused to sit down or move another inch until her objections were acknowledged. Her dark eyes were glaring at Natasha, who in turn, refused to allow it to bother her. "What? You couldn't even stick around for a few minutes longer?"

"I could," Natasha commented airily as she sat back down on the couch, her feet curled up underneath her, now in a comfortable pair of shorts and t-shirt. She blinked innocently, knowing that it would probably infuriate her sister even more, if that were possible. "I didn't want to."

"That's hardly an excuse, Nat!"

"Of course but it's a great reason," Natasha pointed out, her hand gesturing toward the nearby window. "I could be here, enjoying one of the few days left before returning to work *or* I could be in our parent's house, listening to a bitter, miserable woman trying to degrade us both. I chose to avoid the latter and came home. You could've done the same."

"You *know* I couldn't have done the same," Vanessa was quick to object, her hand angrily jutted out, while her face continued to tighten in frustration. "I had to stay there and listen to her rant on about how we humiliated *her* by our numerous 'stunts' and here you were, just chilling in your apartment?"

Her words were accusing, even though there was no basis for that at all. It actually humored Natasha to think that her sister was so brain washed by their mother, that she honestly believed that she had no choice in the matter. Then again, wasn't that kind of sad? Should she point it out or let it go? Live and let live?

"Van, you chose to be there. Nothing was holding you in that house," Natasha pointed out, while still continuing to smile. Her giddy attitude wasn't catching. Scratching her baby toe with one hand and playing with her hair with the other, Natasha couldn't stop grinning. "Your feet weren't stapled to the floor, for God sakes! You could've walked out and said 'buh bye'"

"You know that's not true," Vanessa said with a loud sigh. "She wouldn't have left it alone. It would be putting off the inevitable, as you will soon find out." Vanessa moved a little closer to the couch, but still refused to give in and sit down. "She's going to be on the phone, calling you up within the hour, then you'll see what I mean. She'll be even worse."

"She's already called." Natasha shrugged. "I just didn't answer."

"Then she'll show up at your door."

"I don't have to answer that either."

"Come on, Nat," Vanessa whined, clearly growing more frustrated with her sister. Her hand now rested on her hip in a stance that suggested she was challenging Natasha. "So what? Are you telling me that you'll just avoid our parents forever? Cause you know that if that doesn't work, she'll get dad after you."

"That's exactly what I'm saying," Natasha replied with laugher in her voice. "If I have to, I will avoid them forever. I'm not going to be raked over the coals by those hypocrites, I don't care if they're my parents or not. They don't have power unless you give it to them. I refuse to give them the power to make me feel bad and you shouldn't either."

Something in these final comments seemed to resonate with Vanessa and she silently sat on the edge of the couch, her face dropping into sadness. She turned her attention toward the window and quietly commented. "You really do have an awesome view, Nat."

"I do," Natasha agreed, refocusing her eyes on the skies outside. There were some dark clouds rolling in, but she wasn't concerned. It was nothing she couldn't handle. "You got to let it go, Van. It's not worth it. Their words aren't worth it. It's just an opinion, it doesn't mean they're right."

"I know, but it -" Vanessa's voice caught in her throat, a rare sob attempted to escape but she took a deep breath and it was shoved aside. "It reminds me of when we were kids and mom would comment on sending me back to Cambodia. Every time she starts to scold me now, I'm that little girl again; sitting there, feeling guilty for making their lives so difficult."

"But you didn't make their lives difficult," Natasha reminded her in a gentle tone. She neither attempted to comfort or lecture her sister, but carefully point out the facts. "I've been thinking about that a lot today, as I sat here looking outside at the ocean. You know, Cambodia isn't a terrible place, as if it would be a punishment to be 'sent back' there, but they always made it sound that way. As if it was another version of hell, a punishment when you got out of line."

Vanessa didn't reply.

"It was the way they said it, as if to suggest that as white Canadians they were superior," Natasha said, as she changed positions on the couch, feeling her legs falling asleep beneath her. "That wasn't right. It automatically belittled you. It was a control thing, like everything else with them. They're bullies."

"I don't think I'd go that far," Vanessa injected. "I mean, when you think about it, they were good enough to adopt me. I would've grown up in poverty and maybe never had the same opportunities if I stayed there."

"But don't you get it," Natasha turned and faced her sister. "That's the wrong way to look at it. It should've been a *privilege* to bring you to their home and bring you up, not a sacrifice. They always made it seem like it was the latter and that was wrong."

Vanessa's face softened, while at the same time, it was as if Natasha had hit her with a brick on the side of the head. It was a realization that she perhaps never had before, Natasha considered. Her eyes suggested that maybe hearing those words helped her escape from her own, gripping prison. Her body seemed to relax and she didn't speak, but nervously blinked, as if the comment was too much to process in one sitting.

"Sure, it was kind of them to adopt you," Natasha continued thoughtfully. "But they made a decision to do so, for whatever reason and they shouldn't have played the power game with you."

"But why would they?" Vanessa appeared confused. "I don't understand."

"Because everything is a power game with them," Natasha pointed out. "And that's why we've spent our whole adult lives feeling as though we had no power in anything. But now, I see differently and I hope you do too."

Vanessa didn't reply, but sat beside Natasha on the couch and stared out at the ocean. People could be seen in the water, walking along the beach and children were playing in the waves. They both were silent. The only interruption was the loud buzzing, signifying that someone was downstairs, waiting at the main entrance – but neither of them answered. They sat there and waited for it to pass.

# Chapter Forty-Three

❦

"So what happened when you were there?" Natasha asked breezily, after the two listened to the message that their mother left on her phone. It was the usual – demanding, cold and furious – the theme of their lives and childhood replayed again and again. The situation may have been different, but it invariably came down to the same thing. This time was their response that had changed.

Natasha could tell her sister had a knee jerk reaction to race back to their mother and try to make peace, to allow her to ruin the entire day in worry and anxiety; that's what their mother wanted. It was about maintaining control over her two children and lately, that hadn't been going so smoothly.

"Jesus Christ, it was a fucking bloodbath after you left." Vanessa spoke bluntly; rubbing her temples as if even recalling the commotion was enough to send her into a state of anxiousness and frustration. Leaning against the couch, a sorrowful expression on her face, she bit her bottom lip as her eyes stared off into distance. "Mom was furious that you took off. I think at first she was stunned that you would do that, but then she got angry."

"Make sense" Natasha replied softly, showing no judgment and biting back any comments that were coming to the forefront of her brain. There was a piece of her that was dying to answer the door, to let her mother finally have it! To tell Cynthia Parsons that she was a tyrant while her children were growing up – hot one moment, cold the next – never allowing compliments, praise or affection to be extended.

"She blamed me when you took off and then asked a lot of questions about the trip. What did Aunt Flow say about her? That kind of thing," Vanessa said and closed her eyes, making a small effort to shake her head no. "I told her that Aunt Flow didn't even mention her."

"She may have to me," Natasha said as her fingers played with a stray string that was hanging from her T-shirt, almost as if she was undecided to rip it off or caress it. "Who cares if she did?"

"I think she thought you were reacting to something Flow said," Vanessa slowly replied, her eyes suddenly springing open, they slid in Natasha's direction. "Do you think she knows some big secret about mom?"

"Well, if she does, I'm sure we've burned that bridge to the ground," Natasha commented and let out a small snicker. "Well, one of us did, anyway."

A smile lit up Vanessa's face and she let out a small laugh. "Yeah, I know. But it kind of makes me wonder what the deal is with mom."

"The deal is that our mother is terribly insecure and that's why she tries to control us, she thinks that is the only way to keep us in her life."

"Does she think that being controlling works better than, say, I don't know, being loving?" Vanessa asked and rolled her eyes. "It seems kind of stupid."

"But it's worked, hasn't it?" Natasha couldn't help but point out the obvious. "She has no control with dad, he's running wild, so maybe she thought the only way to keep us in line was to try to intimidate us. Who knows?" We can guess all day. In the end, it's how we deal with her that matters."

"I think it's a short term solution," Vanessa insisted, some confidence returning to her voice. "I don't think it's long term. She is relentless."

"So what else did she say," Natasha returned to their original conversation. "Other than ranting about me."

Vanessa thought for a moment. "Well, I guess Aunt Flow called her and said that not only did one of us steal her perfume, that you created a huge scene in her driveway with 'some guy', then I came along and was up to something 'inappropriate' with the 'married' neighbor in my car-

"She *knew* about that?" Natasha screeched, sitting up straight and leaning toward Vanessa. "She *knows* you *did* Chase? Seriously?"

"Yeah, I mean, I don't know if he told her or if she saw something, but she somehow knew about it," Vanessa replied, her eyes lit up as she turned to face Natasha. "He must've told her that he 'cheated' on her." She let out a small laugh.

"Ironic, since he's cheating on his *wife*, but I guess that's the 'boys will be boys' and 'they can't help themselves' mentality," Natasha rolled her eyes. "It's always the woman's fault isn't it? Even when you hear about celebrities who cheat, it's the woman that is ostracized not the man. Have you ever noticed that? *He* made a mistake, says he's sorry and we all move on. She's officially a whore for the rest of her life."

"I know, right? I didn't even know this guy was married at the time," Vanessa shook her head. "I mean, he was wearing a wedding ring, but it was the middle of the night and after driving forever, I wasn't in the state of mind to look for a ring."

"Regardless, *he* knew he was married." Natasha pointed out and shook her head in frustration. "Such a double standard. So mom knew about you and the married man, did she know about Aunt Flow and the married man too?"

"Of course not," Vanessa laughed and her eyes filled with a devilish glimmer. "But I did!"

"You didn't? You told mom about Aunt Flow and Chase?" Natasha asked with a giggle catching in her words. "That's awesome!"

"Not only did I tell her about it, I *showed* her," Vanessa flashed her iPhone past Natasha's eyes. "I still have the picture you sent me."

"Oh my God! No wonder mom is so fucking pissed now," Natasha let out a squeal of delight. "That is so fucking awesome! I'm glad you did that."

"It had to be done," Vanessa replied as she scanned through her phone. "I got tired of her calling me down. After the fact, I kind of regretted it. She looked completely stunned with the information, it threw her off her game."

"Isn't that what we want to do?" Natasha asked, her eyes looking up, her lips pursed. "Don't we want to throw mom off her game a little bit?"

"Yeah but now she's twice as mad," Vanessa sighed, her body collapsed back on the couch and she stared at the ceiling. "She was mad you took the picture and shared it with me. She was mad that we still made spectacles of ourselves and it's a small town, so it will connect her to everything."

"Well, that part is probably true, but then again, who's going to tell?" Natasha replied thoughtfully. "I mean, we aren't going to tell anyone. I doubt Flora is going to advertise the fact that her married lover is humping someone else in her own driveway."

"Unless she's mad at him for 'cheating' on her," Vanessa pointed out, her dark eyes on Natasha. "Which is what it sounds like."

"But what does mom care, that's all back there? That has nothing to do with her here, in Vancouver. Some hick down in Alberta isn't even on her friend's radar."

"Something about Uncle Arnold's campaign and finding dirt about the family blah blah blah…"

"Ohhh!!!" Natasha grinned and sat right up in her seat. "That gives me a fabulous idea. We should leak some bad stories about Uncle Arnold to the media, so he doesn't get voted in!"

"Seriously, how are we going to do that? We don't know any bad stories, other than the fact that he has a bad political angle," Vanessa said and let out a loud sigh. "Telling stories about his relatives to make him look bad, also makes *us* look bad."

"I don't mean that way," Natasha insisted. "I mean, there has to be something that we can do that will throw him off guard."

"He has another political fundraiser this weekend," Vanessa commented in a mocking tone. "You could fuck some other guy in the bathroom and make another big scene like last time."

"Okay, so that's not going to happen," Natasha replied jovially and pretended that she was about to throw a nearby ornament at her sister. "But I still think we should go to that party."

"What do you have planned?" Vanessa's eye narrowed and her lips seemed to jump between a smile and no expression, as if they were indecisive on how to take this suggestion. "Or do I want to know?"

"You probably don't want to know," Natasha replied cautiously. "Just put on your best party dress and meet me here on Saturday night."

# Chapter Forty-Four

❦❧❦

"Do you remember the creepy twins that I used to work with in high school?" Vanessa's question came from nowhere, throwing Natasha's concentration completely off the task at hand. The two were walking through the ladies department of a major department store, checking out potential outfits for the upcoming fundraiser. Silently turning her attention to Vanessa, she shook her head.

"Come on, Nat, I used to work with them at the mall? I couldn't tell them apart and they used to pretend to be one another and switch shifts?"

"What in God's name are you talking about?" Natasha finally chimed in, almost running into a lady who stormed through a nearby set of doors, screaming into a phone. "I don't remember that at all. When did this happen?"

"When I was in high school!"

"You barely talked to me when you were in high school, so *no*, I don't remember," Natasha sternly made a point, as the two headed toward the exit.

"I know I told you about it," Vanessa ignored her accusation, as the two stepped out of the store and back into the mall. "I used to talk about them all the time, remember? One of them tried to break me and my boyfriend up?"

"The Chinese guy that you were too scared to break up with on your own?" Natasha calmly asked, glancing from side to side at the various stores. "Now *that* I remember you telling me about."

"But yet, you don't remember the twins? Come on!"

"Whatever, Van, why are you bringing this up?" Natasha said as she suddenly stopped in the middle of the mall, growing irritated with this conversation. "What's the deal? Why do I care about these creepy twins from your high school or whatever?"

"Cause they're over there," She gestured toward a group of mimes performing on a small stage, in the middle of the mall.

"They're *mimes* now. Now *that's* creepy," Natasha replied and started to walk again, only to have Vanessa grab her arm and pull her back.

"No, not performing, I mean they're there, in the crowd."

Natasha raised her eyebrows and shrugged. "So?"

"If you would just look," She gestured again and Natasha continued to shake her head no. "They're there. The people with the missing arms."

"What the fuck? You didn't say that they were conjoined twins." She commented, noting that both women were missing the opposing arm. It was bizarre and Natasha's expression didn't hide her feelings on the matter. "So, were they both in an accident together?"

"I don't know, I have no intention of asking," Vanessa replied, her nose crinkled up in disgust. "I hate them."

"You don't even know them now, plus aren't you curious?" Natasha asked. "You should go and start a conversation and find out what happened. Maybe they were tied together in a bizarre kidnapping situation and had to cut their arms off to get out of-

"What the hell are you talking about?" Vanessa asked as the two continued to stroll along and in the opposite direction of the twins. "It could be something simple. Besides, they were so attached and weird, my guess is one got her arm cut off somehow and the other did the same out of compassion."

"No one does that, Van," Natasha said as she rolled her eyes. "I love you, but if you get your arm cut off, you're on your own!"

"I'm telling you," Vanessa whispered to her sister, as if they were sharing a big secret. "One would break up with her boyfriend and the other would do the same. One would have a cut on her finger, the other one would suddenly have a cut on the same finger, the very next day."

"Can we not talk about this right now?" Natasha asked and put her hand up to indicate it was time to stop the pointless conversation. It somehow had little meaning in that moment. "I want to get this over with and get out of here, okay? You know how I feel about malls."

"Hey, you never worked in one," Vanessa reminded her.

"Yes, I know, I didn't work in a store with a creepy set of weirdo twins. Instead, I was part of the glamorous pizza restaurant industry. I got to come home smelling like pepperoni every night," Natasha said and twitched her nose, before pulling Vanessa into a men's wear store. "I got to get one thing here."

"Are you going to the party in a suit and tie now?" Vanessa teased as she glanced toward a mannequin of a male, wearing a pair of boxer briefs. She momentarily reached out to touch his crotch, but only for a second before Natasha pulled her hand back.

"For God sakes, Vanessa, can you keep your mind off of sex for a few minutes, while we're in public?" Natasha teased and rushed ahead to find a sales clerk. Pushing these thoughts aside, there was one more thing she would need before the fundraiser that weekend and after a brief conversation with the consultant, she made her purchase and turned to leave. "Its taken care of now."

"What are you doing? I don't get it?" Vanessa asked, briefly glancing at the mannequin on their way out. "You bought more products for men today than yourself, unless there's something you're not telling me?"

"It's a surprise." Natasha said, attempting to sound casual. If her sister sensed that she was up to anything more, there was a chance she would report her concerns to their mother in order to regain some lost brownie points.

"I'm nervous cause you've been acting weird lately," Vanessa continued to coax her. "If you're going to do something odd, can you at least give me some kind of indication? Maybe a thoughtful heads up would be nice?"

"Don't worry, it's nothing that will affect you and it's not bad," Natasha insisted as they walked toward the exit, past coffee kiosks and various merchants located in the middle of the mall. A man selling some kind of lotion was attempting to get their attention, but their previous retail experience had long ago taught them to keep walking or get caught up in an endless marketing campaign to buy a product that neither had an interest in.

"Then why is it top secret?" Vanessa teased, but her attempts fell flat, as they walked down the street toward a nearby parking lot, where she had left her Jeep. The sun beamed down on them and it made Natasha smile. It was so good to be back in BC.

A brief sadness crossed her heart, but she took a deep breath and pushed it aside.

*It's not the time to think about this, not right now.*

"... me and then at least maybe I could help you prepare?" Vanessa continued to ramble on and Natasha met her with a smile. "Seriously? Nothing?"

"There's nothing to tell besides the more you know, the more that mom will try to get out of you," She replied. "This way, you can honestly say you know nothing."

"Give me some credit," Vanessa insisted as the two got into the vehicle and Natasha threw her bags on the floor. "I obviously didn't tell mom that you're planning to go. She encouraged me to go and not to tell you."

"I would still feel better if you didn't know," Natasha insisted as she pulled on her seat belt. "Trust me, please. It'll be fine."

"You got your ticket?"

"Yup."

"Pretty pricey, aren't they?" Vanessa huffed as she turned the ignition and shifted the Jeep into drive. "For an average meal and the honor of hanging out with that fucking asshole for the night."

"Wow, did he go from 'Uncle Kramer' to 'fucking asshole' that quickly?" Natasha quipped as they drove out onto the street and she turned down her window.

"I honestly wasn't paying attention before and now that you've told me a few things regarding his policies, I started to read up and I see what you mean," Vanessa replied, shaking her head and squinting her eyes.

Reaching for her sunglasses, she quickly pulled them on and continued to talk. "He's a sly fucker and I don't trust him, but the scary thing is that he has a lot of rich friends who are backing him up."

"What we need to do is make the average person see what's going on and the problems is, that most people *aren't* paying attention. They're going by a few snapshots in local ads that highlight what he *claims* he will do for the people."

"I think you described every election ever."

"It's true," Natasha agreed. "People don't pay attention anymore, cause they assume politicians are all dishonest."

"It's unfortunate," Vanessa agreed and sighed loudly. "Stephen is moving out next week."

"What?" Natasha asked and pulled off her sunglasses. Turning to her sister, she shook her head. "We've been together for at least a couple of hours and you're only mentioning this now."

"It's not a big deal, we both knew it was going to happen," Vanessa remarked with a cool tone that seemed unlike her sister. "If he wants to go, then he can go."

"Does mom know?"

"No, and I'd like to keep it that way." Vanessa replied in a stiff tone, but the hurt in her voice was clearly lingering behind the words.

"No need to tell her," Natasha reached out and patted her arm. "It's going to be fine, Van. We'll get through this and when you want to tell mom, then you tell her."

"I think she knows something is up," Vanessa confessed. "She dropped by the apartment unexpectedly the other day and some stuff was in boxes in the living room. I told her it was stuff I wanted to donate to charity, but I don't think she bought it."

"You *let* her in?" Natasha asked. "I mean, you shouldn't have let her in."

"I'm not like you," Vanessa reminded her. "It bothers me to pretend I'm not home, when I am."

Natasha didn't reply. She stared out the window and from the review mirror, noted the apathetic smile on her own lips.

# Chapter Forty-Five

❧✦❧

Exhausted from a morning of organizing some last minute details, Natasha decided to take a quick 'cat nap' before getting ready for the event scheduled for that night. She would need her energy to get through the evening without erupting into a fit of anger, finally telling her uncle what a self-indulgent hypocrite he was – even though she knew that such a scene would prove less effective than what she had already planned.

A grin erupted on her face as she considered his reaction.

It was a shame to have such despicable relatives. She felt very much like the black sheep wandering through a field full of white, painfully aware of the differences between her and the others and yet, not sure who decided which was better. It almost felt as if public opinion swayed the weak, making them mindlessly follow the larger of the two groups. The numbers were more powerful than she originally had considered.

And yet, her uncle chose his words carefully, smiled in the right way, finding a nice balance of kindness and strength that made him appear endearing and strong, yet down-to-earth and approachable. Natasha was aware that he had a whole team of people telling him exactly how to stand, what to say and of course, how to approach the media.

Natasha was wondering if any journalists would be at the event that night, as she began to drift off to sleep. She could see herself immediately go into a dismal, cold place, almost as if dreams and sleep were a temporary death that no one could find the strength to fight, but merely reawaken later and come back to life – if you were lucky. And was she lucky?

She entered a world unlike her own. It was dank and still, in fact, the lack of sound felt like an echo running through her entire body that landed at her feet. She breathed in stale air; it was almost suffocating, vile to the senses and yet, it wasn't like there was any other option, as Natasha roamed through a dreary room. It took her a minute to realize that it was familiar, as she slowly trudged ahead, she realized it was her childhood home – the one before her parents bought their mini mansion on the 'nice' end of town – it was before they allowed both their lives to spin completely out of control.

The house was much more modest in comparison, yet more homey than their current residence would ever be - authentic and warm - it felt like an actual family home as opposed to a place they wanted to show off to impress others, who were equally as superficial and power hungry as Gerald Parsons. With average furniture, blinds you could buy at any department store and dishes that later would find their way to a donation bin on the 'bad' end of town.

The last time Natasha walked through this particular place, she was a child of maybe 3 or 4, and so she could barely remember it. However, in her dream, it was as if time had returned to those days, as her bare feet touched the cool, morning floors.

Cynthia Parson was seated at the kitchen table, reading a newspaper, as she entered the room. She glanced up only briefly, not allowing a smile to touch her face, hardly glancing at her daughter; she carried on with what she was doing as if her child was of no significance. Reaching for an elegant cup, part of an antique set that the children were never allowed to use, she scrunched up her nose as if something offended her and turned toward her youngest daughter.

"You stink," Her comment was hate-filled, with no regret to her abrupt attack, she only continued to say more to Natasha. "You smell as if death took over your body, you vile little girl. Go wash yourself! What would the neighbors think?"

Natasha didn't reply, but chose instead to stand still, permitting the words to sink in. A single tear slid down her emotionless face and dripping from her chin, it fell to the ground, barely missing her toe. She was dirty, Natasha decided, her feet were black as if she had finished walking through soot in order to get to the kitchen. In fact, as she inspected closer, her entire body was ash tone and bleak, as if the color of life had been drained from her limbs and leaked into the earth.

"I never understood you, Natasha," Her mother continued. "You were always the rebellious one, you had to be such a strange little girl. It was as if we were being punished for our sins." She hesitated and took another drink of her tea and continued to glance over the paper, as she spoke. Cynthia Parsons sat up a little taller, her white, silk blouse flowing over her body as if it were flawless, while her black pants were smooth as she pulled her legs back, entwining her ankles under the chair. "First we adopt a little immigrant child who doesn't seem to appreciate what we've done for her, all the expenses we paid to get here in this country. How much did it cost for so many to look the other way and allow her here, to have her turn out as she did. And then, there's *you.*"

"But, I-

"Embarrassing us in such a way at the party! A vile child, trying to hurt your uncle's chances in politics for your own ignorant beliefs about how the world works, talking about things you don't understand." She paused for a moment, as if to compose her position. "Your father was horrified."

"I am not vile." She couldn't remember speaking and yet, Natasha heard her own voice flow through the room.

Her mother appeared alarmed by this comment. Glancing in her direction, if only briefly, she shook her head in denial. "You most certainly are an evil child. You always were and you always will be. Why couldn't you be normal? Dress and act like other kids? You became this hippie, like the people I despised growing up. Unclean, unfit, going against society, as if that was the most normal thing to do. Repulsive. You're repulsive."

Her mother continued to speak in an even tone, as if she were merely talking about the weather or a news story in the paper, a local event that caught her eye or possibly a sale at her favorite store. It was her casualness that repulsed Natasha more than anything. It was her lack of caring, her coldness that caused her anger to slowly build, with each word, every breath, she grew furious, but managed to keep it in line.

"It's unfortunate," Her mother commented and with one abrupt move, grabbed a large carving knife and began to viciously chop up an apple, as if the anger she had was behind that blade. Her face was expressionless, as she tore into the apple, creating perfect, bite sized wedges. She then lifted one to her mouth – slowly, almost seductive in nature, as it gently graced her lips and slid across her tongue, she bit into the piece of fruit and stared at her daughter, as if to see her reaction. Finally, after chewing the apple, it seemed to disappear without her swallowing it. "Would you like some, Natasha? Would you like a piece of the forbidden fruit?"

With this, her mother erupted into laughter, as if she made the most hilarious comment, her head fell back in absolute glee and Natasha moved closer to the table. Reaching toward the apple, she almost had a small wedge in her hand, when her mother reached out and slapped her. "This is how it all started. If anyone should know that, it should be you."

Without even thinking, without even realizing what she was doing, Natasha was reaching for the knife; power surged through her veins, changing her from the frightened, hesitant child to the strong, powerful adult that her mother couldn't dominate. She grabbed the smooth handle with a strong grasp and in one, quick swoop, Natasha gritted her teeth and dug the sharp object into her mother's chest. Blood absorbed into the white material rapidly, as her mother gasped, as if the words were caught in her throat, shock filled her dark eyes and Natasha felt light, lighter than she ever felt before, as if she could float out of the room and into another world.

The scarlet liquid poured on the floor, dripping on Natasha's toes and felt sticky as she rubbed them together. She quickly dropped the knife and jumped back.

Suddenly, she felt as though her soul had jumped back in her body and Natasha's eyes flew open and for a moment, she couldn't breathe. Jumping up from the couch, she recognized a panic attack was coming on and managed to stay calm, to the point where it became clear that it was only a dream.

The apple. It was symbolic of Eve from the Bible, of the supposed evil that she brought to the world, by simply biting into the forbidden fruit.

*Even in the fucking Bible, it was always a women's fault. No wonder I'm not religious.*

But she couldn't avoid the fact that it was an odd dream to have and it made her nervous. Had her thoughts got out of control?

Glancing at the clock, she quickly realized that she didn't have the time to think about this further. She had to get ready for the political fundraiser and to teach her uncle a very valuable lesson.

# Chapter Forty-Six

❦

Red had always her best color. People complimented Natasha when she wore it and in fact, since she was a kid, many would rave about how it brought out her eyes, her hair and made her skin glow. Even her mother had to acknowledge that it was a good color for her, but Natasha somehow doubted she would receive the same compliments on that particular night.

Truth be known, she could've shown up in an expensive gown or completely naked and her mother would've been equally offended by her presence. For all the times she attempted to call Natasha since returning from Hennessey, the fundraising dinner would definitely be one place she would not want to speak to her.

The venue where the dinner was to be held was part of an expensive hotel chain, overlooking some of the richest parts of the beautiful city. People were greeted by a young Chinese lady, who accepted their ticket, took their coats and gently ushered them into the room, pointing to the specific table where they were to sit. Even from a distance and in fact, even without looking, Natasha somehow assumed she would be seated at the reject table. She was right.

Back in the corner, in fact, if she had been any farther away, she would've been out of the room completely. She was seated with three men; one was a young, nerdy type guy who refused to make eye contact with anyone else at the table. He had dark hair, a pale complexion and blue eyes, shielded with somewhat stylish glasses. He stared at his Blackberry and ignored everyone else.

Another man, this one older, stared through her from the other end of the table, but he didn't say a word. She considered saying 'hello', but decided against it. She wasn't there to make friends.

The man sitting beside her, wearing a turban was definitely the person who stood out in the room. Most of her family was closet racists, so it would be interesting to see their reaction. Glancing around, she noted that the majority of people were actually white, with a few Asians in the mix, a couple of black men and one Latino. Other than that, it was a sea of white people. Just as she suspected, the only person with a turban was at her table.

"Hello again," His dark eyes were friendly, filled with relief upon seeing her. "How are you today, Miss?"

"I'm good, Rasul," Natasha smiled and noticed he appeared nervous, perhaps because he sensed judgment within the room. She couldn't blame him for feeling uncomfortable. "Thanks for doing this for me."

"You were most friendly to me in my cab when we met," He offered and glanced around the room and displaying some uneasiness, continued to speak. "There are a lot of people here tonight."

"Yeah, I'm surprised," She commented and wrinkled her nose. "Who knew he was so popular."

"Oh, yes," Rasul gave a slow nod and calmly replied. "Some will listen to anyone who dares pick up a microphone."

"That's a good point," Natasha replied with a laugh and she relaxed. "His words have no value."

"Oh really?" Rasul replied, tilting his head slightly, a grin slid across his lips. "Then why would you be here at this dinner?"

"Hopefully, to ruin his night" Natasha said with a devious laugh, while her friend joined in. He watched her as her eyes glanced toward the door and suddenly she jumped up from the chair. "I see another friend has just arrived, I better go introduce him around. See you in a bit, Rasul."

Grabbing her clutch, she hurried toward the door, her heart racing steadily. Before arriving at her destination, someone caught her arm with a tight grip, immediately stopping Natasha in her tracks. It was her mother.

"What are you doing here?" She hissed, squeezing Natasha's arm tightly, as if it was the most appropriate way to stop her daughter from humiliating the family. Natasha immediately had flashes of her bloody dream earlier that day; her heart started to race and her throat went dry. "You haven't returned my calls, now you decide to show up at this event? Are you cooking up another scheme to humiliate the family? Haven't you done enough?"

"I'm here for the same reason as you," Natasha answered in an innocent, childlike voice that would've disarmed many, but not her mother. Her cold eyes shot through Natasha and there was little question that she suspected her youngest child was up to something, but what could she do? "I'm here to support Uncle Arnold, of course, and I see my guest has arrived, so if you want to stop digging your claws in my arm, I'm going to say hi."

Her mother let go and immediately turned toward the door, to see a young man wave at Natasha. She was clearly sizing up the stranger to see what was amiss with him, but at first glance, it wasn't as if she would find anything wrong; he was young, handsome and dressed properly. Had she found an issue, Cynthia Parsons wouldn't have had a chance to comment, because her daughter was long gone.

Slipping through the crowd, Natasha reached Andre and gave him a quick hug. He was tall, standing at around 6'3", with dark curls, a pale complexion and huge, brown eyes that appeared as nervous as Rasul's had a few minutes earlier. It was funny, Natasha considered, how her uncle had a way of creating a room of tension for those who were not soul-sucking vultures like him.

"Andre, thanks so much for coming," She whispered before letting him go and standing back. He wore a suit and the tie she had purchased for him earlier that week. "You look great."

"I feel like a fish out of water," He confessed, his body awkwardly leaning forward and in a quiet voice, asked her a question. "Are you sure this is a good idea?"

"I definitely think it's a good idea." Natasha muttered and led him away from the crowd. "Trust me, I know what I'm doing here."

"I do trust you, but I was thinking-

"Natasha!" Vanessa's voice interrupted them and Natasha was surprised to turn and see her sister with Stephen. Narrowing her eyes in his direction, Vanessa rushed over to her and didn't allow her to comment. "I know what you're thinking, but just go with it, please."

"Ok, I'm-

"Just *go* with it," Vanessa repeated and turned to Andre. "Who's this?"

"Andre, this is my sister, Vanessa and her...husband, Stephen." Natasha introduced the three to one another and watched them awkwardly shake hands and say their hellos. Spotting her mother's evil glares from across the room, she felt her throat become dry again and quickly grabbed a glass of wine when it was offered, drinking it in one gulp. Then she noticed everyone staring at her.

"What? It's one drink of wine." Natasha immediately became defensive.

"Well, after last time," Vanessa said and let out a small grin. "I would-

"Don't worry about me," Natasha interrupted and grabbed Andre's arm. "We should get to our table before the dinner starts."

Unfortunately, before they managed to even step away, she turned around to come face to face with her aunt Sylvia. Her red hair was in strange kinks; as if it never could be smoothed out properly, while her small, dark eyes darted through Natasha with disgust. Her thin lips were pursed so tight that tiny lines were meeting the red paint that awkwardly covered them.

"What are you doing here?" Her voice was barely audible, causing Natasha to lean in slightly, before realizing that it was a trick. To observers, it might have looked like an intimate discussion between family members, rather than an outward threat that was soon to follow. "If you do anything to embarrass the family this time you little slut, God help you when this night is over."

"What?" Natasha felt herself snap a little louder than she had planned, startling a few people nearby. She stood back and bit her tongue, wanting nothing more than to tell her aunt off, she instead gave a smug smile, leaned in and with a smile whispered in her aunt's ear.

"Fuck you."

Then, with a grin on her lips, she reached out and grabbed Andre's hand. "Now, if you will excuse me, I have some people to talk to."

Before her aunt could retaliate, she pulled a dumbfound Andre aside and her eyes narrowed.

*The party is just getting started bitch.*

# Chapter Forty-Seven

It wasn't a surprise that Vanessa brought Stephen along to this event. After all, she had always been the conformist when it mattered; which was the only time her parents actually cared. That was the thing with 'society people', as long as you made a proper impression in public, it was apparently okay to do pretty much anything you wanted behind closed doors.

There was a brief second – just as she walked away from her aunt – that Natasha felt a sharp stab of loneliness creep into her heart, a small tear form in the back of her eye, one that would not escape until later that night. It was difficult to accept that she was completely alone in the world. Even if your parents were cold, disconnected and only contributed conditional love, there was something very shattering about having no one to count on in the world; and after that night, she knew that this would be the case. Her sister would feel torn between two worlds, but there was never any doubt which side she would ultimately choose. She wouldn't stand up to their parents.

Taking a deep breath, Natasha decided to concentrate on the task at hand. She couldn't live with herself if she didn't stand up for the poor and troubled people of the downtown eastside, something that her uncle intended on destroying. His campaigns were slick, only suggesting that he would 'revitalize' the area and 'clean it up' – but the fine print was clear and those who paid attention knew that he wanted to close down the supervised injection facility and make the homeless less visible. He had no intentions on creating low income housing, opening more shelters or preparing a program to assist those in need, so what was the plan? "Create more police presence" was just a nice way of saying, he desired to throw everyone in jail – that is, those who didn't first OD on the street.

Natasha had made numerous efforts to talk to Uncle Arnold about this issue, but it never got through. He instead threw her a condescending smile as he showed her the door. Although Arnold hadn't said the exact words to her, she had overheard a conversation with her dad, where he explained that it was time to 'get the scum off the streets; once and for all.'

It was deplorable and inhumane. It was so easy to categorize and judge. It was also ironic that her family saw her as a disgrace, when she saw them the exact same way.

She knew her actions and words would put her out of the family circle, but it was a decision that Natasha knew had to be made. A poster from her teenage years flashed through her mind – *Stand up for something or you will fall for anything* – it was so true.

From the other side of the room, she saw her uncle and father giving her discerning looks, as if they were wondering if security should take her out, kicking and screaming.

*Nah, they know I would make a scene and there's media here. They have to be careful.*

She slowly headed in their direction, her eyes challenging Gerald Parsons', with Andre silently in tow.

"Natasha, my dear girl, how *are* you?" The older man that she vaguely remembered from her childhood gave her a good-natured pat on the arm and she stalled her original plan – but just for a moment – and smiled back. When this was all over, she didn't want everyone at the party to think she was some kind of loon. A smile eased on her lips.

"Frank? How are you?" She recognized the old man as someone who liked his Scotch and cigars, who wasn't beyond a good, dirty joke and if he hadn't been a judge, would've never been invited to this party. He had come to some of her parent's Christmas party's years earlier and usually stuffed himself with food, then left. "I haven't seen you? Wow, it's been over ten years?"

"At least, my dear, at least," Frank ran his hand through his limited strands of hair and shook his head, glancing around the room. He had inadvertently dismissed the people he had been speaking with moments earlier, a couple that gave Natasha a dismayed look as they walked away. "I was invited here tonight, but it's a bit of an *unusual* crowd for my taste."

"My uncle is a bit of an unusual man," Natasha spoke curtly, not attempting to hide any resentment in her voice. The judge appeared to pick up on that and nodded.

"I don't think I agree with some of his politics, at least, not the ones I've heard so far." He muttered to Natasha and glanced over her shoulder. "And who do we have here?"

"Oh, Frank, I'm sorry," Natasha smiled and heat spread across her cheeks. "This is Andre, he's my guest for tonight. Andre, this is Frank."

The two chatted quietly for a moment, Frank appeared to be intrigued by what Andre said, while Natasha's mind was across the room, where her uncle seemed to be moving farther away from her. Could that be on purpose? Did he think he was going to make an escape this time?

Not a chance, you fucking-

"..wouldn't you say, Natasha?" Frank was asking her a question. "Being part of the medical profession, you must see a lot of that, I would think?"

"Ah, sorry, what was that?' Natasha shook her head. "I was off in my own world for a moment."

"Hey, as long as you aren't sitting in a judges chair during a trial, I would say you're within your rights to do so," He joked and they all laughed politely. "I was just saying that some of these notions your uncle has about health care are quite ridiculous. Plus, eliminating the injection site will only increase the volume going through the legal system, when many of them could be helped."

"He doesn't think that the site is helping many people." Natasha curtly commented, wrinkling her forehead. "He believes that we are encouraging drug use and making it easier."

"Well, they certainly aren't going to stop taking drugs just because they don't have access to clean needles" Frank said, his face turning a light shade of red. "It's only putting a stack more of paperwork on my desk every day and more people in the morgue."

"I think that's what he wants," Natasha muttered softly as her mother eased by, one eye on her daughter. "It takes care of *the problem*."

"I disagree." The judge shook his head. "I can see that a 'free' ticket for an event like this is never really free is it? I may have to have a word with him before I leave."

"You should." Natasha encouraged and started to walk away. "Now, if you'll excuse me, I have to go have a word with my uncle before the dinner starts."

Frank nodded in understanding. "It was lovely seeing you again, young lady. Maybe you should be having this kind of party yourself, one day."

Glancing at Andre, his smile strong, his eyes intense, she knew it was time to talk to Uncle Arnold. However, before she got there, she saw Rasul on the far end of the room waving, attempting to get her attention. He was pointing at her chair, where someone else now sat. Rushing over to meet her and Andre, his dark eyes were large, full of concern.

"Miss, shortly after you walked away," Rasul pointed in the general direction of their table. "Someone else came along and took your seat. The woman, she says that you are leaving? Not staying for dinner? I did not know what to tell her, but I thought she was quite rude."

"We aren't having dinner?" Natasha asked, perhaps a little more loudly than she planned.

"That is what she said, yes." Rasul replied and pointed to the table again. "They said I had to leave too, that my ticket was invalid, but how could this be so? It was the same as other tickets."

"Wait, he's kicking us out?" Andre let out a short laugh. The same man who was originally hesitant to enter the fundraiser, who quietly swept through the crowd with Natasha was metamorphosing before them. His eyes full of defiance, his face cringing as he spoke, a sense of justified fury was setting in and Natasha could sense that Andre suddenly saw that he had the right to be in that room; and maybe, she decided, that was the most important factor of all.

"Is that a reporter? Rasul prompted, leaning his body slightly forward, as if to converse in secret. "Wouldn't this be a remarkable time to make a point?"

"It would be," Natasha replied, her lips curving into a mischievous smile that suddenly made her feel free, no longer tied down by the restraints of her family. "It would be the perfect time."

It didn't matter that her mother was lurking about, much like a shark in the water or that her father was throwing her a warning glare as he stood beside Uncle Arnold, who was having a spirited conversation with a local reporter. Natasha feared that this person from the media had been selected carefully, rather than allowing true freedom of the press. These kinds of people tend to not permit reporters in if they thought they might ask unpleasant questions. Then again, at the end of the day, reporters wanted the big story, didn't they?

Natasha was about to give this one something she could sink her teeth into.

# Chapter Forty-Eight

❦

Much to Natasha's surprise, she managed to approach her uncle without being pulled away, dragged out the door both kicking and screaming, but as if it was the most natural thing in the world. Neither he nor her father did a thing to stop her, acting perfectly normal, as if she were simply congratulating him for his efforts within the community.

That didn't happen.

"So, I guess I was sold an 'invalid' tickets?" Her voice was strong when she confronted Arthur, who appeared surprised by her comments. "Does that mean I get a refund when I'm escorted from the party?"

Her abrupt question caught the attention of the reporter, who suddenly was very aware of Natasha's presence. She was a young lady, pretty, who seemed to favor Gerald Parsons over the actual candidate in the room.

*He's probably fucking her.*

The thought turned Natasha's stomach; revolted by everything they secretly stood for, she couldn't believe she was a product of such a despicable family with such a low moral fiber. It was beyond comprehension how she turned out so incredibly different than the others. Even Vanessa, who wasn't a blood relative, to a certain degree was the same. It was a rude awakening: a sad realization.

"Oh, there must be some mistake," Arthur said with an awkward grin, attempting to play stupid. He shuffled from one foot to another and looked hesitant to continue, so Natasha did.

"That's okay, I don't think I have the stomach to stay for long anyway," Her comment was sharp, although not to the level that would've caused a scene. She was careful to not misrepresent herself, something she assumed this crowd would've favored. "I wanted to talk to you about the drug injection center and homeless on the downtown eastside."

"Oh don't worry your pretty little head about that," Arthur said as he recovered his composure and appeared full of confidence again. He gently patted her arm as if she was a child of eight, frightened of the bogeyman. Natasha narrowed her eyes and stepped back from his condescending gesture. "We will make sure to take care of those people."

"How? You have nothing on the agenda that implies you plan to create more shelter space. You certainly aren't speaking about getting these people into much needed programs, and I don't see how closing the injection center is helpful." Natasha raised her voice ajar, noticing that the people in their vicinity, including the reporter, were indicating some interest. "So, I'm a little confused about what you have in mind. Increased police presence suggested we should be scared of people in that area, rather than doing the humane thing and helping them."

Even as she said the words, Natasha felt a combination of energy and frustration. She knew they were falling on deaf ears that couldn't possibly realize what it was like for people in that world. It was devastating abyss for those who had come under the spell of addiction. No one ever chose to be on the streets and no one ever thought they would become an addict.

"With all due respect, I don't think you understand this situation. It's much more complex than I think you realize." He spoke slowly, almost as if she couldn't possibly grasp his words if he were to speak any faster.

"With all due respect, you're forgetting that I'm a doctor and I do understand and you're right, it *is* very complex. Unfortunately, I think you've made the decision to write off these people without thoroughly examining all the factors involved." Natasha noticed that more people were gathering around and listening to their discussion: even though some were attempting to make it less obvious than others.

"Of course and I plan to look into it more in the future, now if you excuse me-

"I would like you to meet someone, Arthur." She purposely didn't throw the 'Uncle' part in because she no longer considered him family. It was like a slap in the face, as his mouth fell open ajar; she recognized it was time to move in for the kill. She gestured behind her at the tall, young man that was trailing behind her most of the night. "His name is Andre and he used to frequent the injection site and now he's clean. He's clean because the people who work there reached out and got him the assistance he needed."

"I owe them my life," Andre spoke solemnly, gathering more attention in the group. "I wouldn't be here if they hadn't been there for me."

"Can I speak with you?" The young reporter moved toward Andre, almost pushing Natasha aside as she did, leaving Arthur with a stunned expression on his face. "I would like to quote you on that, if you don't mind?"

"Of course." Andre agreed and followed her lead away from the crowd.

Her uncle shared a dumbfounded expression with Natasha's father, who quickly moved in with his suave smile, while checking the reactions of those around him. "Natasha, we should go outside and get some air. This might be a little confining to you, you know, since your accident."

"No, I'm fine." Natasha said, making sure she sounded assertive, without allowing any aggression in her voice; even though it was clawing at the door to get in, she had to be careful in this crowd. "I also wanted to introduce you to Rasul. His family moved to Canada in 2009 and they had to live in the downtown eastside because they couldn't afford anywhere else in the city. His entire family was crowded into a small, one bedroom apartment. Ironically, it's one of the buildings you were hoping to tear down."

"It was not ideal." Rasul spoke evenly. "But it..it was fine. It was mostly safe. The building, it was in need of some repair, but it was a home."

"You want to tear down these old buildings down and build new ones, but yet, you have nothing planned for the people who are low income and can't afford high rent. Even people working full-time and sometimes two jobs struggle with the prices, let alone someone who is starting from the bottom. There has to be better answers."

"Yes, yes and we are taking all that into consideration," Arthur said hurriedly. "Now, if you'll excuse me, I have to go make a speech." He gently tapped her arm and rushed away, while her father gave her a look of disapproval. People were muttering around them, suggesting that after listening to everything that was said, nothing was really heard.

"...but that's the rare exception, not the rule..."

"..I don't think this was the time and place..."

"...invalid tickets, probably a scammer..."

Sighing, she turned to Rasul, who gave her a sympathetic smile and shrugged. "You tried Miss, you tried."

"Okay, well, I can't handle this anymore." She muttered to him. "Want to go get a cup of coffee?"

"Yes, I would." Rasul agreed. "What about him?" He pointed to Andre.

"I think he'll be fine." Natasha replied, following Rasul's eyes to across the room. "Let's get out of here."

Without saying good-bye to her father, after passing her mother's dark glares and Vanessa's cowardly glances, she walked out the door with Rasul and felt a huge weight immediately being lifted from her, when she finally exited the building.

"I didn't accomplish anything tonight, Rasul." She said, suddenly feeling exhausted, as if she could fall to the ground and sleep forever. Her body was heavy, even though her soul was light. "I thought I would make a difference, that people would stand up and listen."

"Do you think, maybe, that those people in there," He gestured toward the ritzy building they were walking away from and frowned. "Do you think that maybe they are there because they believe what your uncle also believes? Maybe they aren't interested in hearing a different idea?"

"I think you might be right, Rasul." Natasha replied, fighting off tears that were threatening to explode at any moment, as they wandered through the Vancouver's downtown area. People were all around, going in every direction and completely unaware of their presence. "Thanks for helping me, even though we didn't get far."

"Not yet, we might though. You never know what is the future." Rasul reminded her. "Even when things are at the darkest, sometimes there is light we just haven't found yet."

"I like that." Natasha replied. "I guess I thought…" Her voice caught in her throat and her eyes began to water and Rasul placed his hand on her arm. "I thought that in these last few days, I would be able to make a difference, you know? But it feels like nothing I did worked."

Rasul didn't reply but nodded, his eyes full of compassion He ushered her to an empty bench. They sat down and she reached for a tissue in her clutch. For a few minutes, it was as if the world stopped, as she gazed at the mountains in the north. It didn't matter that people rushed past, or that traffic continued to move forward. Calmness filled her body and the tears stopped.

"I thought I'd make a difference." Natasha repeated and stared forward, at nothing in particular. "I guess we always want to think we can make the world a better place, but that's often not the case, is it?"

"It is, sometimes." Rasul quietly replied. "And sometimes, all we can do is try. We do not control the faith or the minds of others, just ourselves."

"Can we influence them though?"

"Sometimes, but not always."

"I thought people would listen to me in there." Natasha said as she started to shred the tissue. "Just like I thought my sister would listen to me, or my parents, but no one did. I don't know if I should be angry or insulted."

"You should not be either of those things." Rasul insisted. "You did all you can and they must learn their own lessons at the time when they are ready."

"They may never be ready."

Rasul didn't reply.

# Chapter Forty-Nine

There's always a part of us that believes we could've done more: if only we had that one last chance. If we hadn't been daydreaming at 11 then maybe we would've had all our work done by 5. Perhaps if we made one, last ditch attempt to make that special person understand, they'd still be in our lives. If we had studied just a bit harder for that exam, maybe we would've had the life of our dreams.

It doesn't work that way. All the extra effort in the world doesn't always change circumstance, particularly when those circumstances involve thoughts and ideas of other people. That is when we overstep into their world, their lives and their own personal journey. Sometimes they're on a totally different path than us and are setting out to learn lessons the hard way, if they learn anything at all.

Natasha Parsons wanted to do the right thing for those who lived in a dismal, hopeless world. She wanted to help the addicts who lived their own personal hell everyday. She wanted to assist the people who lived so far below the poverty line that they had no concept of how to claw their way out. She wanted to help the children who felt that life was about survival at any cost.

Possibly it was Hollywood that fed her the unrealistic dream that it would just take a confrontation at her uncle's fundraiser to change his mind. Perhaps her gullibility believed that someone would overhear their conversation and reach out, to make an effort to help societies most vulnerable people. That it would end in a 'happily ever after' scenario and all would be right with the world.

It was naïve. *She* was naïve. Perhaps it was the consequence of growing up in a rich family that caused her Pollyanna attitude that somehow overlapped into adulthood. Hadn't she always been a bit credulous though? Wasn't she the same girl who blocked her parents' arguments while growing up? How many times had she watched her sister sneak a boy in the basement and pretended they were just innocently hanging out, watching TV? Hadn't she believed that her father had hired the immigrant women in order to help them, rather than to take advantage of their vulnerable circumstance?

*And now I want to save the fucking world? As if it were simply magic?*

It was too late now. Her time was up.

*I ran away for so long: from the truth, from reality, from my own life.*

Outside, dark clouds loomed overhead, warning the city that rain was never far away. It was part of the magic of life and although people complained about it, hated the very thought, they knew it was necessary. It had to happen.

Inside, Natasha was sitting comfortably on her couch, when she suddenly felt serenity flow through her body. Pure acceptance and forgiveness surged from the top of her head to the tip of her toes, like a warm current that caressed her soul and brought her peace.

*Everything is exactly how it is supposed to be.*

Getting angry, getting upset or crying a million tears wouldn't solve anything; it was merely disappointment in one's self that brought on such desperate emotions. She saw that now. It had never been so crystal clear to her as at that moment, if only she had seen it sooner. What would she have accomplished in her time?

Taking a deep breath, she rose from the couch and crossed the room. Clicking through the music on her computer, she finally found the song that had been in her head all day. A smile curved her lips, as it jumped out to her, begging to be played and she felt a giggle crawling up her throat, sliding out at the same time that tears sprang to her eye. She cried for everything that could've been. She laughed at all that it was – and really, had any of it mattered?

Music filled the room and she started to dance – her usual, geeky, terrible, silly dance that no one else understood except for her. It was the free, uncomplicated movements that had neither rhyme nor reason, but simply fit her mood at the time. To someone watching, it was the center of jokes and teasing, her terrible dancing was legendary.

But did it matter? Who was she dancing for anyway? She was hardly attempting to be a professional, elegantly flowing on a stage, but just moving to the music as it felt right. The Facebook posts that suggested you dance like no one is watching obviously aren't people who have attempted this spirited gesture, because people's eyes and ridicule made her hesitate. Chances were good, they did their subtle, unnoticeable moves awkwardly, concerned with how they would seem to others and never really enjoyed the music, but Natasha did. She just usually chose to do so alone in her apartment.

She sang to the words – mostly with the wrong lyrics, stuttering through and muttering the parts she had no idea about – but she sang. She showed no grace or vocal talents – but with the passion and energy of someone who cared about the spirit behind the music. It ran through her like blood in her veins, it was as much a part of her as it could be as a listener, rather than the artist that created it. Music was everything and she couldn't imagine a day without it.

The song ended and another one came on. This time it was Nicki Minaj and once again, Natasha danced around her room, knowing she would look ridiculous to anyone, had they been watching, but she didn't care. She needed to feel alive for one more moment before reality set back in.

Eventually, she collapsed in her office chair and turned the music down, as it moved on to a classic 70s song that she loved, even though she didn't understand the lyrics and could never remember the name, it was a song that always made her smile.

Images sprung up on her computer screen, the natural reaction of her computer after it sat idle for so long. It was photographs from her life; from the day she was born right up till the previous week, when she and Vanessa were driving home from Alberta. Had that only been a few days earlier? It felt like years ago. How much her relationship with her sister changed since then – or was it in the course of those days that her perception of Vanessa changed forever?

Her sister had been right when she once remarked that we were all different shades of the same color. The Parsons acted as if they were great, socialites with class and elegance and yet, when the truth came out, they were of less virtue than those they considered of a lower class. People weren't so different from one another, even though they wanted to believe that they were worlds apart. They were much closer than they wanted to admit.

If she could do it all over again, Natasha would've spent her time since the accident doing something useful, helpful and make her own efforts rather than grow angry at her uncle Arthur for not having the same belief system as she did; it was easy to get frustrated with people who thought differently, but it was much more difficult to do your own thing and try to be part of a solution. Even if it was just a small piece of the puzzle, at least you knew that you had tried.

Acceptance was a gift you had to give yourself sometimes. We do the best we can, she decided. These thoughts flowed through her head as photos of her and Vanessa sprang up on the screen. It was an image from the previous Christmas. So many secrets were hidden behind those smiles, she considered. What if she knew then that-

It didn't matter now.

She picked up her phone to find no messages from Vanessa. Her heart sunk, but not for herself, as much as her family. Would they regret it? Would they someday wish that they reached out to her, even though they had very different points of view?

She had three text messages. One was from Andre, telling her that the reporter was intrigued by his story and wanted to do a feature on him for one of the local papers.

*Maybe I made a difference after all.*

The second message was from Rasul. He simply inquired if she felt better after a night's sleep. She only knew him as the cab driver that drove her home after a confrontation with her mom. They started to discuss social issues on the way home and saw they were on the same page. On a whim, she got his business card and would later call him to explain her plan.

The fact that he was part of an ethnicity that her uncle despised somehow seemed like a good idea at the time. In the end, perhaps it was a rebellious choice that only ended up victimizing Rasul, by having him thrown out of the event. Unfortunately, this wasn't the first time someone had judged him unfairly, so Rasul merely shrugged it off. That fact only made Natasha feel even worse.

The third message was one she had been expecting since she left Hennessey. In fact, it was a message she had been ignoring in the weeks following the accident. It was unavoidable at this point, but she was ready to face the music. It was time.

Sitting her phone down, she briefly considered contacting her family, but decided against it. Perhaps this was how things were supposed to end, she decided and instead closed her eyes and thought back to the positive memories, back when her opinion of her family hadn't been tainted. She saw the fun Christmases; the rare snowfalls when she and Vanessa rushed outside, as children, throwing snowballs at one another – then again as adults, hadn't they enjoyed the same thing? She thought of brief moments of pride her parents showed her and the laughter they sometimes shared, but then again, was any of it ever real?

It was history now and that was fine. She made her peace.

Looking outside, she realized that the sun was attempting to make its way out, after what amounted to a brief shower. Walking to the window, she looked over the horizons and smiled. It would clear up just in time for her to go to the beach once again.

# Chapter Fifty

It was like a scene out of a movie. A beautiful movie that you never wanted to end, even though you knew the time was up. Natasha Parsons was walking along the beach – quite possibly her favorite place in the world – her thoughts a million miles away. She stared at the heavens above and wondered what was really up there? Was it beautiful? Were there angels watching from the clouds or was that merely a myth, something that gave the living comfort during difficult times.

*Times like this one.*

She knew this was the day. How long had she put it off and waited, hoping that something would mysteriously change, that she would awake from a terrible nightmare and laugh at the ludicrously of it all, but it never happened. Each day was just one less in her life and no one else could know. It was a secret she couldn't share, even during times when it was on the tip of her tongue. She swallowed it back, understanding that things just simply didn't work that way.

"Natasha." He said her name gently, carefully, as if she would suddenly run away, as if it mattered if she had tried. It wasn't his fault and it was time she stopped avoiding her destiny.

Turning around, she saw Clifford walking toward her, a hesitant expression on his face, as if he didn't know quite what to say. His eyes were kind, caring, letting her know that he wasn't a terrible person, but simply a man who was trying to make her face something she preferred to ignore; like so many other things in her life. Unfortunately, some things were unavoidable.

"I knew I would find you here," His voice was soft, velvety like the most delicate silk that ran through her fingers on her sister's wedding day. It was Vanessa's dress: expensive, designer, elegant, as she swirled around and Natasha held back from asking her if *this* wedding was what she really wanted. Instead, she went on with the role she was supposed to play, saying all the things that sisters were supposed to say to one another on that significant day.

A small tear slid from her eye and down her face. She nodded and quickly wiped it away. Their eyes met, his full of compassion and understanding, the two traits he had shown her from day one, even though she definitely didn't deserve his kind treatment. She had always been so rude, even though he could've chose to not listen to her at all, demand she go with the flow, as it was expected she would do.

"I'm ready now," Her voice was shaky and she quickly cleared her throat and took a deep breath. "I know I've been cruel and terrible to you. I wouldn't listen to you. I thought…I thought if I had more time, I could make a difference that things would be tied up neatly, like it would be better. But I think, I actually made things much worse."

"I don't think so," Clifford shook his head and reached for her hand. "You did what you felt you needed to do, in order to complete your journey. I'm sorry it didn't work out as you had hoped. I know how difficult that must be for you."

Natasha nodded and stared at the ocean. "I was hoping to have that series finale type ending, you know? The kind where everything comes together nicely and everything suddenly makes so much sense." She paused and took a deep breath. "It was actually the complete opposite. Nothing makes sense now. Everything is more mixed up. I'm farther away from my family, I didn't do the good that I had hoped I would, nothing worked out quite right."

"It seems like that now," Clifford replied and held her hand tightly, despite all the tears that flowed down her cheeks when he did. "But you never see a miracle when it happens and even though you think nothing changed, something radical could be happening right now. It might be some words you said, that you thought never really connected, but maybe they did. You just never know how you change someone's path. We're all in this together, Natasha. We want to separate ourselves, but we are *so* deeply connected."

"Why did you do it?" She whispered and used her sleeve to wipe the tears away. "Why did you give me more time?"

He didn't answer at first; he seemed to think carefully before answering. "Because you asked."

"That's the part that I never understood." Natasha said and took a deep breath, glancing down at her toes and wiggled them to remove the smidgen of sand caught between them. She had done this a million times before and yet, something so simple suddenly felt miraculous. She felt like a baby that was in awe of a brand new world. "Doesn't everybody?"

"No." His answer was simple and unexpected. Wouldn't everyone ask for more time, when faced with death? Clifford wasn't the boyfriend that wouldn't let go – like Natasha had led many to believe – he was the man who took people from this world. She had once referred to him as the grim reaper and he wrinkled up his nose in distaste, as if she were naïve on the subject of life and death. "Most people are actually ready long before their day arrives. They don't have a death wish; they just feel like they've done all they set out to do. They've accepted that it's just a matter of time."

"But you always hear stories about people begging for their lives or fighting for their lives…."

"They're mostly just stories." Clifford gave a gentle smile, causing her to think back to a boy from junior high. His name was Randy and he approached her at a school dance and she played dumb, as if she thought he walked over just to say hi and nothing more. She changed the subject, made an excuse and fluttered off to the other side of the room, leaving him standing there. Regret filled her. "You probably see them on television."

"I do." She nodded.

"And when you hear about people fighting for their lives, is it usually that person telling the story?" Clifford softly asked. It was only after she nodded, that he continued. "If they were there to tell the story, then it was because they asked for more time."

It didn't make sense to Natasha and she wasn't sure if she should believe him. Yet she felt very comfortable in his presence. He didn't send fear and shivers down her spine, he wasn't horrific in appearance; in fact, most people would be frightened to know that he looked amazingly average. He could've been the guy sitting beside you at the mall, eating a burger and fries, reading the weekend newspaper. He saw himself as the escort to the next world. He made it sound poetic and beautiful, but yet, he was taking her to her death.

"So if I asked for more time?" Natasha asked carefully, as if her words would somehow piss him off, but in reality he showed no emotion.

His eyes were pensive, probing and yet showed no signs of judgment. "Is that what you want to do?"

It wasn't a question she was expecting. It wasn't even something she had considered until that moment. Did she really want this to continue? It wasn't that she was suicidal or hated her life; it was more that everything felt finished, completed, kind of like writing a book and sensing when the final chapter has come along. If you were to continue to write, it just would become redundant. And yet, was it acceptable to ever see your life that way?

She shook her head no, not knowing how to put her thoughts into words. It was hard to explain something that made so much sense in her soul, but on a logical level was complex. How do you explain that you just felt ready? Hadn't she been handed extra time? Would more really be helpful at this point?

"You have to ask yourself if *your* journey complete? Have *you* grown?" His voice was beautiful and calm, soothing and she found herself nodding. Originally, she asked to stay in order to have some fun. She wanted to really *live;* but she quickly found out that she squandered most of those days and acted silly, like a spoiled child trying to stay up a little later past her bedtime and so she attempted to run away, but Clifford reminded her that this wasn't possible. It was then she took things seriously, attempting to get to know her family, understand where they were coming from, but that didn't leave her with the answers she searched for, but seemed to push them farther apart. Then finally, Natasha attempted to make a difference with her remaining days, but it didn't work either. What more could she do now?

"I don't know if you are aware of this, but there are five stages of grief." Clifford said and gave her hand a little squeeze. He didn't have to say another word. She had lived them all. At first, she denied that death was unavoidable, playing the role of the wild child, careless and free. Then she grew angry, lashing out at Clifford when he made another attempt to get her, while in Hennessey. The third was bargaining, when she decided to save the world, by attempting to talk to her uncle. The fourth was depression, which quickly followed the party and finally, acceptance. This was it.

"I know all about them. I am…was a doctor." She whispered. "I know them well. I just didn't see them in myself."

"We mourn our own death." Clifford reminded her. "But it should come second to living our own lives."

His words floated, as did she in that moment. Natasha closed her eyes and felt a warmth flow through her body, lightness surrounded her as everything heavy that had anchored her feet to the ground for over 30 years was suddenly removed and she was free.

We are all dark. We are all light. We are all different shades of the same color.

Love the book? Write a review☺

To learn more about Mima and her books, please go to www.mimaonfire.com

Thank you for reading my book! xo

Printed in the United States
By Bookmasters